OLD ROOSTER'S LAST CROW

STORIES FROM AN UNSETTLING WORLD

OMER ERTUR

Omer Ertur is a retired senior official of the United Nations and a former professor of Community and Regional Planning at the Iowa State University, Ames, Iowa. He has published many research articles in academic journals and several books, mostly historical narratives in four languages: English, Turkish, Japanese and Arabic.

ISBN: 9798390340257

Published by Amazon Kindle Direct Publishing

South Carolina, USA

May 2023

THE LIST of STORIES

Omer Ertur

Stories from an Unsettling World

OLD ROOSTER'S
LAST CROW

[MALAWI]

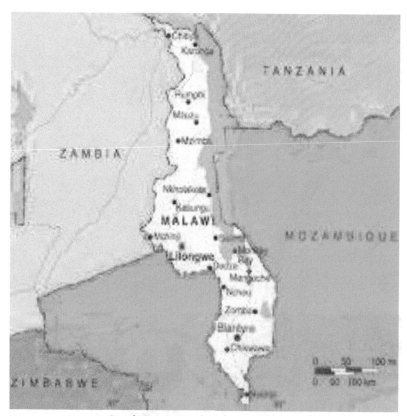

South-Eastern Sub-Saharan Africa

OLD ROOSTER'S LAST CROW

By spring of 1915, nearly nine months after the beginning of the First World War, the European nations' armed forces were fiercely fighting each other. As the bloody war effort continued in Europe; British, French, German and Portuguese colonies in sub-Saharan Africa received orders for much-needed mineral transfers and instructions to draft young men for possible military action against the neighboring colonies loyal to their European foes. Because the British colony of Nyasaland had no known natural minerals at that time, only a single set of instructions from London were sent to Nyasaland's capital city Zomba to enlist local young men to be trained for military action against the German East African Colony along the northern border. The British Colonial Administration in Zomba thus dispersed instructions to all district centers in Nyasaland for the immediate drafting of qualified young men into military service.

It was almost midnight in the British colony of Nyasaland. The full moon shone down upon the large thatched-roof hut in the middle of a small village in the vast, barren Central Region plateau. Almost everyone inside was sound asleep. A short, skinny, seventeen-year-old man walked quietly to the outdoor cooking area and hurriedly packed a few pieces of boiled cassava and a small water pouch into his shoulder bag. Returning to the sleeping area that he shared with his siblings, he laid down on his cot. As he drifted into sleep, he reminded himself to wake before sunrise.

Just before dawn, young Chewa tribesman Kamuzu Banda was awakened by a loud rooster crow. Grabbing the shoulder bag next to his cot, he walked out of the family hut and left his village Chiwengo without a backward glance. As he began his journey, he proclaimed to the empty dirt road ahead: "I have better things to do than fight for my colonial masters." Driven by a strong determination to avoid the military draft, he commenced a six-week, six hundred kilometers trek from the Kasungu District of Nyasaland, through Salisbury, Southern Rhodesia to Johannesburg, South Africa.

Upon arriving at Johannesburg, young Kamuzu found a job as a janitor at a local health clinic. After this exposure to the medical field, he decided to do whatever it takes to become a physician and return to Nyasaland to help his people. Realizing that to acquire the necessary formal education to reach his goals, he would need assistance from the church missions in South Africa; Kamuzu adopted the moniker 'Hastings' after his Scottish schoolmaster at the Kasungu Presbyterian Mission where he learned English.

He spent the following five years working various menial jobs across South Africa, mostly in mining establishments. He saved most of his earnings for travel to the United States of America. During that time, he met and gained the confidence of an American Episcopalian Bishop in South Africa, who promised to support his higher education aspirations, provided that he could get himself to the State of Ohio in the United States of America. Hardly a year later, Hastings Kamuzu traveled to Cape Town and secured a deckhand position on an ocean steamer bound for New York City.

After a long overseas journey, Hastings Kamuzu Banda entered the United States as an immigrant in spring of 1923. He quickly made his way to the State of Ohio, reaching out to the Episcopalian Church for help. With the congregation's generous assistance, he received his high school degree in 1928 from Wilberforce Academy in Xenia, Ohio. After graduating from high school, he was admitted to the University of Chicago to study political science and history. However, a university degree in history was not what this aspiring young East African student had in mind. Hastings had not forgotten his dream to become a medical doctor. He immediately transferred to Meharry Medical College, a predominantly black university in Nashville, Tennessee, where he received his medical degree in 1937.

Soon after receiving his medical degree, Hastings moved to Edinburgh, Scotland to practice medicine. Discovering that his medical degree from a black American university would not qualify him to practice medicine in the United Kingdom, he attended the Universities of Glasgow and Edinburgh and earned the necessary medical degrees in 1941. During the World War Two, Dr. Hastings Kamuzu Banda practiced medicine in various private clinics and treated wounded soldiers in public hospitals around Edinburgh. Toward the end of the war, he opened a private clinic in a suburban neighborhood of London.

***

When the bell rang, Mrs. Merene French, a tall, attractive, sensuous woman in her mid-thirties, rushed to the door and welcomed the visiting doctor into her mother-in-law's apartment. The doctor, dressed in a dark-blue three-piece suit, entered the apartment. Removing his black homburg hat, he greeted the much taller lady, "How do you do, madam? I am Doctor Hastings Banda, Mrs. French's physician. I presume you are the daughter-in-law."

Trying hard to hide her great surprise to see a black doctor at the entry hall, she replied nonchalantly, "Yes, I am. My name is Merene. Presently, my husband is at the warfront. I am here to help Mrs. French."

"Yes, I know. She told me about you a few days ago. She also informed me that you are a trained nurse. Are you presently employed?"

"I volunteer at various hospitals to help recovering soldiers."

As he approached the old lady's bed, Doctor Banda commented, "Once I finish checking on Mrs. French's condition, we'll then talk about a nursing job available at my clinic."

That was the beginning of a long-lasting relationship between the bachelor East African black doctor and the unhappily married white British nurse with a four-year-old son.

A few weeks later, in early 1944, Merene became Doctor Banda's nursing assistant and, a short while later, his trusted secretary. Soon thereafter, Doctor Banda rented the extra bedroom in Merene's apartment. These mutually supportive activities between the doctor and the nurse lasted until Merene's husband William returned home at the end of World War Two. Merene was able to convince her husband that working for Doctor Banda and renting him a room in the apartment enabled her to improve the family's strained finances. The French family and Doctor Banda thus became cohabitants with occasional secret conjugal visits between Merene and Hastings Banda.

By 1945, Hastings' medical practice was flourishing. He bought a car and a large Victorian house in Brondesbury Park, a respectable residential area of London. He and the entire French family moved into the new house, continuing their mutually agreed cohabitation. Later that same year, Banda heard about and decided to attend the International Pan-African Conference in London. Upon discovering that nobody from Nyasaland was attending the gathering, he nominated himself as the representative of Nyasaland. During the conference, he met many dissident African leaders campaigning for decolonization of Africa.

Banda's cohabitation with the French family lasted only a few more years. One day, Merene, as she removed her wedding ring, informed her husband that she was in love with Hastings. Soon thereafter, William French moved out and started divorce proceedings. Following her husband's departure, Merene took full responsibility for the day-to-day operations and financial affairs of Banda's clinic. Similarly, she assumed full control of the house: cooking, cleaning and sleeping with the doctor whenever he wished. To Merene, these actions stemmed from her sincere affection for Banda, free from expectation of receiving anything in return. She even helped Hastings with his political activities, assisting him in organizing several house-gatherings of African leaders including Kwame Nkrumah of the Gold Coast and Jomo Kenyatta of Kenya. Both leaders were in London prior to starting their anticolonial activities in their respective countries. She diligently took notes during these meetings and advised Hastings on how to appear elegant, confident and knowledgeable.

***

One late afternoon, Doctor Hastings Banda ushered his last patient from the examination room and went straight to his personal office. He stood for a long time in front of the window, aimlessly watching the busy street below, agitatedly ruminating over the news he received yesterday from Nyasaland's colonial government, informing him that he could establish a medical practice in his homeland as long as he promised not to mingle with the country's white medical community.

Loudly mumbling, "Racist pigs!", he turned away from the window and approached his desk. Noticing an envelope from the Presbyterian Church of Scotland, he grabbed it to open. The letter informed him that he had become a lifelong elder of the Church. Smiling, he reminded himself, "I should thank Doctor MacPherson for this good news. I'd best forget about returning to Nyasaland for now. I must remain in England to build up my medical practice."

Putting on his black homburg hat and beige trench-coat, he joined Merene at the reception desk to go home for dinner.

During the late 1940s and early 1950s, Dr. Banda accumulated considerable wealth from his flourishing medical practice and investments in the London stock exchange. Also, by becoming a freemason, he used his affluence to finance the college educations of forty African students in various English universities. In late 1951, he received a letter from his friend Kwame Nkrumah in the British West-African colony of Gold Coast. Nkrumah invited Banda to join him in his efforts to gain independence from Great Britain.

Having spent several decades in the United States and the United Kingdom, the prospect of returning to Africa excited the fifty-four-year-old doctor. Seriously considering moving to the Gold Coast, he spent considerable time in London establishing contacts for an eventual return to his home country of Nyasaland. Through these contacts, he learned of the fledgling anticolonial movements in Nyasaland, the Gold Coast, Kenya, Nigeria and Zambia. After careful considerations and in-depth discussions with Merene, he decided to accept Kwame Nkrumah's offer. He sold his medical practice and moved to Accra, Gold Coast in 1952.

Soon after Banda arrived in Accra, the Gold Coast gained independence from the British Empire and formally changed her name to the Republic of Ghana. When the newly independent country was established, President Kwame Nkrumah offered Hastings Banda an important government position. Still hoping to return home to Nyasaland one day, Banda declined the offer. Instead, he moved to the city of Kumasi to establish a medical clinic. Similar to his former lifestyle in London, he practiced medicine, while his partner Merene ran the office and took care of their home. As time passed, depressed that his return to Nyasaland seemed to have stalled, the old doctor began focusing less on his medical practice and spent less time with his longtime partner Merene.

One day in late October 1957, Merene confronted Hastings about the noticeable increase in the clinic's abortion activities. She loudly declared, "In London, you wouldn't do that for any price. Now, most of the time you do it for free! As an elder of the Church of Scotland, how could you partake in such sinful activity?"

"Merene, you are not being fair," Banda firmly replied. "You are forgetting that in London young unmarried British women rarely get pregnant. It is quite the opposite here: local women get pregnant too frequently. This isn't a moral issue in Ghana; it is a social menace."

"Sooner or later, you will get into trouble with the authorities."

"I don't think so, but if it happens, I'll handle it."

Hardly a few months later, government ordered a court action against the clinic for conducting abortions. The court action against his clinic disturbed Doctor Banda's peace of mind, leading him to consider returning to London. It was during this time of uncertainty that an unexpected letter arrived from Nyasaland. It was from Henry Blasius Chipembere, the leader of a group of anticolonial dissidents active in NAC, Nyasaland African Congress. Chipembere invited Doctor Banda to take over the Congress' anticolonial activities against the Nyasaland-Rhodesia Federation.

Chipembere's letter sent Doctor Hastings Kamuzu Banda into a mental tailspin. He was indecisive because he knew nothing about these young dissidents and definitely did not trust them. He repeatedly discussed the matter with Merene, becoming frustrated when she told him that he did not truly understand the mindset of these young revolutionaries because he was more of a British gentleman than an African dissident.

"You are a soft-hearted, generous medical doctor," she emphasized. "If you join these young political vultures, you will be devoured in no time. I have always respected your wish to return to Nyasaland to practice medicine. If you go back as a doctor, I will be next to you. I don't think you realize that if you return to Nyasaland to start an anticolonial uprising, as your white British partner, I cannot join you."

During the following months, the relationship between Merene and Hastings had soured. One day, after hours of intense and bitter discussions, Merene, in the heat of argument, revealed her true opinion on his planned political adventure in Nyasaland.

"Hastings!" she loudly hissed, "After nearly forty-five years away from your homeland and spending great amounts of time in America and England, you ignore the obvious fact that you act like a white man in black skin. You should accept the fact that this obvious stark reality will not mold you into a revolutionary African leader that you hope to become one day."

After that heated argument, they did not speak for quite some time. As this was going on, Hastings went to Accra to visit his friend President Kwame Nkrumah to discuss his plan to return to Nyasaland and lead the ongoing anticolonial activities. Emboldened by Nkrumah's blessing, he returned to Kumasi having decided to accept Chipembere's offer. During the next few days, he crafted his acceptance letter wherein he clearly set forth a set of conditions that must be agreed by the dissident leadership. The very next day, another visitor from Nyasaland brought another letter from Chipembere, requesting an answer. Banda handed the visitor his written response.

At the beginning of summer in 1958, Banda received a reply from Chipembere that his conditions had been accepted by the Nyasaland African Congress. The elderly doctor was now ready to start his journey home, but he first wished to visit London to establish political contacts to help him take a strong political stance against the existing pro-colonial Federation of Nyasaland and Rhodesia. Banda was certain that the colonial Federation, in existence for the six previous years, would prevent the actualization of his plans to acquire independence for Nyasaland.

***

Hastings, opening the door, asked the taxi driver to load his luggage into the car. Turning towards Merene, standing gracefully in the hallway, he gruffly mumbled, "You don't have to come to the airport. We will bid our farewells here."

Avoiding eye contact, she replied sternly, "Hastings, I insist on accompanying you to the airport."

It was a long, silent ride to the airport. As they stood before the immigration desk, she looked at him and murmured, "I will remain here in Kumasi, waiting for your return. Goodbye Hastings and good luck!"

Hastings Banda, choosing not to respond, turned around and walked away from her without a backward glance.

Merene serenely watched him disappear into the crowd ahead. With a sad smile on her lips, she bowed her head down.

"It is so sad to end a long trusting relationship in this fashion. But I am sure he will return to me when his political adventure results in failure. I pray that he will remain safe and stay away from the harms' way!"

After concluding his planned visit to London, Banda took a flight to Blantyre, Nyasaland on July 6, 1958. When he landed at Chileka Airport in Blantyre, he received an uproarious welcome by thousands of people. After nearly forty-four years away from his homeland, the old doctor was greeted as a returning hero. Ascending to the podium, he announced to the crowd, "In Nyasaland, we mean to be masters of our land. If that is seen as treason by the colonial authorities, to be free we will make the most of it."

The sixty-year-old doctor toured most of the regions and districts in the country and visited many towns and cities together with the young dissident leaders who had invited him to lead Nyasaland to independence. Wherever he went, he was welcomed jubilantly by spectators loudly calling him 'Ngwazi', the conquering lion.

This tremendous public excitement baffled Henry Blasius Chipembere and Dunduzu Chisiza, who accompanied him on his countrywide tour that included Banda's birth place in the Kasungu District. The young dissidents marveled that this little old man, dressed in a dark-blue three-piece European suit with a black homburg hat and dark sunglasses, was able to ignite the public's nationalistic sentiments. They congratulated each other for selecting the old doctor as the ceremonial head of Nyasaland's anticolonial movement. Soon after the completion of the countrywide tour, Chipembere and Chisiza helped Banda to be elected as president of the Nyasaland African Congress. This marked the official beginning of Nyasaland's bid for independence.

As he prepared for his newfound political responsibilities, Banda opened a medical clinic in the town of Limbe near Blantyre. He hired a twenty-year-old qualified nurse, Cecilia Tamanda Kadzamira, as his medical assistant. This tall, attractive and elegant young woman, already engaged to be married, fell in love with the impressive doctor, almost forty years her senior. Thus, began a close, lifelong relationship between the medical assistant and the practicing doctor, soon to become president of a newly established republic.

During the rest of 1958 and most of 1959, Banda practiced medicine in his clinic in Limbe. He spent considerable time with Nyasaland African Congress members to organize public demonstrations against the Nyasaland Rhodesia Federation. In August of 1959, following intense street demonstrations in Blantyre and Zomba, Banda was arrested by the British colonial authorities. He spent the following thirteen months in Gwelo Prison in Southern Rhodesia.

Upon his release and return to Nyasaland in early 1960, he received two letters that strengthened his conviction to consolidate political power. The first letter was from Merene, who had written from Accra in late 1959 to inform him that his imprisonment was an inevitable proof that his political adventure in Nyasaland would end in failure. Assuming that as a political prisoner, Hastings would remain in custody for an unforeseeable future, Merene informed him that she had decided to return to England.

The second letter was from his friend Kwame Nkrumah, the President of Ghana. Nkrumah warned Banda to be extremely careful in his upcoming political life. He ended his letter with the following statement: "As a political leader, if you don't get rid of the opportunistic vultures surrounding you, sooner or later, they will eliminate you!"

After his release from prison, Kamuzu Banda led a well-organized anti-federation political struggle, finally resulting in Nyasaland's separation from the Rhodesia Federation and her establishment as a semi-independent British Protectorate in 1962. Still remaining under the jurisdiction of the Queen of England, Banda was elected Nyasaland's first black African Prime Minister.

Four years later, in 1966, Nyasaland became fully independent and Hastings Kamuzu Banda was elected as her first President. Upon becoming the President, he immediately renamed the country as Malawi, after an ancient Chewa Kingdom from the Central Region and adopted a red, black and green flag emblazoned with a rising sun at its center.

At the pinnacle of his political power as Malawi's first president, the elderly doctor became a well-respected and admired national political leader. However, at a cabinet meeting a few months after independence, he noticed his ministers' overwhelming efforts to override many of his policy suggestions, particularly several food-security and higher-education recommendations. Ensuing heated arguments reminded Banda of Kwame Nkrumah's words and made him realize that if he did not take action, he would soon be politically sidelined by the young dissidents who originally invited him to Nyasaland. Controlling his deeply felt anger and frustration, he decided not to react during the heated proceedings of the cabinet meeting. A few days later, taking a tremendous political risk, he purged his cabinet and several elected members of the Parliament. Most of the young dissident group and some members of the Parliament were arrested. Within a short time, he was able to remove almost all of the founding members from the ruling political party positions. Some of his political opponents, escaping arrest, tried to leave the country. Dunduzu Chisiza died in a car crash while trying to reach Mozambique border while Blasius Chipembere fled to the United States as a political refugee.

In the midst of the ongoing political turmoil in Malawi, Banda received news of a military coup d'état in Ghana that overthrew President Nkrumah. He again remembered Nkrumah's cautioning him against the surrounding political vultures.

With a sad smile, he mused, *"Dear friend, you should have practiced what you preach. It seems that you didn't purge the vultures surrounding your throne."*

The news of Nkrumah's overthrow, convinced Banda to create a community-based quasi-military organization, the Young Pioneers, to control all forms of opposition to his now ironfisted rule. The Malawi Young Pioneers Organization was originally formed as a community-based agricultural extension program to assist small landholders to increase agricultural productivity. Structured around the Kibbutz model of community improvements originated in Israel, the Young Pioneers, as they helped increase in subsistence-crop production, became, in time, the providers of information to the one-party state. Soon afterwards, they acquired arms to help consolidate Banda's political authority in local communities.

In 1971 the legislature declared Kamuzu Banda 'President for Life'. His full official title now read 'His Excellency the Life President of the Republic of Malawi, Ngwazi Dr. Hastings Kamuzu Banda'. After declaring himself 'Life President', he strengthened the institutional structure of the one-party state and took complete political control of the country. Now comfortably settled in the Sanjika Presidential Palace in Blantyre, President Banda declared Cecilia Tamanda Kadzamira, his former nurse in his clinic in Limbe, as the presidential hostess. After her move into the presidential palace, she officially was referred to as 'Mama Kadzamira'. Over time, with the introduction of Mama Kadzamira into the immediate configurations of the political power structure surrounding Banda, many opportunities were created for the presidential hostess to implant many relatives, including her maternal uncle John Zenus Ungapake Tembo into important government positions.

During the following years, President Banda successfully accomplished many of his political aspirations. Malawi was now independent and many of her citizens, while retaining their ethnic identities, were unified under their new Malawian identity. For future development purposes, Banda concentrated public investments and foreign aid activities on agricultural production. In due time, Malawi became almost fully self-sufficient in subsistence agricultural production and substantially increased export of cash-crop products, such as tea, coffee, tobacco, sugar cane and cotton. In the meantime, by establishing a cordial relationship with the Republic of South Africa, Malawi began receiving considerable development assistance, including funds for the construction of a new capital city in the Central Region.

***

Toward the end of 1976, Banda received a letter from London. It was from Merene's son Peter, informing Banda that Merene had passed away. He was saddened with the unexpected news. Placing the letter on his desk, he remained silent for a while. Then, standing up, started pacing the floor of his large office.

"Poor woman!" he mused. *"She waited for a long time for my political failure and expected my return to her bosom. She never truly understood that I loved my country and my people more than I ever loved her. Mothers and daughters of this land would have never accepted me as their leader with a white British woman at my side."*

Back to his desk, he sat down, closed his eyes and whispered, "I'll always remain thankful for our wonderful times together. Rest in peace dear Merene, rest in peace."

Early in June 1977, Banda visited, for the first time as President, Mzuzu and Nkhata Bay Districts in Malawi's Northern Region. The warm welcome he received from the local communities was so impressive that he was overwhelmed, especially when many colorfully attired local women, called *mbumbas,* chanted and danced in his honor.

Upon arriving at the new capital city Lilongwe, still under construction, he was welcomed at the airport by an entourage of his cabinet ministers and a group of ambassadors. After the end of the welcoming ceremony, Banda and his official hostess, Mama Kadzamira, entered the presidential car that was surrounded by a group of chanting mbumbas, wearing colorful cloth emblazoned on breast and bottom with the Ngwazi's smiling face. As the black convertible Rolls Royce moved slowly through the crowded streets, Mama Kadzamira, tapping Banda on the shoulder, handed him his favorite ivory handled, lion-tail flywhisk to wave at the thousands of people enthusiastically welcoming him to Lilongwe. After reaching the newly constructed presidential palace, Banda asked Mama Kadzamira to prepare for a visit from an old friend from his days in Edinburgh: Doctor Fergus MacPherson, a highly respected member of the Presbyterian Church of Scotland.

A few days later, Doctor MacPherson was greeted at the airport by an official of the Ministry of Foreign Affairs and taken to the presidential palace as President Banda's special guest. Later that afternoon, Banda welcomed his friend in the official meeting room. MacPherson's first impression of his seventy-nine-year-old friend was that the President appeared frail, was hard of hearing and had poor eyesight. Doctor MacPherson initiated their long conversation with a pointed question about Banda's efforts to eliminate all political opposition in Malawi.

Banda responded to his friend's politically charged question carefully, "If I don't eliminate the opposition, they would eliminate me. It was obvious from the beginning that the young dissidents who invited me to lead their anticolonial movement were not serious about creating a unified country under my complete guidance. They were more interested in formulating and establishing various self-serving agendas. Leaving them with their highly disruptive political aspirations would have resulted in civil wars as has happened in many newly independent African countries. I was not about to allow that to happen in Malawi."

Not satisfied with this explanation, MacPherson further inquired, "You are a western educated man, who has lived in the United States and England for a long time. With that background, how could you declare yourself president for life?"

"After returning home to Nyasaland," Banda sternly replied, "if I held fast to my acquired western cultural and political values, I would be long dead. After my demise, the young dissidents would have organized themselves against each other and started a never-ending cycle of civil wars, which would have ruined the country for good. For the time being, as the president for life, I will continue to retain absolute power to guide my country toward proper development direction. Under my guidance, we have identified the much-needed aspects of development: unity, loyalty, discipline and obedience. These aspects, when fully established, will clear the path toward socioeconomic development and political stability. Only when that happens, the people of Malawi will be ready for playing the rigorous political games of democratic choice."

Softening his tone with a weary smile, Banda continued, "Please understand that for the masses of starving people without feasible socio-economic opportunities, the game of democratic politics is a dangerous luxury."

With a curious look on his face, the Scottish Doctor asked, "Hastings, in order to reach the level of development that is essential for democratization, what kinds of socio-economic policies you're proposing to pursue?"

After remaining silent for a while, President Banda finally replied, "When I arrived in this land-locked country in 1958, there were only sixty miles of paved roads, a grand total of thirty-three college graduates and no significant mineral resource. Our Constitution clearly instructs the state to develop our agricultural resources toward the establishment of basic principles of a policy structure necessary for food self-sufficiency. When most of our people are malnourished and underfed, why focus our attention on matters of political choice and social development? We have to make sure that our agriculture sector will become, first and foremost, self-sufficient in subsistence production to feed our people."

Banda leaned forward to emphasize his point. "The primacy of agricultural development is the first article in our constitution and that article guides the primary objective of our initial development policy efforts. Please don't forget that although Malawi is one of the poorest countries in the world, we have recently become self-sufficient in subsistence-crop production."

Enjoying the momentum that he was building up, Banda leaned back with a smile. "Furthermore," he said, "we produce substantial amounts of cash crops to generate funds for various public projects. While many newly independent African countries focused their development efforts on industrialization by building profitless steel-mills and car factories, we invested our sparse financial resources into subsistence-crop producing farmer cooperatives and large cash-crop agricultural projects. We also built infrastructure, particularly roads and railways, to help farmers get their products to markets. I would also like to emphasize that Malawi is one of the few countries in the African continent that pays its international debt on time. We have a small but efficient and relatively honest civil service. Our new capital city, Lilongwe, is free of the squalor and crime that blights many of the cities of the African continent."

Scratching his chin pensively, MacPherson nodded. "Fair enough!" he said. "How about people's need for education and training?"

"People's need for training and education that will help increase agricultural production will remain our primary focus until a foreseeable future when there will be other economic opportunities for increased employment. Until then, we will not educate our people for the sake of learning and knowledge, which, in the long term, will only increase people's expectations.

Educating the general public without meeting their fundamental needs for food, employment and income will only generate personal frustrations and cause political upheavals in the country.

Noticing his friend's seemingly unconvinced appearance, Banda modified his approach. "It's not as though I'm completely abandoning public education; I'm just carefully directing it. I am the rector of the State University where most of our bureaucrats are being trained and I will soon establish an elite college in my birth place Kasungu. This school will be structured on the principles of British Eton College, with a curriculum in English, Latin and Greek. Let's not forget that Eton College is the school that had carried England into the industrial age. This new college in Kasungu will serve as the place of educational excellence that will train the future leaders of Malawi."

Appearing perplexed, MacPherson further inquired, "I am not sure I can fully accept your public education policy parameters but I understand your rationale. Please allow me to ask you another question: Within the realms of your medical training, do you have specific policies for improving the overall public health in your country?"

Banda pensively leaned back in his chair. "You know, as a medical doctor, this is a very tough question for me to answer. However, as the president of this underdeveloped, poor country, I could only prescribe the following: Similar to what I explained in matters of public education, in a land where food availability is insufficient, why should we invest our limited resources on saving lives through expensive public health projects. At the bitter end, please remember that most of these saved citizens of public health activities will end up dying from starvation or undernourishment."

"However, my dear friend," MacPherson intercepted, "it is globally accepted that education and health care stimulate overall development. Contrary to this trend, your ideas on public education and public health are based on an extremely controversial perspective that agricultural development should precede education and health care. This becomes a matter of chicken or egg question."

"I don't think so. Please remember that our main policy emphasis is food self-sufficiency. Once we are able to feed our people and when there is no more malnourishment and undernourishment in our land, then we will activate policies investing into improvements in public education and healthcare."

"Hastings, I hope you do realize that it may take a very long time to accomplish such an objective. Many have tried and failed before. But thank you for clarifying these important matters. On another note, I have a potentially sensitive question. Your pro-Israeli, anti-Soviet, anti-Communist China stance are much appreciated by the Western Alliance, yet you are the only African leader who recognizes the apartheid regime of South African government. What is the reason behind your appeasing approach to apartheid?"

Banda smiled broadly, appreciating the chance to clear the global misunderstanding behind his approach to South Africa's apartheid regime. "Dear friend, in a nutshell let me tell you this: I would make an alliance with the devil if that would help Malawi. Keep in mind that we cannot influence or instigate change in South Africa's admittedly inappropriate apartheid approach to governance by rejecting its existence. Here in Malawi, our black majority and white minority coexist as equal citizens. In time, South Africa will also realize and understand our model that blacks and whites are the people of the land with equal rights. Sooner or later, political change will come to South Africa. We must be patient and maintain an open political dialog with the South African leadership. We must give them a chance to study our approach to white minority's rights in Malawi while helping us with our overall development via transfer of knowhow, resources and considerable financial support. For example, because of our cordial relationship, the government of South Africa has agreed to help Malawi to build a new capital. Last year, upon completing most of the construction, we moved some of the governmental offices from Zomba to Lilongwe. Here we are in the newly built presidential palace in Lilongwe. Speaking of which, I am greatly honored to welcome you to our new capital city. What do you think of it?"

MacPherson flashed a sincere smile. "I must admit that I'm quite impressed with this modern city with beautiful houses, wonderful gardens and wide streets lined with colorful *jacaranda* trees. Really, this is a tremendous accomplishment especially when you got it financed by the Government of South Africa. Well done, my friend."

"Please allow me to correct you." President Banda gently intercepted. "South African financial assistance is a long-term loan. Future generations of Malawians will pay for their new capital."

As Doctor MacPherson was about to reply, the large French doors to the meeting room were opened and Mama Kadzamira, dressed in a colorful traditional dress, entered the room, leading a group of uniformed servants carrying food and drinks in large trays. When the tall, handsome and dignified Malawian lady gracefully approached the two gentlemen sitting on plush leather chairs, President Banda introduced her to his guest. After guiding the afternoon tea service, Mama Kadzamira respectfully informed the President that upon completion of the ongoing meeting, the Minister of Finance and Treasury, John Tembo, who happened to be her uncle, would like to see him about an urgent matter.

Upon Mama Kadzamira's departure, Doctor MacPherson, after taking a sip from his tea, remarked, "Dear friend, as an elder of the Church of Scotland, I have one last very sensitive question to ask you. I am aware that I may be repeating myself with that question but please, I beg your understanding that this question has been requested by the elders of our church. Before answering, please remember that because of your strict Christian values and your generous healthcare assistance that you had provided to many poor folks in Edinburgh and London, I nominated you to become a life member of our church. We, the elders of the Church of Scotland, would like you to explain your reasons for harshly treating and violently eliminating some of your political opponents."

The abrupt, politically-charged question asked by his guest irked President Banda. Feeling irritated, he got on his feet and started to pace the floor of the large meeting room. Short while later, feeling calmer, he returned to his chair and tried to frame an appropriate reply to his respected friend's inquiry.

"Anyone of the people I imprisoned or exiled, would not have been treated harshly if they stopped organizing activities against the unified political system I've prescribed for the people of this land. Please understand, if they were successful in their efforts to demolish what I've built for the good of the Malawian people, I would not be here today and you would definitely not visit a starving country embroiled in a civil war."

With a stern look on his face, Banda bowed his head down and remained silent for a short while. Regaining his composure, he continued, "A few individuals who failed to recognize the ongoing accomplishments of food self-sufficiency and socio-political stability, deserved to be eliminated. As a good Christian and also as the President of this country, I am the chosen protector of God-given lives of my citizens. Please understand that my political strategy to eliminate the disruptive opposition is primarily based on protecting the livelihoods of my people. I am sure that the God almighty will forgive me for my misdeeds against a few deserving individuals because their eliminations have resulted in a definite and irrefutable public good."

Taking a deep breath, Banda sighed wearily. "I returned to my homeland at age sixty and invested all my time, energy and my life-savings into my country's development. I expect no personal gains from my political activities and the governmental policies I've instigated. I am an old man with a great hope to survive a few more years to see the day that I will take the necessary steps to introduce some form of democracy if and when my people are ready for such political change. I pray every day that the Almighty may grant me a long life, enabling me to see the day of free elections in Malawi."

***

During the following seven years, due to aging related ailments, there was a noticeable decline in President Banda's health and his involvement into day-to-day operations guiding the development of the country. Many of the members of the Parliament and the ministerial cabinet noticed that President Banda has delegated most of the presidential powers to his official hostess Mama Kadzamira and her uncle John Tembo - a forty-year-old, physically slight, ascetic, fastidious and cunning politician from the Dedza District.

By the beginning of 1983, rumors circulated in Parliament that President Banda would soon declare John Tembo, presently the Governor of the Reserve Bank of Malawi, his successor. During an early May 1983 Parliamentary meeting in Zomba, Dick Matenje - a cabinet minister without portfolio and the Secretary General of the Malawi Congress Party - proposed formation of a specially designated parliamentary committee to deal with the matter of presidential succession. The committee, after long discussions, decided to reconfirm with a few minor adjustments the previously agreed procedures of succession when a president passes away or becomes incapacitated. These slightly modified procedures of succession were slated to be presented to Parliament for review.

When Parliament moved to other matters, John Tembo hurriedly left the meeting. Watching Tembo's hasty departure, Dick Matenje turned toward his closest parliamentary allies: Aaron Gadama, the Minister for the Central Region; David Chiwanga, the Minister of Health and John Sangala, a Member of Parliament. Smiling broadly, he loudly announced, "I think Tembo now clearly understands that his hopes to grab power will not be as easy as he imagined. Parliament will not allow him to become president when Banda dies."

Outside, John Tembo ordered his driver to take him to Sanjika, the presidential palace in Blantyre. Upon arrival at the palace, he immediately sought out his niece Mama Kadzamira. To avoid eavesdroppers, they spoke as they walked around the palace gardens.

Clearing his throat, Tembo spoke nervously, "Dick Matenje has taken parliamentary action to curtail our plan to convince Kamuzu to declare me as his successor."

"How did he hear about it? We never discussed it with anyone but Banda."

"I presume the old man mentioned it to someone."

"It is probable that he may have discussed the succession matter with a few cabinet members when they visited him last week. A few weeks back, I told him that choosing you as his successor would be good for the country because you'll uphold his established policies. He seemed to agree."

Suddenly stopping, John Tembo turned toward Mama Kadzamira and asked, "May I speak with him about this issue as soon as possible?"

"I will try getting you an appointment tomorrow morning."

The following morning, Tembo informed the President of Dick Matenje's motion, noting that Parliament would soon decide on whether to prevent Banda from declaring a successor. Concluding discussions over the details of the parliamentary motion, President Banda immediately summoned his administrative assistant and ordered him to invite Matenje to the palace for a private meeting.

The next day, as he drove from Zomba to the Presidential Palace in Blantyre, Dick Matenje was dwelling on the reason why the President had summoned him to the Palace. He was sure that he would be questioned about his parliamentary motion to prevent John Tembo from becoming the presidential successor.

During the tense meeting at Presidential Palace, Matenje was straightforward about the matter, telling the president that there was no need to declare a successor. He convincingly declared, "As General Secretary of the Congress Party, I am guided by the parliamentary regulations and the party bylaws. I pray that the good Lord grants you a long life, but upon your departure, Parliament will see to it that a qualified person temporarily heads the government until the people of Malawi elect their new president."

Raising his head high and looking straight into Matenje's eyes, Banda harshly replied, "You will do no such thing. The people of Malawi are not yet ready to democratically elect a new president. If I want to declare a successor, you have no option but to obey my instructions. Tomorrow, you will withdraw your motion in the Parliament."

That was the end of the meeting between the Life President of the country and the Secretary General of the Malawi Congress Party. The same evening, Banda summoned Tembo and informed him that Matenje is to be relieved of his duties as Secretary General of the party. He then said,

"Apparently, Matenje, through parliamentary procedures, is preparing to get himself declared president upon my death."

Remaining silent for a few seconds, Banda then asked, "Who else supported his parliamentary motion?"

"Gadama, Chiwanga and Sangala."

Banda, raising his voice, bluntly ordered, "Tomorrow, at the end of the parliamentary session, regardless of whether or not Matenje withdraws his motion, get all four of them arrested. Time served in prison will teach them a lesson they'll never forget."

The next morning, when the Parliament had convened, Dick Matenje, following the President's order, prepared to withdraw his motion on the presidential succession. Yet, before he could make his move, he was informed that a presidential directive had been received early in the morning, ordering the Parliament not to consider any motion until further instructions. Troubled about the President's decision to stop him on his tracks, Matenje briefed his friends Gadama, Chiwanga and Sangala about the previous day's meeting with the President.

"I think, Banda has decided that John Tembo is to be his successor. Since we tried to prevent a possible Tembo succession by a parliamentary motion, we are now in serious trouble. The president was extremely irritated by our challenge to his decision to declare a successor. He might already have ordered our detention."

Aaron Gadama, the Minister for the Central Region, shaking his head, responded firmly, "Let's not jump to conclusions. We did nothing wrong against Banda. We only proposed a parliamentary motion to prevent Tembo from becoming president when Kamuzu is gone. I believe we should stand our ground and defend our position. Sooner or later,

Banda will understand that we did this for the good of the country. We should now reach out to the party members to explain our position. There is an election rally tomorrow at the party headquarters in Blantyre. Let's attend that rally to organize support against Tembo's political games."

After a brief discussion, they agreed to follow Minister Gadama's suggestion. With intention to reach the party headquarters in Blantyre, they left Parliament in an official car driven by Dick Matenje. After driving approximately thirty minutes toward Blantyre, they came upon a state security roadblock on the Likangala Bridge near Namadzi. Taken out of the car, the four parliamentarians were unceremoniously arrested. A convoy of police cars took the detainees to the Mikuyu prison facility near the Eastern Division Police Headquarters in Zomba and delivered them for questioning to four policemen on duty. At the completion of the lengthy inquiry procedure, the four parliamentarians were locked in separate cells.

That evening, following his long phone conversation with John Tembo, the senior police officer in charge of the arrested parliamentarians at the Mikuyu Prison approached his three deputies to report the instructions he had received.

"We have to eliminate all four parliamentarians in a way that they'll appear to have died in a car accident as they were driving to the Mozambique border."

After this announcement, the conniving policemen spent the rest of the evening finalizing the details of the plan to execute the four men in their custody.

Early the next morning, the four policemen drove nearly one and a half hours to the Mwanza District's secluded northern areas to find a proper location to accomplish their murderous plan. As they traveled the wide Thambane dirt road near the border of Mozambique, they came upon a densely wooded high hill running adjacent to the Condedezi River. They stopped the car and surveyed the area.

Standing near the edge of the cliff, the senior police officer, smiling broadly, commented, "This is a perfect location: a high hill at the sharp end of the curvy dirt road and very close to the border. If we push the car from this escarpment into the ravine below, it will end up crashing into the river."

After a brief discussion, they decided that they would finalize their bloody plan there on that hillside dirt road. Leaving his three colleagues standing near the ledge, one of the officers went back to the police car and took out a roadblock sign.

Placing it near the ledge, he hollered, "We are approximately thirty kilometers north of the Town of Mwanza. It's best to leave a marker for us to find this spot easily when we come back."

Turning toward the senior officer, he then asked, "When are we to bring the prisoners here?"

Looking at his watch, the senior officer abruptly replied, "Let's get it done this afternoon."

A few hours later, the four policemen returned to the Namadzi Police Station. After a short period of rest, they went to the station's car pool and selected a privately owned, impounded blue Peugeot station wagon to be used as the victims' getaway vehicle. After a long search in the police station's storage room, one of the officers retrieved a sledge hammer and two shovels. He placed them on the backseat of the station wagon.

Returning to the Mikuyu prison facility, the policemen removed the four prisoners from the cells they were kept overnight. Prior to placing them in police cars, they handcuffed the victims and placed hoods over their heads. The two police cars and the blue station wagon, driven by the policemen, commenced the deadly journey toward the Mwanza District.

At the same time in the Presidential Palace in Lilongwe, President Banda was about to conclude a meeting with the representative of the World Bank, finalizing the details of a large cash-crop agricultural project. Afterwards, President Banda asked John Tembo to remain in the meeting room to discuss the World Bank project's implementation.

"John," the President said firmly, "As the World Bank's loan payments arrive, make sure that those funds are diverted toward activities increasing the productivity of smallholders growing subsistence crops. If we are successful in that effort, we will successfully continue feeding our people. Furthermore, if the World Bank loans help us to create an abundant subsistence crop, we will export the surplus to the neighboring countries."

"Understood. I will instruct the Minister of Agriculture to divert these funds to the small farmers producing maize and cassava. However, sir, respectfully, I have a question to ask: Within the coming six months, a World Bank mission will visit Malawi to inspect the increases achieved in the agricultural cash crop production. What do you suggest we do about that?"

"I suggest that you focus on increasing tobacco, tea and coffee production activities on a few chosen nearby sites. When the World Bank mission members arrive, take them to those prepared sites to satisfy their expectations of increase in cash crop production. Make careful preparations for those site presentations; otherwise, we might lose the World Bank loan payments."

"I understand. I assure you that I will do my best. Is there anything else to discuss?"

"Yesterday you reported that Dick Matenje and his three colleagues disappeared before they could be arrested. Did you find them?"

"No, sir. We checked their homes, but their families reported that they have not heard from them. We assumed that they were heading to the Malawi Congress Party gathering in Blantyre. I talked with the police chief in Blantyre a couple of hours ago. He told me that he hasn't seen them in the gathering. We have no idea where they are. Once we locate them, they will be arrested. I'll keep you informed."

Late that afternoon, the three-car police convoy arrived at the northeastern part of the Mwanza District. After parking the police car at the previously selected dirt road on an isolated hill near the Mozambique border, the senior officer approached the blue station wagon behind him and ordered the driver to position the car near the immediate edge of the cliff. After the station wagon was parked close to the ledge, he reached the back seat and grabbed the sledge hammer and the shovels. Placing them on the ground, he turned toward the driver.

"Before it gets dark, we must finish this job. Wait for me here."

He walked back to the police car he had been driving and pulled out Dick Matenje roughly from the backseat.

Handcuffed and hooded, Matenje loudly protested, "Where are we? Why are you doing this?"

The senior police officer, ignoring Matenje's questions, pushed him next to the blue station wagon. He then asked his victim to kneel down. When Matenje started shouting and resisting, the officer, getting behind his victim, kicked his back hard, causing Matenje to fall flat on his face. Picking up the sledgehammer, he stood next to the victim struggling to get on his feet. Placing his right booth on his victim's back, he forced Matenje to fall back on the ground. He then slowly raised the sledgehammer overhead, and with no hesitation, brought it down forcefully on the back of his victim's head. He repeated this action several times until the victim stopped moving. Stepping back, he threw the sledgehammer on the ground and ordered the driver to continue hitting the victim's head with the shovel until he stopped breathing.

He then called the officer standing nearby to bring another victim next to the station wagon to continue with their murderous plan. Within thirty minutes, four bludgeoned victims lay motionless on the blood-soaked ground. After making sure they were all dead, the police officers removed the cuffs and bloody hoods from the corpses. Then, they carried each body into the station wagon, placing them in sitting positions before pushing the car over the cliff. The police officers calmly watched it plunge into the deep ravine, rolling violently toward the riverbed below. As it fell toward the river, the car, landing upside-down on a pile of stubby trees and thick bushes, came to a full stop at approximately sixty meters below the ridge.

Looking at the car's exposed underframe below, the senior officer shook his head side to side and murmured, "Too bad! I was hoping it would disappear into the river."

After shoveling fresh soil over the bloodstained ground, the police officers returned to Mikuyu prison.

That evening, the senior officer called John Tembo and reported the successful completion of the bloody assignment. After hearing the gruesome details, John Tembo commented, "If the car is discovered by a passerby and reported to the police, there might be an inquiry that we cannot control. That should not be allowed to happen. You should arrange with one of your trusted police officers in Mwanza to discover the car and report it directly to your office. When the car is recovered, quickly get it destroyed. You must get the bodies placed in sealed coffins to be delivered to the families with instructions for immediate burial. Stay in control of this situation and don't involve anyone from the press. We will inform the newspapers about the car accident later. You and your team should remain silent about this matter."

John Tembo visited President Banda the night before the news of the car accident that killed four Parliamentarians were published by the newspapers. He informed the President about the incident and suggested that since the fugitives were trying to leave the country to escape police detention, there should not be officially sanctioned burial services for the deceased parliamentarians. Banda agreed.

Before leaving the palace, Tembo stopped by Mama Kadzamira's quarters. Hearing the true story behind the car accident, Kadzamira asked, "Why didn't you let them escape to Mozambique if that was their intention?"

"They weren't going to Mozambique. They were heading for the party headquarters in Blantyre to organize the party members against us. I could not allow that to happen; it would have been the end for us both."

Looking worried, Kadzamira nervously replied, "I don't like what you've done. We could have coped with the political pressure coming from the party members. Now, with this uncalled violence, you placed us in extreme danger. If the old man figures it out, we're doomed. We have to make sure he never learns the truth. Are you sure you can keep the murderers silent?"

"Yes, I can. Just make sure Banda remains isolated and away from our enemies."

"That's impossible. We can only delay the truth coming out in the open. Sooner or later, he will find out!"

That evening, she joined the old president for dinner. It was obvious that the President was disturbed by the fates of Dick Matenje and his parliamentarian friends.

Staring blankly at his half-empty plate, Banda mumbled, "Something isn't right about this accident. They weren't aware that they would be arrested. I wonder why they tried to escape to Mozambique. What do you think about this, Mama?"

"It is possible that someone in Parliament informed them about their upcoming arrest."

Still staring blankly at the plate in front of him, Banda responded, "Let's see what tomorrow's newspapers will say."

The newspapers repeated exactly what John Tembo had already reported to the President. Even so, this bloody incident had a great impact on the President's mind. Though he was not yet aware that the murders were carried out by the police under the direct order of John Tembo, President Banda refrained from nominating him as his successor. Somehow, Banda no longer trusted the man and a short while later, he released Tembo from his duties as the Governor of the Reserve Bank and sent him for an indefinite period to Washington D.C. to learn the basics of the democratic operations in the United States Congress.

Two years later, John Tembo returned to Malawi. Mama Kadzamira, noticing the change in Banda's attitude toward her uncle, slowly distanced herself from her uncle's bloody politics. Instead, she focused her attention on taking care of the aging President. By then, the bloody 'Mwanza Four' incident, as it was called by the national press, had faded from public discourse but it remained strongly etched in the public's mind. During the following few years, when some rumors about the 'Mwanza Four' incident reached Banda's ears, he ignored them as hearsay. But eventually, the truth about the Mwanza Four incident had spread widely all over the country; the effects of which would be felt during the upcoming national referendum and the general election.

***

Over the next six years, because of his declining health, the President was no longer involved in the management of the policies he personally had instigated. He occasionally demanded reports from his underlings about the status of agricultural development particularly related to cash-crop activities and food security. The senior staff surrounding him, controlled by Mama Kadzamira, told the elderly president that everything was fine and the people were happy. In fact, cases of child undernourishment and infant deaths were increasing over the past several years. On rare circumstances, when President Banda requested field visits, properly set and well attended stages with dancing mbumbas were orchestrated to misrepresent the actual reality. It worked and the President was happy with the level of progress while there actually were noticeable increases in the levels of corruption and financial mismanagement of increasingly scarce public funds. Particularly, the unpleasant news about the March 1992 bloody riots in Blantyre, instigated by Irish Catholic priests, never reached Banda's ears.

By early 1993, President Banda was now a ninety-five years-old man with serious health problems. He lived primarily in his own imagination, dreaming that all was well with his country. Feeling his age, he decided it was time either to declare a successor or introduce some form of democracy for the people to choose the next president. For the following months, he remained undecided about which direction to take. He discussed this matter with Mama Kadzamira and a few of his close advisors; they came up with the idea of having a referendum to let the people decide. The suggested referendum would ask the public to choose either the continuation of the existing one-party political system, which would result in Banda selecting a successor, or a move toward establishing a multi-party system resulting in an election to identify the next president. The idea to hold a referendum was an acceptable proposition for the aging President. After indicating that he had agreed to their proposal, President Banda asked, "What do you think the result of the referendum would be? Please be honest about it."

Advisors apprehensively looked at Mama Kadzamira to provide an answer to Banda's question. Smiling broadly, she replied, "There is no doubt about it that the people of Malawi, who respect and admire their Ngwazi, will vote for the continuation of your presidency."

With a stern look on his face, the President further inquired, "What if the people vote for a multiparty democracy?"

Raising their hands in the air, the senior advisors replied in unison, "That will never happen."

Now smiling, Kamuzu Banda replied, "You never know beforehand the result of a referendum. If the people of Malawi are ready for democracy, they will vote for a multiparty option. If that is the result of the referendum, we have to proceed to hold multiparty elections in due time. Believe me, that would not bother me a bit. I said it at the beginning of my presidency that one of my primary goals is to bring democracy to Malawi. Maybe now is the good time to ask people about their preferred choice of government. Please proceed with proper preparations for the referendum to take place as soon as possible."

The referendum was conducted on June 14, 1993. Over sixty-four percent of the people voted for multiparty democracy; overwhelmingly rejecting the one-party state run by its founder, the Life President Hastings Kamuzu Banda. Even though President Banda had resolved himself to accept the people's choice, the rejection of his forty-years-old one-party state model bruised his ego. His senior advisors explained to Banda that the Mwanza Four incident that happened ten years earlier had a substantial negative impact on the public's opinion about his presidency. Hearing the gruesome details of the incident for the first time, Banda was extremely disturbed. The result of the referendum and all other affairs of the state stressed the aging President so much that in early October of 1993 he suffered a cranial hemorrhage and was transported to a hospital in Johannesburg, South Africa for emergency brain surgery.

While the President was away in South Africa, the government's affairs were managed by a three-member presidential commission led by Gwanda Chakuamba, Secretary General of the Malawi Congress Party. In December 1993, the presidential commission, preparing for the upcoming multiparty elections planned for the summer of 1994, had decided to disarm the members of the Malawi Young Pioneers, a quasi-military extension of the Malawi Congress Party. As a result of the executive order coming from the President's office, the army and police forces approached the Young Pioneer's headquarters in Lilongwe to disarm the members of the organization. A bloody battle erupted, resulting in thirty deaths. Following this incident, many Young Pioneer members escaped to Mozambique.

Recovering from his brain surgery, President Banda returned to Malawi at the end of December 1993. Taking the reins of government back into his hands, he issued many executive orders to activate constitutional and administrative changes necessary for the coming free elections, including the cancellation of life-presidency, repeal of the one-party state, turning over the operations of quasi-parastatal and private entities established under his name to the state authorities and abolishing organizations like the Young Pioneers.

Initially, feeling his age, he was not planning to run for the presidency during the coming election. The people surrounding him, including Mama Kadzamira, convinced him that the people of Malawi still adored him and would like him to continue as their president. At first, he brushed those comments aside, but eventually, he decided to travel around the country to test the claims of the cronies surrounding him. Sadly, he again failed to take proper precautions to prevent the cronies from preparing phony, orchestrated stages for him to be welcomed enthusiastically during all his visits to towns and villages across the country.

Following these staged visits, President Banda, mistakenly assuming that his people still believed in him, finally decided to run for reelection. Under the newly established constitutional guidelines, each political party would nominate a presidential and vice-presidential candidate. Banda, now fully aware of the 1983 Mwanza Four incident, decided against choosing John Tembo as his running mate. Instead, he selected a senior Malawi Congress Party member, Gwanda Chakuamba. In the meantime, Mama Kadzamira, noticing that her uncle was effectively removed from the existing political power structure, decided to stay away from her uncle's inappropriate political activities. She remained loyal to the elderly President and continued delivering her caring attention to Banda's daily needs.

The results of the May 1994 multiparty election, though a complete disaster for President Banda and the Malawi Congress party, was actually a victory for the democratization process enacted by Kamuzu Banda himself. A former cabinet minister, Bakili Muluzi, representing the United Democratic Front, won the election and became the new president of Malawi. A few days later, during the publicly televised presidential transition ceremony, former President Kamuzu Banda congratulated the newly elected President Bakili Muluzi for a well-run campaign and thanked the people of Malawi for their devotion to democratic principles. He then delivered an elaborate speech about the policies he and his party had accomplished since the first days of Malawi's independence. He ended his eloquent speech with a heartfelt, sincere apology for the inappropriate and unethical activities that happened during his administration. He bowed his head and said, "I alone am responsible for the wrong doings that resulted in pain and suffering for my citizens."

In January of 1995 - six months after the presidential transition ceremony - Kamuzu Banda, John Tembo, Mama Kadzamira, three former cabinet members and a retired parliamentarian received summons from the High Court of Malawi. In the summons, all were charged with the 1983 murders of the Mwanza Four: Dick Matenje, Aaron Gadama, David Chiwanga and John Sangala. As the trial had progressed, Kamuzu Banda, due to his old age and ailments, was excused from attending the court proceedings. The former president was asked to prepare a written document to be presented to the court through his lawyers. In the document, Banda declared that he had only ordered the arrests of the four parliamentarians. He stated that a few days after he had issued the order for their arrests, he learned from the police that the four parliamentarians, as they were trying to escape to Mozambique, died in a car accident. He further declared, *"Until very recently I was unaware that they were killed by state security forces. Therefore, I have played no role in their murders."*

After months of deliberations, the High Court decided that there was no direct evidence linking the accused to the murders. Though there was clear evidence that the victims were brutally murdered by a special police unit, the High Court decided not to take legal action against the identified policemen, who had declared, without identifying the source, that they just were following orders emanating from a higher authority. For reasons of political expediency, the High Court decided not to identify the higher authority that had issued the order to kill the parliamentarians. By that decision, the High Court of Malawi buried the 'Mwanza Four' assassination files into the historical annals of criminal injustice.

The following day, the High Court's verdict was delivered to Kamuzu Banda, living in a private house he owned in Lilongwe, he asked Mama Kadzamira to read the verdict.

After reading it loudly, Kadzamira smiled broadly.

"Kamuzu, I think this is a very fair judgement; don't you think so?"

"No, I don't. I now know and you have been aware of it all along that your dear uncle was behind this horrible incident. Worst of it all, the whole nation knew about it and the High Court decided to bury it for the sake of political expediency. Even so, I am happy with the Court's decision because it will protect the politically sensitive aspects of our newly established democracy. Sometimes, for the sake of political stability, it is best to forgive and forget."

Staring pensively at Kadzamira, Banda continued, "We both now realize for sure that your uncle should never have a chance to rule Malawi. If I knew what he did in 1983, I wouldn't have sent him to the United States to learn about democratic process. Now I fully admit that I was wrong in not trusting the good intentions of Dick Matenje and his parliamentarian friends. They only wanted to prevent Tembo from succeeding me. It is so sad that, without realizing, Matenje and his three colleagues died for the cause of establishing democracy in Malawi. The High Court's decision now enables us to move forward without digging into past mistakes."

***

Banda spent the following two years peacefully at his home in Lilongwe, with occasional meetings with visitors from the Malawi Congress Party and various national and global journalists. Under the tender care of Mama Kadzamira, he remained relatively healthy until early November of 1997 when he came down with pneumonia. During his treatment at a local hospital, he fell into a coma. He was immediately transferred, together with Mama Kadzamira, to the Garden City Medical Clinic in Johannesburg, South Africa. After ten days of intensive care, he recovered and regained full mental awareness.

Mama Kadzamira, jubilantly reported the former president's recovery to the Malawi Congress Party leadership in Blantyre. A few days later, a committee, comprising three senior Congress Party leaders, visited Banda in the clinic's private recovery room in Johannesburg. They brought many bouquets of flowers and a colorful Party flag with a proud profile of a black rooster in its center. Pinning the flag on the wall next to Banda's bed, they laid the flowers on the adjacent small table. Kamuzu Banda, now smiling broadly, sat up in his bed and thanked his fellow party members for their visit. He then requested a brief oral report on the recent affairs of the Party.

The visitors nervously reported that John Tembo was now campaigning for the vacant chairmanship of the Party. One senior party member cautiously stated, "If Tembo gets himself selected as Chairman, he will be nominated as our presidential candidate for the upcoming election."

This news irritated the former president so much that he raised his voice and proclaimed, "Tembo's attempt to run for president will disturb the democratization process in Malawi. This should not be allowed to happen."

His face now contorted with anger, Banda declared, "I will soon return to Malawi. Please organize for me a meeting with the general membership; I will convince them not to elect that conniving, rotten man as Chairman. Thank you for your kind visit. I'll soon see you in Lilongwe."

Silently sitting in the corner of the room, Mama Kadzamira took mental notes of the conversation. That evening, still hoping that her uncle would become the next president of Malawi, she called Tembo and informed him of Banda's plan to prevent him from becoming Chairman of the Party. She ended the conversation with a warning: "Organize your followers to counter Banda's efforts to block you from becoming Chairman, without which you cannot become a presidential candidate in next year's election."

Three days later, on the evening of November 24, 1997, a lanky clinic orderly brought two dinner trays for Kamuzu Banda and Mama Kadzamira to the private room they jointly occupied. Kadzamira, after helping Banda eat his meal, ate hers as she watched her favorite television program. A short while later, both Banda and Kadzamira were sound asleep.

After midnight, the same orderly quietly entered the room. Locking the door behind him, he first checked on Mama Kadzamira to confirm that she was completely under the influence of the drug he discreetly had added to the dinner hours earlier. He then moved toward the bed where Banda slept. He shook the old man's shoulder to test the effect of the ingested drug. When there was no response, he took the pillow from under Banda's head and placed it over his face. Suddenly remembering that a person killed in that way may have facial contortions, he lifted the pillow and placed it back under Banda's head. He then took out a couple surgical gloves out his pocket. Wearing the gloves, he placed his left hand over the old man's mouth and with his right hand, he squeezed his victim's nostrils shut. Immediately afterwards, a few minor jerky spasms shook the old man's body. Gazing at the colorful party flag pinned on the wall and occasionally checking his wristwatch, he kept his hands on his victim's face. A short while later, he slowly pulled his hands away. Suddenly, hearing the high pitch sound of air being released from the dead man's lungs, he jumped back. Checking his victim's pulse to make sure that he was dead, he smiled broadly and whispered, "Banda, you old rooster! That was your last crow."

On the morning of November 25, 1997, Mama Kadzamira, upon waking up, noticed that Banda was not breathing. She immediately called on the emergency medical staff. A few minutes later, she was informed that Banda had expired in his sleep during the early hours of the night. His body was taken to a special room for further examination. After the death certificate was issued, the body was prepared for the final journey to Malawi.

On the third of December 1997, the Parliament of Malawi declared a day of mourning and ordered the national flags to fly half-mast. During the official funeral ceremony, thousands of Malawians lined up along the streets to honor their former president who had passed away at the age of ninety-nine. A few days later, the former President-for-life, the founding father of the Republic of Malawi, Doctor Ngwazi Hastings Kamuzu Banda was buried in a solid gold casket in his birth village of Chiwengo in the District of Kasungu.

A few days after the burial ceremony had taken place, the manager of the Garden City Medical Clinic in Johannesburg made a phone call to Malawi. On the phone, the manager reported that the doctor, who had posthumously examined Banda, indicated on the death certificate that the former president had died from induced respiratory failure. He then asked, "If I turn in this death certificate to the authorities, there will be a police investigation. What do you suggest I do?"

The manager received a clear and definite reply: "Immediately destroy the death certificate. More money will be transferred for you to pay the doctor to remain silent."

A year later, John Tembo got himself elected as Chairman of the Malawi Congress Party, becoming a presidential candidate in the next two elections. Banda was no longer around to impede this cunning politician from attaining his lifelong ambition to become president. It was prevented by the voters of Malawi, who twice rejected him at the ballot box. Following those electoral defeats, John Tembo retired from public life in 2013. At the time this story was written, John Tembo, now eighty-eight years-old, spends his remaining days in a retirement home in Lilongwe.

After Hastings Kamuzu Banda, a no-nonsense, self-made medical doctor and the hardline dictator of Malawi, had passed away, his longtime partner Mama Kadzamira settled into a calm and tranquil life in her house in Lilongwe. During the following year, she tried to collect Banda's inheritance of approximately four-hundred thousand dollars deposited in various London banks. Because she was not able to present the death certificate, banks refused to pay her. Mama Kadzamira, resultantly, had to survive with the monthly allowances bequeathed to her by Banda until her death at the age of seventy-eight in 2018.

***

From the time when the first democratic elections were held in 1994 and onward, a presidential election successfully has taken place every five years in Malawi. Every one of these elections was freely and fairly conducted. Five presidents, four men and one woman from three different parties, served their country well. When the second president, Bakili Muluzi, attempted to modify the two-term constitutional limit in 2004, the Parliament overwhelmingly rejected his appeal. Furthermore, the questionable results of the general election in 2019 was repealed by the constitutional court. When the election was repeated in 2020, the overwhelming victory by the opposition candidate Lazarus Chakwera clearly indicated that democracy has become a way of political life and rooted itself deeply in Malawi, which still remains one of the poorest countries in sub-Saharan Africa.

No one would have guessed that the old doctor Hastings Kamuzu Banda, who was considered one of the world's worst dictators during his reign, would have played an instrumental role in establishing a deep-rooted democratic governance in his beloved country before passing away in 1997.

A few days before his death, Banda had told Mama Kadzamira, his official hostess and partner for thirty-five years, his last wish: "I hope there will never be another dictator in Malawi."

So far, Kamuzu Banda's last wish seems to hold true for this remarkable country.

One Kwacha Banknote of Malawi

The Emblem of the Malawi Congress Party

THE PALAWA GENOCIDE

1804-1876

in

LUTRUWITA
[10,000 BC – *1803*];

aka VAN DIEMEN'S LAND
[*1803 – 1856*];

aka TASMANIA
[*1856 – Present*]

©Omer Ertur
2021

Australia

Lutruwita; Van Diemen's Land; Tasmania

Flinders İsland, between Tasmania and Victoria Province of Australia

STOLEN LAND AND THE GENOCIDE OF THE PALAWA OF LUTRUWITA

Until we give back to the black man just a bit of the land that was his and give it back without provisos, without strings to snatch it back, without anything but complete generosity of spirit in concession for the evil we have done to him – until we do that, we shall remain what we have always been so far, a people without integrity; not a nation, but a community of thieves.

XAVIER HERBERT

ULURU STATEMENT – DECLARATION MAKARRATA

Proper acknowledgement of the genocide and the necessary due respects must be established towards the rights of the Palawa, the original inhabitants of the Island of Lutruwita.

Dutch Explorer Abel Janszoon Tasman's Ships [1642]
Warship Haemskerk and Transport-ship Zeehaen

THE PALAWA GENOCIDE

Prehistoric Dreamtime of the Palawa on Lutruwita

Approximately 40,000 years ago, many prehistoric tribes lived on and around the crowded shoreline settlements of south Asia and east Africa. From these settlements emerged many brave souls who courageously ventured over the vast oceans to discover new lands to settle and have better opportunities to survive. After centuries of island hopping, these adventurous souls reached the shores of the uninhabited Oceania Continent. These ancient explorers are the actual and true discoverers of the new continent. Over the following 30,000 years, these newly arrived humans in Oceania multiplied as they spread and settled across the continent's mostly arid land mass.

At the end of the last ice age, almost ten thousand years ago, the rising sea level resulted in the disappearance of a nearly 240-kilometer-long strip of land that connected Oceania to its vast southern peninsula, thus resulting in the creation of the island of Lutruwita, as it was then called by its original inhabitants, the Palawa. On this completely isolated island, nature's flora and fauna, including its hunter-gatherer human inhabitants, remained intact and unchanged for the coming ten thousand years without any foreign human interruption until the year 1642.

Similar to the original inhabitants of Oceania, now called the Aborigines, the Palawa of Lutruwita were also pre-historic, stone-age hunter-gatherers who had neither discovered the wheel nor learned how to domesticate plants and animals. Since Oceania and Lutruwita were completely isolated from other continents of the world, their inhabitants remained unexposed to any of the agricultural and technological advancements that had occurred in the primitive societies of the African, European and Asian continents, such as written languages, subsistence agriculture and domestication of plants and animals. No other human society, except the Aborigines of Oceania and the Palawa of Lutruwita, has ever been isolated for such a long period of time, causing them to remain in their stone-age existence until the arrival of the European explorers at the end of the 18th century.

Unfortunately, without realizing that they have discovered a historically and scientifically valuable snap-shot back into the socio-cultural and evolutionary development of humankind, many European explorers and the resultant colonial administrations erroneously assumed that the original inhabitants of Oceania Continent and Lutruwita Island belonged to a certain primitive sub-specie of humankind much closer to primates. Furthermore, toward the middle of 19th century, the European scientific community utilized the missing-link concept of the evolutionary theory to prove their wrong assumptions about the original inhabitants of Oceania and Lutruwita to be members of sub-human species.

European Rediscovery of Oceania and Lutruwita

On August 1642, Dutch explorer Abel Janszoon Tasman, thirty-nine-year-old commander of the two-ship fleet that belonged to Dutch East India Company, namely the 120-ton warship Haemskerk and 200-ton transport-ship Zeehaen, piloted by Ide Tjaerts Holleman and Gerritt Jansz respectively, departed Jakarta for the Island of Mauritius in the Indian Ocean. After spending some time in Mauritius, the two-ship fleet continued its journey first southward and then turned sharply eastward. By late November, the fleet was sailing toward the shores of an unknown island 240 kilometers south of an undiscovered continent.

As dawn broke on November 26th 1642, a sailor, perched atop Haemskerk's main-mast, shouted that he had seen land. Captain Tjaerts immediately roused Commander Tasman. Rushing up to the main deck, Abel Tasman asked the navigation officer to identify the exact location of the sighted land. Moments later, the navigator replied, "East 94th by South 42nd."

The fleet spent a few days circumventing the southern and eastern shores of the island. Commander Tasman then ordered his captains to move safely towards the shoreline on the eastern tip of the island, possibly near today's Port Arthur. After lowering sails and dropping anchor, the Dutch ships faced the virgin eastern beaches of Lutruwita, as it was called since the end of the last ice-age by the Palawa, the indigenous people of the island.

Gazing across the virgin sandy shoreline he was facing, Commander Tasman, smiling broadly, spoke to his navigation officer: "*It seems we've discovered a sizable, uninhabited island. We will place our flag on the shoreline to claim it for Netherlands.*"

Commander Tasman then ordered the captain to send a boat to the shore with a few sailors to plant the Dutch flag on the beachhead. Turning around on his heels, he walked briskly back to his quarters to enter this newly discovered island into the ship's navigation records. As he entered information about the newly discovered and assumedly uninhabited island, he decided to name it 'Van Diemen's Land' after the Governor General of the Dutch East India Company.

As the Dutch ships were approaching the shoreline, two young indigenous Palawa women, diving for oysters and abalone in deep water, surfaced for air. They noticed in the distant horizon two large wooden ships coming toward the shoreline. They were amazed with the size of the ships and the large pristine white sails on their masts that were also adorned with colorful flags of Netherlands. Apprehensive of these immense wooden ships approaching the shore, the divers hurriedly swam to the shore and retreated into a cluster of thick bushes lining the sandy beach. Well hidden, they discreetly watched a small boat land and disembark five sailors. With wide open eyes, they curiously observed the Dutch sailors hurriedly dig a deep hole near the high end of the beachhead. The sailors then securely buried a three meters long wooden post into the ground with a tri-colored Dutch flag fluttering at its tip.

Not comprehending the meaning of the sailors' actions and the unexpected presence of the huge boats, the young women divers decided to return to their campground to report what they had seen: the first ever encounter with a group of white-skinned people traveling on huge wooden boats with white sails surrounded by colorful flags. They rushed to the clan chief's hut and excitedly described what they had been exposed to. They loudly told the old chief that after the big boats moored at the bay, a small boat with fully clothed white skinned people came to the shore and planted a tall wooden post adorned with a colorful piece of cloth onto the beachhead.

Confused about what he had heard from the women, the chief remained silent for some time. For him and his people, the whole world only consisted of the island on which all the Palawa had lived for as long as many millennia; there were no other people and no other places on earth except for the mysterious people and mythical places described in their religious Dreamtime stories.

The old Palawa chief calmly replied, *"It is possible that you came across some roaming spirits from Dreamtime. We shall go to the beach and investigate it tomorrow morning."*

The next morning, the two Palawa women returned to the beach together with the elderly clan chief and several tribesmen. By then, both ships were long gone. There was no evidence to prove what the two indigenous women had reported to the chief except the mysterious flag post. As they gathered around the flag post, the clan chief, now smiling broadly, ordered a tribesman to pull the flag post out of the ground. The young tribesman respectfully brought the flag-post and placed it in front of the elderly chief. After removing the colorful rag from the post, the chief ordered the young man sitting next to him to sharpen the tip of the hardwood pole.

"With that new spear sent by our ancestors," the chief gleefully announced, *"I will be able to hunt the largest kangaroo on the island."*

Throwing the large colorful Dutch flag over his shoulders, he then loudly added, *"Our ancestors sent me an excellent gift to keep warm during the coming winter."*

•••

For the next 130 years, the European explorer Abel Tasman's visit to Lutruwita Island became a local legend, more like a Dreamtime myth for the indigenous inhabitants. Neither the local Palawa nor Commander Tasman could ever imagine that two centuries later the Island of Lutruwita would be renamed Tasmania, honoring the Dutch explorer, who, without realizing that the new island he had discovered had been inhabited for many millennia, quickly assigned the island a name and declared ownership for his country to exploit its natural resources.

Commander Tasman, who somehow missed the chance to rediscover the continent of Oceania just 240 kilometers north, by chance rediscovered Lutruwita Island and named it after his boss Van Diemen working for the Dutch East India Company. After planting his country's flag on the newly found island, he commenced his eastward journey. During the following year, he rediscovered New Zealand, Tonga and the Fiji Islands. Upon returning to Jakarta in 1643, he informed his company headquarters in Amsterdam about his rediscoveries. Although the Europeans had placed the island of Van Diemen's Land on the maps of the time, fortunate for the inhabitants of Lutruwita, the island was completely ignored by the European explorers for the next 130 years.

After the rediscovery the continent of Oceania by the British explorer James Cook in 1770, the French explorer Marc-Joseph Marion du Fresne arrived in 1772 at Lutruwita Island, named by the European mapmakers as Van Diemen's Land. He, like Tasman, mistakenly thought the island was uninhabited and thus felt justified to claim the island for France under the colonial rule of *terra nullius*, 'uninhabited land'. Soon after Marion du Fresne's visit, another French explorer, Julien Crozet visited Van Diemen's Land and ordered his well-armed sailors to investigate the shoreline. Immediately after landing, the French sailors unexpectedly came upon a group of Palawa hunters in search of kangaroos. Surprised and fearful of the naked black hunters with spears and hefty clubs, the sailors shot and killed several Palawa tribesmen and rushed back to their ship.

Shocked with the slaughter of their comrades by roaring sticks, a Palawa term for rifles, the surviving hunters ran away in horror into the bush to hide.

The French sailors, who had wrongly assumed the island was uninhabited, reported the incident to their captain that they were attacked by a large group of wild naked black men with spears and clubs. Captain Crozet opted to sail away from Van Diemen's Land immediately. Upon returning to France, he reported to philosopher Jean-Jacques Rosseau that the savages living on Van Diemen's Land were definitely not the famed noble savages assumed by the philosopher; they were more like grotesque, ignoble savages looking and behaving like orangutans.

Soon after the French explorers' visits, the British explorer Captain James Cook also decided to visit Van Diemen's Land. His sailors landed on a small island's sandy shore across from the main island near today's city of Hobart. The Nuenonne clan of the local Palawa lived on this small island. Assuming that the white-skinned sailors were the ghosts of their ancestors, a large group of local Nuenonne clan members apprehensively but peacefully approached the British sailors on the shoreline. When several sailors indiscreetly molested several Palawa females by touching their breasts and buttocks, the tribesmen became agitated. The tribe's elderly chief, realizing that these were real people not the ghosts of their ancestors, quickly and firmly ordered everyone to withdraw from the beach.

Captain Cook, watching this unusual incident from the ship's deck with an amazed curiosity, assumed that these almost naked original inhabitants of the island were simple-minded sub-human species without dignity or any social responsibility. Upon returning to London, he reported his wrong conclusions about the inhabitants of Van Diemen's Land to the British Colonial Government.

Also in 1792, another French explorer, Captain Bruni D'Entrecastenaux visited the same location and reached a similar conclusion about the inhabitants of Lutruwita. During those visits, both the French and British explorers erroneously assumed that the local inhabitants belonged to a primitive sub-human species. A similar wrong conclusion was also reached during the latter part of the 19th century by the European scientific community; that the original inhabitants of Oceania and Tasmania belonged to a group of subhuman species that warranted further studies to possibly discover the missing link of the Darwinian evolutionary theory.

Because of the oversimplified and inappropriate Euro-centric superiority-based racist justifications and assumptions about the indigenous inhabitants of the newly discovered continent of Oceania and the island of Van Diemen's Land to be members of a sub-human species, the British Government decided to fully colonize both places during the latter part of the 18th century to initiate British settlements and to establish correctional facilities.

At the time of French and British explorers' landings, Lutruwita had an estimated population of over ten thousand inhabitants in nine tribal groupings that spread across the island's 68,000 square kilometer land mass and the 334 small surrounding islands. Prior to the end of the Ice Age, sometime around ten thousand BC, the original tribes of the island, the Palawa People, presumably walked from the continent of Oceania onto Lutruwita, which was then a peninsula. When the Ice Age ended, the sea level rose and formed the 242-kilometer-wide Bass Straight isolating Lutruwita from the continent of Oceania.

The Palawa were an ecologically dependent and environmentally conservative, stone-age hunter-gatherer people who respected and preserved their natural environment. They survived for the next ten millennia within the natural and ecological capacity of their immediate island environment. The arrival of the fair-skinned people during the 18th and 19th centuries exposed the Palawa to racially demeaning attitudes of the French and British explorers. The Palawa slowly began to realize and consequently acknowledged the existence of a broader, threateningly violent world beyond the boundaries of their isolated island.

Before the arrival of the British, Lutruwita Island's territory was divided among several Palawa tribal groups, who spoke different dialects and controlled their own hunting-gathering areas. Tribes survived by gathering edible vegetables, fruits and roots and also by hunting land animals, sea mammals and diving for shellfish. During the warm summer months, the Palawa tribes moved in bands or family groups of 15 to 50 people through the open forests and moorlands to roam the island's interior. During the colder winter months, they relocated to coastal areas. Occasionally, tribal bands gathered for a Corroboree, a dance and chant ceremony celebrating important community and spiritual events. During these Corroborees, Dreamtime stories were told to children, teaching them to respect their natural environment, the elderly and share food with others.

In this primitive, patriarchal stone-age society, tribal members utilized various hunting weapons that were produced by the local craftsmen: wooden spears, large wooden clubs and flaked-stone knives. Bone cooking implements, basketry and bark canoes for coastal travel were also produced by the local Palawa craftsmen. On Lutruwita today, there exist several Palawa traditional rock carvings depicting animals, natural objects and conventionalized symbols of their Dreamtime religious beliefs.

The Arrival of the British Convicts and Settlers

In 1803, the British Colonial Office in London decided to establish correctional facilities on Van Diemen's Land. The intent was to relocate the excess prison populations of England, Scotland and Ireland to various locations far away from the motherland. Meanwhile, different from the ongoing British colonial involvements in Africa and India, the Christian communities of England appeared uninterested in sending missionaries to Oceania and Van Diemen's Land primarily because they had assumed teaching Bible to sub-human species living on those places would have been an impossible task.

The first group of British ships full of British convicts, prison guards and military personnel landed on Van Diemen's Land in 1804. This landing marked the beginning of a series of violent encounters between the dark-skinned Palawa and the pale-skinned British, whom the Palawa referred as *'raege'*, devil incarnate.

The first permanent British penal colony was established near Risdon Cove on the island's southeastern shore. Due to the aggressive acts of a drunk, racist officer, the British military slaughtered nearly 60 indigenous Palawa men, women and children soon after landing at the shore; thus, launching a series of bloody attacks against the indigenous people to clear the land of their original owners while sexually abusing Palawa women and girls.

Since the early days of British military and the convict population's arrival at Lutruwita, the lack of females among the white settlers was a great mystery for the Palawa. In 1805, a group of Palawa men were invited to visit a British warship, referred by the Palawa as a 'floating wooden island'. On board the warship, the Palawa visitors only noticed many male sailors and plenty of dogs that did not exist on Lutruwita of that time. Noticing that there were no women on the ship, the visitors were highly perplexed. Upon returning to their tribal campground, they reported to their chief that on the warship they noticed many men and plenty of strange looking animals that were smaller than a kangaroo but bigger than a possum. They then abruptly informed the chief that since there were no females aboard the warship, they wondered aloud about the white people's reproductive ways.

Soon after their arrival at Lutruwita, several groups of the freely roaming convict settlers and military personnel formed violent gangs called the 'Bushrangers', who kidnapped, raped and killed local women and girls. Unfortunately, the British Government's permissive attitude toward these horrific acts of predation and cruelty toward to Palawa women clearly indicated the beginning of a state-sponsored extermination policy toward the indigenous people of the island. Unfortunate for the Palawa, many of the frequently occurring violent encounters with 'raege', pale-skinned people with evil intentions, soon evolved into a desperate sense of hopelessness and a long-term defensive stance. Such a defensive stance soon turned into 'David versus Goliath' type of bloody conflicts within which there were no chances of survival for the small number of unarmed indigenous inhabitants, save a miracle. A possible miracle would have taken place if there was a violence prevention policy supported by the State that was formulated with a strong law-enforcement potential by the presumably civilized British Colonial Administration to protect the rights of the indigenous people of Lutruwita. If such a morally and historically sensitive public policy toward the indigenous cultures was ever formulated, the British colonial rulers would have assumed a more responsible attitude toward protecting the rights of the newly discovered primitive stone-age people rather than treating them as wild animals. Establishment of such a civilized, humanistic public policy in the expanding British Empire would have become the miracle that might have marked the beginning of global policies to preserve and protect the basic human rights of the indigenous peoples on all continents including the Aborigines of Oceania and the Palawa of Lutruwita.

The British Government's disregardful and uncaring attitude toward the indigenous inhabitants of Lutruwita caused substantial increases in violence against the Palawa, resulting in a stark realization by the local tribes that these pale-skinned evil people invaded their island with an intention to completely eliminate them. In time, multiplicities of horrific violent experiences with the invaders had become deeply etched into the living memory of the surviving Palawa. Nearly a decade after their island was invaded by the pale-skinned British, the dark-skinned Palawa decided to fight against the occupiers to protect their lands and families.

During the beginning of the first decade of the 19th century, Van Diemen's Land was being fully colonized by the British Empire. A new form of colonial administration was introduced to create safe havens for the roaming convicts and newly arrived British settlers, who were primarily interested in land-intensive agricultural, animal husbandry and forestry logging businesses. The British colonial administration also allowed several sealer establishments, who were hunting seals in the seas around the Bass Straight and the coves of Lutruwita, to establish temporary seasonal camps at the northeastern beaches of the Island. The Palawa tribes, because of the negative impact of the earlier encounters with roaming convicts, undisciplined military personnel and aggressive male white settlers, stayed away from the occasional sealer campsites. Yet, despite their efforts to remain away from the evil intentions of the sealers, many Palawa campgrounds were attacked, resulting in many local Palawa men being killed and many tribal women and girls taken to sealer camps as sex-slaves. Except for a few municipal ordinances that were introduced by local colonial authorities, there were no efforts by the municipal administrations to curtail these frequent violent acts that were regularly instigated by the convicts, settlers and sealers against the local Palawa families. Sealers, livestock-keepers, lumbermen and especially prisoners, coming from the lowest of income classes of England, Scotland and Ireland lacked education, cultural sensitivity and religious insight to treat the indigenous people of Lutruwita with the usual human affinity, understanding and care.

By 1810, as an extension of the earlier penal settlements in Australia, the British Government also decided to establish convict-labor based agricultural and pastoral settlements in the southeastern parts of Lutruwita, near today's Port Arthur. These sex-starved and often violent convict settlers regularly raped local women, took over Palawa hunting grounds, attacked indigenous campgrounds and indiscriminately killed male members of the Palawa.

Most of the newly arrived convicts were placed under minimum security supervision by the colonial authorities and allocated plots of viable land in the southeastern part of the island to grow essential subsistence crops and graze thousands of livestock. This policy of land distribution to convicts and the newly arriving British settlers resulted in obvious physical encroachment into Palawa living space and their tribal hunting-gathering grounds. Particularly, the arrival of white agricultural settlers, livestock-men and lumbermen, who were allowed to settle in wide-open plains and forested lands in the central and northern parts of the island, resulted, within a period of two decades, in the complete destruction of the indigenous inhabitants' natural environment suitable for hunting-gathering.

Palawa tribal family groupings traditionally survived in temporary campgrounds of 15 to 50 individuals who were well-aware of the ecological carrying capacity of the immediate natural environment. To protect the existing ecological balance, they were in constant movement and regularly utilized land-burning techniques to revitalize the natural capacity of the soil and encourage proliferation of game. The land grabbing white settlers and convicts focused instead on land-intensive agricultural and animal grazing activities, destroying nature's capacity to provide life sustaining proliferation of game, plants and roots that were essential for the survival of the hunter-gatherer Palawa people.

As more settlers and convicts arrived, the frequency of deadly clashes between white men and local tribes increased substantially. Many Palawa warriors, bravely but unsuccessfully defended their families with spears, clubs and knives against well-armed white settlers. The Palawa braves, armed with primitive weaponry, were no match for the white settlers armed with rifles and pistols. Resultantly, the surviving Palawa families sought to protect themselves and their families by moving away from the lands recently occupied by white settlers and convicts. Two decades after the arrival of white people to Lutruwita Island, almost all of the Palawa tribes in the southern parts of the island were forced to relocate to various inland plateaus and hilly northern regions with less natural capacity for foraging and hunting, resulting in malnutrition and starvation of many indigenous families. Starving Palawa tribes, now barely surviving in the central and northern parts of the island, had no choice but to raid the British farming, sheep-herding and forestry logging communities to acquire food, clothing and blankets.

After colonizing the Australian continent and subduing its indigenous inhabitants, the British Government in London was astonished by what was going on in Van Diemen's Land, particularly with the indigenous Palawa people's strong desire to be free. Unfortunately, rather than recognizing the natural rights of the local people and respecting the Palawa for their desire to be independent, the Royal Government instead chose to completely eliminate the local inhabitants. In time, this highly improper and immoral decision would become an embarrassing skeleton in the dark corners of the British Colonial closet.

The British colonial government's aggressive settlement policies between 1805 and 1825 clearly indicated that the Palawa people's resistance had begun successfully impending the colonization effort. Subsequently, many state-sponsored policies were introduced to support or simply to ignore the settler's violent attacks against the local inhabitants to make land available for new settlements. As the newly arrived settlers noticed that they were being allowed by the colonial authorities to eliminate the indigenous resistance mostly through terror and violence, the numbers of attacks on the local Palawa families substantially increased. As the Palawa lost their natural hunting and foraging lands, their women were also under constant threat of being kidnapped, raped and murdered. It was obvious from the beginning that the Palawa people, the original inhabitants of the Island, did not matter at all in the British colonial mentality, which considered the local inhabitants to be a group of primitive subhuman specie with no rights of existence.

...

The most well-known and one of the last surviving Palawa was a woman named Truganini. She was born in 1812 to the family of Rescherche Bay Nuenonne clan chief Mangerner. The clan lived near Oyster Cove on the western side of the D'Entrecasteaux Channel located at the southeast part of the island of Bruni, where Nuenonne clans of the Palawa tried to survive the arrival of prisoners and the land grabbing white settlers in 1804. Bruni was a very beautiful little island full of mutton birds, penguins, crayfish, abalone, oysters, scallops, swan eggs, wallaby and fur seals. Within a period of seven years after the arrival of sex-hungry convicts and the sealers, the vast hunting and gathering grounds of Nuenonne clan were considerably reduced and shoreline diving for shellfish by the clan women became prohibitively dangerous. It became nearly impossible for tribal hunters to find kangaroos and possums that were once plentiful on their pastoral lands. Furthermore, clan members were unable to roam their land to gather whatever nature offered them to eat. Obviously, the lifestyle with abundant food supply that the members of the Nuenonne clan were used to for thousands of years was now disappearing under their feet. They were actually being forced out of their own small island that was called Lunawanna Alonnah in the Nuenonne dialect of the Palawa language.

Regardless of what was happening on the Island of Lutruwita and the nearby small island of Bruni, [named after the French explorer Bruni D'Entrecasteaux], Truganini, as a child, grew up in a secure, peaceful tribal family atmosphere. Together with her parents and two sisters, she lived within an extended family of several uncles, aunts and cousins. She enjoyed her productive times with her mother gathering plants, roots and fruits for the family and loved teaching her male cousin Paraweena how to swim and dive underwater to gather shellfish near the rocky deep seashores of the Bruni Island. As she grew up to be a healthy young woman, her friendship with Paraweena grew closer. When she was almost fourteen, their relationship was accepted by the extended family for future marriage.

One warm summer day in 1826, Truganini was helping her fiancée dive for oysters. A small boat with four sealers from a ship near Bruni came to the shoreline and forced Truganini into their boat. As the sealers pulled away from the rocky shoreline, Paraweena surfaced and saw Truganini struggling with the sealers. He quickly swam to the boat to save his friend. Reaching the boat, he tried to get inside the boat to rescue Truganini. One of the sealers in the boat hit his head with a heavy piece of wood. Despite receiving several blows to his head, Paraweena kept on fighting to board the boat. Finally, another sealer drew his knife and stabbed the young man several times on his neck and shoulders. It was the last time Truganini saw her fiancée Paraweena.

Truganini was forcefully taken to the sealing ship near Bruni and was sexually assaulted by many sealers during the following several days. Late one night while everyone on board was heavily intoxicated, she quietly slid herself into the dark sea and swam back to shore.

What happened to Truganini during her kidnapping was not an unusual affair: since the arrivals of the British convicts and sealers to Van Diemen's Land, local women were regularly kidnapped and raped by convicts and sealers. If there was any resistance by Palawa men to kidnapping of their womenfolk, perpetrators viciously attacked and killed them. The kidnapped women were kept in chains as sex-slaves and worked as domestic servants for long periods of time. A few of the women who were able to escape and return to their tribes carried with them a host of infectious diseases that spread to other members of the clan. By the time Truganini was kidnapped and raped in 1826, nearly ninety percent the indigenous Palawa population of the island of Lutruwita was decimated by indiscriminate killings, starvation and disease.

In mid-1827, a group of land grabbing convict settlers attacked Truganini's clan and killed many, including her mother and uncle. The attackers also kidnapped her two sisters, Lowhenunhue and Maggerleede, selling them as sex-slaves to local sealers. Truganini never saw her sisters again. Truganini and her father Mangerner survived many onslaughts by the convicts and settlers. Later that year, Truganini, a small but handsome and shapely young woman with short curly hair, a pronounced brow and high cheek bones that framed sorrowful brown eyes, married a Nuenonne clansman named Woorady.

One summer afternoon in 1828, there was commotion near Truganini's camp. She, her husband Woorady and her father Mangerner rushed to the scene where three white men were surrounded by a group of spear-wielding clan warriors. Noticing that the white men did not bear arms, Truganini got in front of the young warriors and prevented them attacking the white intruders. Truganini, now speaking a few words of English asked the leader of the group, *"Why are you here? What do you want?"*

The leader of the group, a tall, thickset, middle-age man, bowed his head down respectfully and introduced himself, *"My name is George Robinson". These two young men are my sons."*

He then asked in local Palawa dialect Truganini her name. This was the beginning of a long-lasting friendship between the friendly Englishman and the Nuenonne clan. Thereafter, Robinson regularly met with clan members to learn more about their language, culture, spiritual beliefs and daily habits.

•••

George Augustus Robinson was born in 1791 in London England. His father trained him as a builder. After arriving in Van Diemen's Land in 1824, he found work as a storekeeper on Bruni Island. A man of solid religious values, he became increasingly disturbed by the ongoing violence against the indigenous Palawa. It appears that George Robinson was the only Englishman who showed a sincere curiosity and a desire to mingle with the local People. He exhibited genuine interest in the Palawa cultural values, religious beliefs, traditional lifestyle and language.

In letters written to friends in England, he complained about the mistreatment of the Palawa who lost their hunting-gathering grounds to white settlers and convicts. He reported that many of the sex-starved British convicts, settlers and sealers regularly raped Palawa females and took them away as servants and sex-slaves. He also started to write letters of complaint about his impressions of the inhuman treatment of the Palawa to various governmental authorities, including Lieutenant-Governor George Arthur. When the British Government in London granted 2000 hectares of Bruni Island's prime land to a wealthy British citizen named Richard Pybus in 1829, Robinson became extremely irritated. As the result of this land grant, the Nuenonne clan were forced to relocate and give up access to their usual hunting-gathering grounds and to the shoreline to dive for shellfish.

By the time of Robinson's arrival at Lutruwita, the population of Palawa had been reduced to fewer than one thousand. The survivors were mostly men because their womenfolk were either killed or taken as sex-slaves by the settlers, convicts, sealers, livestock-men and lumbermen. The surviving Palawa tribes courageously decided to defend themselves against the well-armed British occupiers.

...

The newly appointed Lieutenant-Governor George Arthur, a former British Army officer, arrived at Van Diemen's Island in 1824. He immediately activated an aggressive land distribution scheme, opening the central and northern parts of the island for the recently arrived settlers. The new Lieutenant-Governor, a tough, ambitious and unflinching administrator, succeeded in turning the island into a hell for the few remaining Palawa families who were barely surviving in the central and northern parts of the island.

George Arthur's policies and military actions that were initiated against the indigenous people of Lutruwita marked the beginning of the end for the remaining Palawa tribes. Palawa tribal leaders, having lost their lands and many men, women and children, decided to stand their ground and fight. These tribal warriors were fully aware that with the constant influx of white settlers, they had no chance to regain their lost lands or their lost honor and dignity. Between 1825 and 1827, a small number of Palawa warriors commenced regularly attacking white settlements to murder men, women and children indiscriminately to revenge what was previously done to them. Particularly, in response to the indiscriminate killings of thirty Palawa men, women and children in Cape Grim in 1828, a large Palawa warrior group, seeking vengeance, attacked and killed several settlers, livestock-men and their families.

Seeing that the Palawa were strongly resisting his policy of pacification, Lieutenant-Governor Arthur declared martial law in 1827 and organized a comprehensive military campaign, named the Black Line, against the remaining Palawa tribes. He ordered a battalion of 5000 soldiers and thousands of local armed convicts and settlers to march in clusters of close proximity in a cordon line across the island from southeast to northwest. The purpose of the Black Line was to indiscriminately eliminate indigenous Palawa people wherever they were found. Although a few Palawa families were eliminated particularly during several night attacks, this murderous military action was ultimately unsuccessful in fully exterminating the remaining Palawa tribes.

The Black Line was an overzealous, poorly designed and improperly implemented military campaign and it failed for several reasons that were not taken into consideration by the colonial administration. First, there were only a few hundred Palawa families who had survived two decades of murderous attacks, starvation and exposure to various diseases. The loss of their natural hunting grounds was amplified by widespread killing and enslavement of their women, who did much of the foraging and shoreline diving, resulting in substantive increase in starvation and reduced birthrates. With sharp decline in birthrates, Palawa tribal leaders realized that they faced an imminent extermination.

The Second reason of the Black Line's failure was because there were only a few Palawa warriors to eliminate in the southern parts of the island. Most of the surviving tribes had already escaped into the vast central plateaus and disappeared into the chilly and snowy mountains in the northern part of the island.

The third reason of the failure of the Black Line was due to the nature of the guerilla war tactics that the Palawa successfully implemented against the army. The elusive tactics of the tribal warriors who remained away from the Black Line incursions, turned them into a highly ineffective military strategy. Unfortunately, these evasive Palawa guerilla tactics made life unbearable for the Palawa themselves. To remain unnoticed, campfires were forbidden, resulting in malnutrition. Furthermore, surviving in colder northern regions they regularly needed animal fat to insulate their bodies for warmth. Without fire, they were not able to eat meat regularly and use fat to cover their bodies to keep warm. Their evasive tactics may have saved their lives against the Black Line military forces but because of cold weather and lack of nutrition, Palawa families lost many of their young and elderly members.

After nearly two years of mostly fruitless military efforts to exterminate the local inhabitants and killing only a few straggling Palawa tribesmen, the twenty thousand strong Black Line army was finally dismantled. As the failure of the Black Line military campaign became clear to the colonial government, Lieutenant-Governor George Arthur in 1829 considered a new and cost-effective way to completely pacify the remaining Palawa tribes. He determined to settle them in a concentration camp, preferably on an isolated island. He soon opted to forcibly resettle the surviving Palawa and accordingly he created a new position called the 'Protector of the Aborigine People' to manage his newly initiated local indigenous people resettlement strategy. Obviously, the Lieutenant-Governor had no intention to properly protect and humanely resettle the Palawa; his thinly-veiled intention was to orchestrate circumstances that would eventually guarantee their extermination.

Remembering the letters that he had received from one conscientious storekeeper named George Robinson who had requested in his letter that the local inhabitants should be treated more humanely, the Lieutenant-Governor decided to ask him to assume the newly created position as the protector of the indigenous people. Robinson's primary task was to negotiate the surrender of the remaining Palawa tribes and convince them to relocate to a government designated area.

George Robinson received the news of his being selected for this unique responsibility in 1829 while working as a storekeeper on Bruni Island. Accepting the Lieutenant-Governor's offer, he immediately requested the help of the local Nuenonne Clan members, including chief Mangerner, his daughter Truganini, her husband Woorady and an upcoming young warrior Kickerterpoller to convince the remaining Palawa tribes to give up fighting and settle in a safe location chosen by the government. He tried to explain to his Nuenonne audience that because presently there were more than 100 well-armed white men on Lutruwita for every surviving Palawa warrior, they had no chance for retaining their lands. Emphasizing that fighting against such a formidable force was suicidal, he told them that now is the best time to make peace and survive. Realizing the hopelessness of their situation, many clan members silently wept.

As the lone British supporter of the Palawa people, Robinson accepted the Lieutenant- Governor's offer with the hopeful intention to convince the government to allocate a viable piece of land on the island that was suitable for hunting and foraging for the remaining small number of Palawa families to securely relocate and safely survive under a guaranteed governmental authority.

To accomplish this unusual, tough assignment, George Robinson first had to convince Truganini and her now much reduced Nuenonne clan to help him arrange meetings with the few surviving tribes scattered across the island's central and northern regions. Truganini, was initially apprehensive about joining Robinson in his peace-making responsibility because basically she did not trust any white man. However, realizing that the Palawa people were in a losing battle against the superior forces of the invading white people and having many long discussions with her husband **Woorady** and her father **Mangerner,** she finally accepted Robinson's offer.

...

Over the next five years, Robinson and his Nuenonne clan guides undertook a total of six expeditions, eventually making contacts with every remaining Palawa tribes on Lutruwita. First, with assistance from Truganini and her husband Woorady, Robinson was able to convince all the Nuenonne clan survivors around Bruni Island and Oyster Cove to move away from their hunting grounds and relocate to areas in the northern shoreline of the island with promises of a secure and healthy existence. Soon after death of her father Mangerner, Truganini, her husband Woorady and several other clan members accompanied Robinson as the 'Protector of Aborigines' on his various missions between 1829-1834 to reach the remaining Palawa tribes hiding in the central and northern parts of the island with an intention to convince them first to capitulate and then relocate to a government chosen area. On two separate occasions Truganini and her husband Woorady saved Robinson's life when he was threatened by various Palawa warriors.

At one his initial peace-making efforts in 1830, Robinson was able to convince the well-respected Chief Mannalargenna of the Plangermaireener Clan of the Big River Tribe to capitulate. Afterward, the great chief Mannalargenna willingly joined Robinson's mission to convince the remaining Palawa tribal leaders to seek a peaceful settlement with the white colonial government.

During his extensive travels with the Nuenonne guides and Chief Mannalargenna, Robinson tried consistently to convert them to Christianity. Although everyone listened intently, Robinson was not able to convince them to abandon their traditional Dreamtime spiritual beliefs within which a pantheon of spirits as humans, animals, landscapes, heavenly skies and natural forces infinitely coexisted in forms of good and evil. The Palawa Dreamtime belief is based on a multilayered existence consisting of the physical world and spiritual realm. It provides the believers with a rationale for worldly custodial responsibility to protect environment and keep it in balance with nature's forces.

After explaining the basic precepts of Dreamtime spiritual beliefs, Truganini and Woorady simply told Robinson that their beliefs also included a divine figure called Wandjina that encompassed similar Christian concepts like the good and evil.

Realizing the impossibility of converting the Palawa, Robinson for the time being decided to curtail his religious crusade; though, he later would try again to convert them upon settling in Wybalenna concentration camp on Flinders Island.

Woorady's Dreadful Dreamtime Dance with the Devil

After the termination of Black Line military campaign by the colonial authorities and during one of his final missions to pacify the last remaining members of Mairremmener Clan in 1831, Robinson and his Nuenonne guides camped next to a wide, roaring river in the northeastern part of the island. Robinson, noticing how beautifully rich the nature was around this particular location, told his Nuenonne guides that this would be a perfect area for the remaining Palawa to settle.

This particular area was located across Swan Island and around the little Musselroe Bay where the roaring river, after forming a lagoon, ran into the sea near a wide, curving sandy beach full of pink-and-gray granite boulders. The area was full of ducks, pelicans, swans and various shellfish that would provide all year-round nourishment for the Palawa. Hoping that

Robinson's suggestion would become a reality, Nuenonne guides gleefully celebrated except Truganini, who nonchalantly whispered to her husband, *"This area has been one of our best feasting sites for many millennia. Raege will never agree to give us this beautiful piece of land."*

To approach Lieutenant-Governor Arthur with such a proposal to grant this secure piece of land for the Palawa to live and flourish, Robinson decided to take a trip to Hobart. First, he decided to take Chief Mannalargenna with him to meet with the Lieutenant-Governor. But then he changed his mind and decided to take Truganini, Woorady and Kickerterpoller with him.

The meeting with Lieutenant-Governor went exactly as Truganini predicted: he completely rejected Robinson's proposal and stated that he was contemplating placing the remaining Palawa on Swan Island or the Gun Carriage Island, or even possibly on the distant Flinders Island.

Soon after returning to Swan Island, Robinson successfully arranged the capitulation of Chief Umarrah, a respected tribal leader who had been surviving with a few followers on the vast hills of the northern region. Responding to a request from the Lieutenant-Governor to meet with Umarrah, Robinson decided to take Mannalargenna together with Umarrah to Hobart. During this meeting, Robinson and the two former Palawa chiefs were not able to acquire an agreement from the Lieutenant-Governor to grant the Palawa survivors a viable piece of land on the main island.

After returning back to Swan Island with the discouraged former chiefs, Robinson and his large entourage moved inland in search of the evasive Mairremmener tribe. After many days of search, Kickerterpoller reported that he had located the whereabouts of the tribe. Hearing that the chief of the Mairremmener tribe agreed to negotiate, Robinson, hoping to convince the chief to give up fighting against the white occupiers, asked the former chiefs Mannalargenna and Umarrah and the well-respected young warrior Kickerterpoller to join him during the negotiations.

The next morning, on August 6, 1831, the remaining members of the Mairremmener tribe, 16 men 9 women and one child, peacefully entered Robinson's camp. Robinson and his negotiations team welcomed the worn-out tribal members. After long negotiations, they were able to convince the Chief and the surviving members to capitulate by promising that they would soon safely settle on a piece of land of their own. During these negotiations, the Mairremmener Chief stated that because of white men's cruelty and their never-ending attacks on Palawa womenfolk, his tribe was forced to fight the white men. Looking directly at Robinson, he solemnly concluded, *"But now, we no longer have any means to defend ourselves. We must now entrust ourselves to you."*

That evening, Robinson entered into his diary this very special agreement that he reached with the last remaining Palawa tribe. He wrote:

"In the presence of tribal members Mannalargenna, Umarrah and Kickerterpoller, I informed the Mairremmener *chief that I was commissioned by the Governor to inform them that, if the natives would desist from their wonted outrages upon the whites, they would be allowed to remain in their respective districts and would have flour, tea, sugar and clothes, so that good white men would dwell with them who would take care of them and would not allow any bad white men to shoot them."*

This was wishful thinking by Robinson, who would soon realize that the Lieutenant-Governor, his boss in Hobart, would never agree to such a settlement strategy allowing the Palawa tribes to return to their home districts. He would not even consider giving a decent piece of land on Lutruwita for the surviving Palawa to settle; he would only agree to settle them on a barren island where they would slowly die out.

On the evening that followed the successful negotiations, Robinson, his Nuenonne guides, two former chiefs and the survivors of the Mairremmener tribe celebrated the hard-earned peace settlement with a Corroboree of dances, chants and Dreamtime stories around the campfire. After locating several cider gum trees and sucking their intoxicating juices with rolled bark straws, they dined on the usual roasted kangaroo meat. After a sumptuous meal and before traditional dancing ceremony, the warriors covered their bodies and hair with mutton-bird fat mixed with ground red ochre and black charcoal. Several Nuenonne warriors, Chiefs Mannalargenna and Umarrah joined Woorady to perform the traditional dances around the well-lit campfire.

After dancing for nearly two hours, all of the exhausted performers collapsed on the ground except Woorady. He was now in a complete Dreamtime spiritual trance. As he loudly chanted a Dreamtime story, he continued dancing wildly around the campfire.

Robinson had been intensely watching the whole dancing and chanting ceremony. He asked Truganini about the meaning of the words that her husband kept on repeating. Truganini, without interrupting her back and forth movements that followed her husband's gyrating dancing motions, coldly replied, "*I am not so sure you really want to know what exactly he is saying in his Dreamtime chant.*"

Robinson, getting impatient, firmly replied, "*Of course I want to know.*"

Truganini hesitantly replied, "*If you insist, I will tell you the true meanings behind his words. These words emanate from the spirits of Dreamtime. His words indicate that the Palawa of Lutruwita will soon exist only among the spirits of Dreamtime; they will no longer roam the fields of real-time because no future generations of Palawa will remain on this island. The spirits of the slain Palawa will ensure that the same end befalls upon the future generations of the evil white men who caused the extermination of the Palawa People. They are cursed forever and will one day suffer the same evil destruction that they unleashed on the Palawa of Lutruwita.*"

Eyes locked on the campfire burning wildly, Robinson whispered, "A *curse of divine justice; we reap what we sow.*"

Robinson was so much disturbed with what he had heard, he remained awake most of the night. After a sleepless night, as the sun rose in distant eastern horizon, he convinced himself that he will do whatever necessary to guarantee the survival of the Palawa.

The next morning before dawn, Truganini, Woorady, Kickerterpoller and Chiefs Mannalargenna and Umarrah sat around the campfire and discussed the agreement that had been reached with the Mairremmener one day prior.

As he stared at the campfire, Chief Mannalargenna loudly inquired, "*Do you expect that Robinson will ever deliver us a piece of land of our own on Lutruwita?*"

Woorady quickly replied, "*I hope so! He is our last hope. Most of our people have been decimated since the arrival of white people. Only a few of us survived the decades long onslaught. We just hope that Robinson's boss will agree with Robinson's promises."*

Truganini, shaking her head side to side, spoke her mind, *"I don't trust any white man, they always say one thing and do something else. Yet we have no choice in the matter; we just have to wait and see if Robinson will be able to convince his big boss in Hobart."*

After years of intensive efforts, Robinson was able to persuade the surviving Palawa tribesmen and their families to surrender with assurances that they would be protected and provided for. However, he personally guaranteed without government authorization that eventually the surviving Palawa people would be allowed to settle on a large viable hunting-gathering land on the main island. Despite Robinson's best intentions, unfortunately for the Palawa, such a promise was politically unrealistic because the white colonial government would never allow it to happen. With this unrealistic promise that long-lasting peace was now at hand and the remaining Palawa families would soon settle on a protected piece of land of their own, Robinson was able to convince the chiefs Mannalargenna and Umarrah to support his peace-making efforts.

Following the capitulation of the remaining Palawa warriors and a few of their surviving women and children, Robinson took all of the tribal members to Hobart. As requested by the Lieutenant-Governor, they were required to dress in western clothes and forced to parade through the crowded streets of the city.

The parade had ended near the Hobart Port. Seeing their island Bruni in the distance, Truganini and a few Nuenonne women discarded their weird looking blanket attires and jubilantly jumped into the water to swim. When they came out of the water, Robinson, who was surrounded by policemen, told the Nuenonne women to put their attires back on and warned them not to swim naked in an urban area ever again.

After the Hobart parade of 1832, Robinson received orders to move all 200 remaining Palawa to settle temporarily on Swan Island. He tried again and again to convince Lieutenant-Governor Arthur to grant the remaining Palawa families a large piece of land across the Swan Island that was suitable for hunting-gathering. Unfortunately, the Lieutenant-Governor had no inclination to provide anything to the remaining Palawa people to have a decent chance to survive; he therefore repeatedly rejected Robinson's proposal for a large land grant for the remaining Palawa people and he instructed his government for the establishment of a concentrated settlement camp for the Palawa on the inhospitable, wind-swept island of Flinders. In 1834, Robinson was ordered to relocate the remaining Palawa to the designated Wybalenna aboriginal settlement camp on Flinders Island.

Before he was relocated to Flinders Island, Chief Umarrah became ill with a serious lung infection. Robinson asked Kickerterpoler to take Umarrah to a hospital in Hobart. Chief Umarrah soon died in the hospital. The young warrior Kickerterpoler also died from a lung infection soon after returning to Swan Island.

By mid-1834, Robinson began transporting the few Palawa still remaining on the Swan Island to Flinders. Chief

Mannalargenna, before boarding the boat, cut off his beard and hair in anguish. When disembarking the boat in Flinders, he sternly reminded Robinson of his earlier promises. Robinson, unfortunately replied with an obvious lie that the trip to Flinders was just a temporary measure. Hardly a year later, Chief Mannalargenna, who had lost two wives, four daughters and all of his tribal land to invading whites, died from a respiratory disease without ever setting foot back onto his beloved Lutruwita.

In 1835, only a few new expeditions were undertaken by Robinson to gather the few remaining Palawa families still surviving in the wild. During one of his last expeditions, he came across a young Palawa couple with a seven years old boy. Robinson took the family to Wybalenna settlement. The young boy named William Lanne, grew up on Flinders Island. In time, when all remaining Palawa men died from disease and malnutrition, he became the only surviving male of the Palawa People.

After Robinson's final official trip, Truganini, **Woorady** and the remaining Nuenonne guides were also relocated to the Wybalenna indigenous concentration camp on Flinders Island, a barren piece of land in the middle of the ocean far away from Lutruwita. Immediately after landing in Flinders, Truganini begged Robinson that they all should return back to Lutruwita. *"Otherwise,"* she sadly said, "we *will all die on this miserable island."* She was correct because Flinders had limited agricultural capacity, only a few animals to hunt or shellfish to dive for. Despite the island's inhospitable terrain, Robinson decided to remain with the Palawa to help them to survive by becoming subsistence farmers.

Despite Truganini's constant warnings, Robinson ignored her and attempted to make farmers and Christians out of the remaining Palawa. As expected, all of the surviving Palawa completely disregarded his instructions to change their traditional ways to become exactly like the white settlers.

As time passed, Robinson became increasingly disturbed by the realization that he was becoming an instrument of the government's hidden extermination policy. He took solace in the assumption that he could transform a group of hunter-gatherers into Christian subsistence farmers. He wrongly assumed that if he was successful in such a social transformation, he might generate a chance for them to exist and thrive within the rules and regulations of the white society. His attempts on establishing a viable subsistence agricultural settlement on a windswept island and his efforts to convert Palawa to a Christian way of life were definite failures from the beginning. Over the coming few years, most of the Palawa on Flinder's Island died of malnutrition and disease.

...

In late 1837, feeling guilty about what was going on Flinders Island, Robinson decided to get away. He accepted a new job in Melbourne, Australia. To offer a better life opportunity to his longtime Nuenonne clan guides, he took fourteen of them with him to Melbourne, including Truganini and her husband Woorady.

After nearly two years of living in and around Port Philip near Melbourne, a few of the Nuenonne clan members became outlaws, stealing from settlers around the town of Dandenong. Immediately afterwards, six of them, including Truganini, escaped to Bass River and then to Cape Paterson. In the spring of 1841, they murdered two whalers at Watsons near Cape

Paterson. Later they shot and injured several other settlers in the same area. A long-lasting police pursuit followed the six criminals responsible for the murderous attacks. After they were captured, a gunshot wound to Truganini's head was treated by Dr. Hugh Anderson of Bass River Town before she and her party sent to stand trial in Melbourne. On January 20, 1842, four Nuenonne men were hanged in Melbourne. The two women members of the Nuenonne crime gang, including Truganini were found not guilty by the court and were ordered to return to Flinders.

Before being shipped to Flinders Island, Truganini met with Robinson; they had a heart-to-heart talk. Robinson, who felt bad about the hanging of the four Nuenonne men, looked directly into Truganini's pitch black eyes and said, *"You know very well that with a set of good intentions I brought some of you to Melbourne so that you would find a way to establish productive lives for yourselves. You and several others instead have chosen a criminal lifestyle that caused four of you to be hanged. Most of you are now on your way back to Flinders Island. You have failed me badly. What did I do wrong?"*

Truganini, as she stared back at him, firmly replied, *"You did many things wrong from the onset by taking us to an isolated barren island so we would become agricultural settlers. After being with us for such a long time you should have realized that we only know how to dive for shellfish, hunt for game and search for plants, roots and fruits to eat. Because of our thousands of years old traditional ways of living with nature, we simply don't fit into white people's life styles. Also, please remember that no white men who killed many Palawa and raped many of our women were ever punished for what they did. But when we defend ourselves and do what we can do to survive, white-men's justice delivers us a very harsh punishment by hanging my male compatriots."*

When Robinson attempted to reply, Truganini firmly asked him to let her finish.

"Please remember that we know that you are genuinely interested in helping us; you studied our ways of life, learned our language and our traditional and cultural habits. You also made us understand that we, the Palawa and the white people exist in different Dreamtimes, thousands of years apart. When we were traveling in Lutruwita asking our tribes to give up fighting and turn themselves into the hands of the white authorities, you promised us a viable piece of land where we could hunt and gather whatever nature bestowed upon us. We believed in you and expected that you would fulfill your promise. But you and your big white boss imprisoned us on an island where there was no chance for us to survive. When you realized the fact that we were being slowly exterminated and feeling sorry for us, you took a few of us with you to Melbourne. Now, Mr. Robinson, you say that we failed you. No, we did not; you simply were unable to convince your boss who completely failed to recognize the possibility of coexistence of two different people in two different Dreamtimes by sharing whatever the nature offered to all of us. The white people's decision to eliminate us was based primarily on selfishness and greed, because the white people do not want to share anything with anyone who does not look or talk like them."

This honest reply by Truganini was the last words she uttered to Robinson. She, her husband Woorady and eight remaining Nuenonne clan members were shipped by the government back to Flinders Island. On the way, Truganini's husband Woorady, ailing from an upper-respiratory infection, died on the ship. Upon arrival at Flinders, against Truganini's insistence that her husband should be cremated, Woorady body was unceremoniously buried in a Christian cemetery.

...

By the summer of 1847, only 34 Palawa remained alive on Flinders Island. During that year, the surviving Palawa, including Truganini and William Lanne, were relocated to a designated aborigine settlement area at Oyster Cove, south of Hobart. Soon after arriving at Hobart, the young Palawa man, William Lanne, became a sailor on a whaling ship and worked for several years. The remaining Palawa were forced to settle in an old, decrepit, sparsely furnished prison building. Because they were provided only minimum rations, they had to hunt small marsupials and dive for shellfish for additional nutrition.

After settling in Oyster Cove, Truganini was not allowed to visit her birthplace on the island of Bruni right across the Oyster Bay because the Island now belonged to two wealthy British landowners. Ignoring the instructions not to visit Bruni, on many occasions she swam with her friend Dray to the island to visit her birthplace. Usually upon arriving at Bruni, she and Dray went to Woodcutter's Point on Richard Pybus' land where Truganini was born. For memories sake, they walked around the beach on the channel side of the island. There, they would dive to catch some shellfish to take home.

In the Oyster Cove indigenous settlement area, Truganini and all other Palawa were required to wear western clothing. Truganini and Dray were issued dark-blue serge petticoats to be worn under an ankle-length, woolen sack dress tied at the waist with a rope. Truganini and Dray wore these clothes with red peaked caps and placed many dangling, colorful and luminous shell necklaces around their necks. They were occasionally seen walking around the Port of Hobart, strolling confidently with tobacco pipes hanging from their mouth.

On his way back home to England in 1852, Robinson stopped by at the Oyster Bay's Palawa settlement to bid farewell to Truganini. When she heard that Robinson was in town, Truganini decided to disappear.

Not finding Truganini in her hut, Robinson took a boat to Bruni to finalize the sale of his small land holding on the island. After completing of the transaction, he walked into the heavily wooded area of the island where he had first met the members of the Nuenonne clan, all of whom, except Truganini, were already dead. He sat on the ground and leaned against a tree trunk. Closing his eyes, he contemplated his ineffectiveness in preventing the extermination of the Palawa.

As he buried his head between his knees, he loudly hissed, *"The decision to exterminate the Palawa was made in London and in Hobart. I had no choice in the matter. I was forced to take the surviving Palawa to Wybalenna on Flinders. On that miserable piece of barren rock, I just simply failed in my attempts to convert them into becoming Christians and farmers. Perhaps it would have been better if they died fighting rather than slowly perishing from starvation and disease on that damned island."*

Overwhelmed by guilt for having assisted the government in their extermination of the Palawa, he wept silently. Remembering Woorady's fireside trance and his Dreamtime prediction that raege would be cursed forever and one day in the future they will also suffer the same fate. After wiping his tears and taking a deep breath, he murmured, *"I should leave this cursed island and never come back."*

He walked to the Bruni Island's western beach, which faced Oyster Bay. Near the shoreline, he noticed two swimmers approaching the beach. Recognizing Truganini and her friend Dray, Robinson, as he waved his arms, started to shout and ran toward them. Recognizing Robinson, Truganini coaxed her friend back into the water. They quickly swam away from the shoreline before Robinson could reach the beach.

Swimming for nearly an hour, the two Palawa women approached the shoreline at Oyster Cove. As they emerged from the water, Dray asked Truganini, *"Why don't you want to see Robinson?"*

"Why *should I speak with him or with any white man? Nothing good comes out from any interaction with raege. I want to live the rest of my life in peace and tranquility until I join my ancestors.*"

A few days later Robinson, his wife and two sons left Van Diemen's Land for good, never to return. He died in 1866 in England. His written notes, memorandums and various collections of Palawa art and drawings are the only remaining scientific and artistic notations including many photos and artifacts he collected about the prehistoric Palawa culture, religious beliefs and traditional ways of the hunter-gatherer people.

In 1856, the island of Lutruwita, which was improperly called Van Diemen's Land since its discovery by European explorers, was officially renamed Tasmania by the local government. This was the final British insult to the ancient memory of the Palawa, the exterminated people of Lutruwita. After Van Diemen's Land became Tasmania, the Royal Society of Tasmania were allowed to exhume the corpses of the Palawa to be utilized in so-called scientific research on theories of evolution. Many Palawa skeletons and skulls were removed from many burial grounds and were placed in museum collections. In 1864, when ethnological studies in Oxford University in London requested male and female Palawa remains, Hobart Museum transferred a few of their collections to England. With the increase of demand for Palawa remains, grave robbery became a common practice in late 19th Century Tasmania.

...

William Lanne, the little boy Robinson brought to Flinders Island in 1837, now a thirty-one-year-old sailor on a whaling ship, returned to Oyster Cove Palawa settlement in 1866. He was the last remaining Palawa man. Soon after his arrival at Oyster Cove, he refused to go back on his whaling ship. He explained to Truganini that he was badly treated by his shipmates. Feeling sorry for him, Truganini married him and shared her residence and rations with this lonely suffering man who was now heavily drinking.

Truganini for a long time was referred to mockingly as 'the queen' by the white inhabitants of Hobart. Her marriage to this troubled young man had resulted in William Lanne also mockingly being called 'King Billy'. When the Duke of Edinburgh of that time was visiting Tasmania in 1867, the Tasmanian Government decided to present to the visiting British Royalty the presumed royalty of the Palawa People: Queen Truganini and King Billy. This was basically another crude insult to the memory of the exterminated Palawa People. Truganini promptly refused to attend such a ridiculous and phony ceremony. Unfortunately, Billy accepted the invitation and was introduced to the Duke as the King of the Palawa. It is a great wonder if the Duke of Edinburgh ever knew that he did not really meet a king but, in fact, the last surviving male of an exterminated people.

By 1862, only eight Palawa, including Truganini remained alive in Tasmania. During the same year, after her friend Dray's death at the age of 75, Truganini spent many lonely days in her old crumbling hut at the Oyster Cove's Palawa settlement until her marriage to William Lanne in 1866. Unfortunately, her marriage to Lanne did not improve her life-style because the young man was an unemployed alcoholic.

Three years later, after suffering many illnesses including cholera and dysentery and also because of his heavy drinking, Billy Lanne died at the age of 34. As the last remaining Palawa male, his corpse was taken by the authorities to be dissected for scientific analysis. A local surgeon from Hobart, named Dr. Crowther, who became the prime-minister of Tasmania in 1878, made several illegal arrangements to ship Billy Lanne's body parts including his skull to Royal Surgeons Society of London for further scientific analysis to investigate the missing-link assumptions of the evolutionary theory that generated many false racist premises of the 19th century Social Darwinism. William Lanne's stolen body parts remained a mystery until several body parts sent by surgeon Crowther were eventually repatriated back to Tasmania in the 1990s, William Lanne's skull among them.

In 1869, due to what had happened to the last Palawa man's remains, the Tasmanian legislation passed a new law prohibiting such future medical experimentations on Palawa remains. Seven years later, that law had prevented Truganini's body from being dissected.

After the death of her husband William Lanne, Truganini was occasionally seen on the streets of Hobart and Oyster Bay's indigenous settlement area walking confidently alone with a tobacco pipe hanging out of her mouth and many colorful seashell necklaces dangling on her neck. She was well aware of what had happened to her husband's corpse. She made up her mind not to be dissected like her husband. To prevent such gruesome fate, she decided to be cremated.

Soon after she was taken seriously ill in 1872, Truganini was moved by the local government to a care home in Hobart managed by the Dandridge family, a Christian missionary couple. During the following four years, the missionary couple took good care of Truganini. In the spring of 1876, at the age of 64, Truganini became bedridden with various illnesses. On her deathbed, she requested from Mrs. Dandridge and Reverend Henry Atkinson that she wanted to be cremated and her ashes be scattered across the waters of the D'Entrecasteaux Channel.

After she died in May of 1876, she was buried, against her last wish, at the Christian cemetery of the former Female Prison Facility at Cascades, a suburb of Hobart. Soon after her burial, her body was exhumed by the Royal Society of Tasmania and, after a mummification process, was placed on a public display in Hobart Museum. It remained there until 1951. Only in April of 1976, approaching the centenary of her death, with political pressures emanating from the newly established Tasmanian Aboriginal Center, Truganini's mummified body was finally removed from the museum's storage area and ceremoniously cremated. A few days later, fulfilling her last wish, Truganini's ashes were scattered across **the waters of the D'Entrecasteaux Channel.** A Nuenonne princess, the daughter of Chief Mangerner, Truganini finally joined her ancestors. May she rest in peace in her everlasting spiritual existence in Dreamtime of her forebearers...

Truganini was incorrectly considered to be the last remaining Palawa woman. Actually, there were several Palawa women who survived her. By the beginning of the 20th century, the departure of the remaining a few Palawa women marked the end of the British genocide of the Palawa people of Lutruwita.

Mixed-race Palawa Community in Today's Tasmania

In today's Tasmania, there exists a large mixed-race Palawa community of 20,000 people. There is no evidence that any Palawa tribesman ever raped a white woman during the period between 1804 and 1866 when the last remaining Palawa man had expired. Therefore, it may be assumed that today's mixed-race community likely emanated exclusively from male European and female Palawa lineage. To be fair, some British men willingly and lovingly took Palawa women as life partners and raised good families. Unfortunately, many more British men violently raped Palawa women who mostly ended up pregnant. These unfortunate Palawa women, in many occasions, were able to raise singlehandedly their mixed-race offspring.

One special mixed-race Palawa woman, Fanny Cochrane, born in 1837 on the Island of Flinders, willingly married in 1854 to a white settler named William Smith, had eleven children. Many of today's mixed-race Palawa community of Tasmania may be the descendants of Fanny Cochrane Smith who greatly contributed to the preservation of Palawa culture by recording many of Palawa traditional songs in 1899 and 1903.

Much of the surviving mixed-race Palawa community has sought to preserve what remains of the island's original indigenous culture, arts and language. In 1966, the Tasmanian Information Centre, later renamed the Tasmanian Aboriginal Centre (TAC), was formed and commenced activities for heritage protection, land return, the recognition of Palawa identity, and the return of stolen human remains.

By the 1970s, a Tasmanian movement for Aboriginal rights started gaining steam. It was led by several activists who pointedly identified themselves as Palawa rather than as the "descendants" of indigenous Tasmanians. Soon thereafter, the movement's goals evolved beyond simple recognition of Palawa identity to the pursuit of land rights. Judging from the adoption of the Aboriginal Lands Act of 1995, it seems that these efforts by Tasmanian Aboriginal Center resulted in positive legislative responses by the Australian and Tasmanian authorities.

During the following few decades, there were many substantial efforts by the local Palawa community organizations, including Tasmanian Aboriginal Center that was established in 1966 by Michael Mansell, a well-respected Palawa leader, activist and lawyer. He instigated many social, political and legal changes to improve the lives and social standing of the Tasmanian Palawa People. Since the establishment of the Tasmanian Aboriginal Center, he worked hard to convince the governments of Australia and Tasmania to recognize the mixed-race community's civil rights to establish memorial monuments and conduct traditional ceremonies of remembrance on the lands of their forbearers. Unfortunately, by 2015, Michael Mansell decided or possibly forced by the Australian Government to withdraw from active political life.

Before any further efforts that could legally establish a complete recognition of the full rights of the remaining mixed-race survivors of the extinct Palawa People, there is an urgent need for a sincere global public apology from the British, Australian and Tasmanian governments for disregarding the inalienable human rights of the unique indigenous people of Oceania and for completely exterminating the Palawa of Lutruwita Island with ten thousand years old stone-age cultural habits, arts and languages. Such a global apology is essential especially when there was a complete inhumanity in the British Colonial Government's disregard for the Palawa People's rights to self-determination and their inalienable rights to their own land. Furthermore, there is a need for an historical explanation of the reasons behind the British Government's improper and unfair decision to foist England's unwanted criminal classes and vicious sociopaths onto the lives of undeserving indigenous inhabitants of Australia and Van Diemen's Land.

After delivering a worldwide public apology for the unjustified Anglo-centric actions and misdeeds of past British colonial administrative policies that were implemented against the indigenous peoples of Australia and Tasmania, both governments should fully extend civil and political rights to remaining mostly mixed-race aboriginal peoples of the continent and to the mixed-race Palawa of Tasmania. The surviving mixed-race and full-blooded Australian Aborigines and the existing Tasmanian mixed-race Palawa of today must be given equal access to socio-economic opportunities through establishment of a broad comprehensive compensation package covering their basic socio-economic, cultural and educational development needs.

ILLUSTRATIONS

A Palawa Gathering c.1810

Robinson and the Nuenonne Clan c.1826

[Truganini, the young lady with necklaces in the right center]

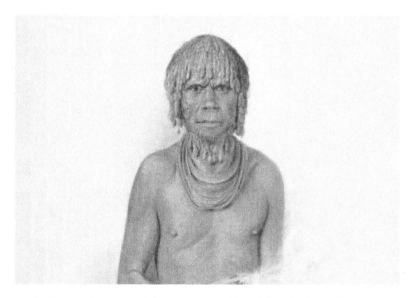

Chief Mannalargenna, Plangermaireener Clan of the Big River Tribe c.1830

William Lanne, the Last Palawa man c.1865

The last four Palawa of Lutruwita c. 1860
[William Lanne second from left & Truganini last one on right]

A Bust of Truganini c. 1836

Stories from an Unsettling World

THE LAST TRAIN TO TAKARAZUKA

[JAPAN]

Hankyu Lines, Umeda Station, Osaka

THE LAST TRAIN TO TAKARAZUKA

It was a warm and windy early September morning in Ikeda, a small suburban town on the outskirts of the city of Osaka. At the Ikeda's local hospital, Kenji Zenda—a tired-looking, thin, short man in his late sixties—had been informed a day before that he was terminally ill and would only live a few more weeks, if that much. It was his last night at the hospital. He remained awake during most of the night. At almost dawn, he finally fell asleep but the same recurring nightmare woke him up immediately. In the nightmare, Aum Shinrikyo's leader Shoko Asahara was guiding him into a metro train where he was asked to deposit a large bag full of poisonous chemical sarin. Sitting upright in the bed, Kenji Zenda, wiping the sweat on his forehead, mumbled, "Why do I keep on dreaming of something I did not do? Damn you Shoko! You're a cursed monster."

Sun was about to rise. He quietly dressed up, packed his belongings into a small bag and got ready to leave the hospital. Before departing from the hospital, he called his older brother's home with whom he has not spoken for nearly twenty years. His sister-in-law informed him that her husband had a stroke over a month ago and has been in coma in the Osaka City University Hospital. Deciding to visit his brother at the hospital, Kenji took the Hankyu Lines Takarazuka semi-express train to Umeda, where he transferred to a subway connection to the Tennoji neighborhood. After a short walk he entered the University Hospital and found his brother in a private room.

He sat next to the bed and murmured, "My dear brother, it is sad to see you in this condition. I came to say farewell. I don't know which one of us will die first, but it doesn't matter. Soon, we both will be gone forever."

Closing his eyes, he tried to remember the good old days when they were both growing up. He whispered, "During our carefree childhood we had a few happy moments. Didn't we?"

Suddenly the door opened and a short, skinny young man with long, dyed blond hair in a ponytail, wearing a dark purple jean and a loose, long-sleeved pink shirt entered the hospital room. Placing the guitar in his hand next to the patient's bed, he stared at Kenji.

"Who are you?"

Pointing at the patient, Kenji replied, "I am his younger brother."

"My name is Yoshi and I am his son. You must be Uncle Yosuke. I've heard about you: the infamous brother who disappeared many years ago."

As Kenji got to his feet, Yoshi bent his head respectfully and said, "Uncle Yosuke, finally we met. Thank you for visiting my father. I hope he was able to feel your presence and hear your words."

Without answering Yoshi, Kenji left the room hurriedly. As he was leaving the hospital, he murmured, "A nice-looking, effeminate young man; a musician, I presume."

Returning to Ikeda, he walked to his small one-bedroom apartment. As he took the keys out of his pocket to open the door, he suddenly changed his mind and went straight to his landlady's apartment across the hallway. When the landlady, Mrs. Morimoto, opened the door, the old man greeted her with a deep bow and profusely thanked the middle-age, plump woman for saving his life nearly ten days prior.

As she mirrored his bow, she replied, "You're quite welcome, Zenda-San! How lucky that I noticed your living room lights were on all night."

Her mind conjured up an image of unlocking his apartment to find him crumpled unconscious on the kitchen floor. Genuinely happy to see him on his feet, she flashed a friendly smile. "I presume the hospital just released you. Are you fully recovered?"

Kenji Zenda pursed his lips. After his emergency treatment, the hospital had informed him that he was terminally ill with a rare, fully-metastasized bone-marrow cancer. He wanted to tell her that he would soon be dead, but instead told her what landlady expected to hear: that he had fully recovered.

Hearing his answer, Mrs. Morimoto smiled.

"Harumi-San would like you to help with her garden work this coming weekend. Are you available?"

"This is good news indeed, Morimoto-San! That will help me pay you what I owe for the last month's rent. Thank you! I'll call Harumi-San. Have a good day!"

Before entering his apartment, he discovered an official note in the mail box. It had been left there by a visiting police officer, Seiji Nishimura of the Ikeda City Police. The note asked him to report to the police office immediately.

...

Later that evening, a tall, slim, middle-aged police sergeant disembarked from the Hankyu lines semi-express train coming from Takarazuka at the Ikeda Station and walked hurriedly toward the nearby police office. Sergeant Takashi Ishihara had recently been assigned to night duty and thus expected a tranquil, uneventful evening at work. After changing into his dark blue uniform, he reported for duty on the main floor. At the reception area, he found the short and portly new recruit, Seiji Nishimura, staring intently at his computer screen. Stopping behind Nishimura's chair, Ishihara noticed that he was peering at an old map of Asia, colorfully displaying the boundaries of countries.

"What is so special about that map?" Sergeant Ishihara asked curiously.

Without turning his gaze away from the screen, Nishimura replied, "My father-in-law mentioned that there were only two independent Asian countries in 1939: Thailand and Japan. It turns out that he was correct."

"So, what does that mean?"

"When I looked at the map of Asia today, I noticed many more independent countries."

"What's your point?"

"Almost all of those new countries became independent after World War II. They were able to do so because during the war we kicked the European colonialists out of Asia. Obviously, it was the Japanese blood that freed those countries."

Sergeant Ishihara frowned but remained silent. He was from Hiroshima, born to parents who survived the atomic bomb attack that forced Japan to sue for peace. He stepped away to get a cup of coffee.

Officer Nishimura, originally from the Island of Okinawa, scooped up a dossier from his desk and joined the Sergeant standing next to the coffee machine. Before handing the dossier to the sergeant, he vented his thoughts: "We definitely kicked the colonizing Europeans out of Asia, but in return we became an American colony. I dream about the day when these rapist American soldiers leave Okinawa."

A crooked smile appeared on Sergeant's sanguine face.

"Nishimura-son, that may remain a dream for a long time to come. But if by chance it happens, I hope you'll live long enough to see it."

The two police officers stood in tense silence as Ishihara sipped his coffee. After a moment, he gestured with his mug at the dossier in Nishimura's hand.

"What's that?"

"Last week we were informed by the local hospital of a discrepancy in a patient's social security records. I went to the address to interview the individual but he wasn't there. His landlady told me that the man renting the unit had been living there for the past two years and had recently been hospitalized. I left him a note asking him to come to the police station as soon as he returns home. However, late this afternoon I received a message from Tokyo headquarters that this individual, Kenji Zenda—also known as Yosuke Oki—is one of those un-apprehended suspects of the Aum Shinrikyo terror organization responsible for the March 1995 sarin gas attack on Tokyo subway trains that killed many innocent people."

"If that is the case, we should detain him for questioning as soon as he gets out of the hospital."

As he handed the report to the Sergeant, Officer Nishimura replied, "That is exactly my recommendation to our supervisor. In the morning, please make sure someone checks with the hospital about his expected date of release. Have a safe and quiet night Sergeant!"

...

Kenji Zenda noticed that it was getting late and he was the last remaining customer in the local pub. He quaffed his drink and left the bar, wobbling toward his nearby apartment. Ten days ago, the hospital had requested his true identity to continue with his treatment. He was sure that the police would soon catch up with him, and in previous occasions they did exactly that. In the past, whenever his identity had been questioned, he simply moved to another town, changed his name, found a place to live and went on with his life. But this time it was different; he soon would die after suffering excruciating pains. He was now sure that he no longer needed to run away and hide.

Waiting for the traffic light to change, he muttered drunkenly, "Why wait for such a bitter end? Why go through such agony? I must end my miserable life soon, very soon indeed!"

He opened the door and entered his apartment. After pouring himself a glass of whisky and placing it on the kitchen table, he went to the *tatami* room to retrieve his prescription painkillers from the floor beside the futon. Back in the kitchen, he emptied the medicine bottle onto the tabletop and counted the pills.

Giggling, he whispered. "Enough to kill a horse!"

He stared at the glass of whisky and the scattered pills as his mind wandered. Imagining his poor landlady discovering his dead body the next day, alerted him to remember that he owed her a month's rent. Reaching into his back pocket, he took out his billfold. He removed all the bills out of the billfold and placed them on the tabletop.

"At least she'll receive a part of what I owe her," he murmured.

He then stared for a long time into the darkness outside the kitchen window. Suddenly raising his head, he looked intensely at the shiny ceiling light. A bright new idea had just entered his mind. Given his present circumstances, a home suicide would be a fruitless way to end his life.

"Killing myself in this apartment would not be publicly noticed," he mused. *"The justice system that has been chasing after me for such a long time will unceremoniously dispose of my body."*

He started to walk around the dinner table, his agitated steps matching his nervous thoughts. After a long while, he suddenly stopped and exclaimed, "Why didn't I think of that before?"

Stretching his imagination, he wondered, *"Rather than killing myself in this miserable apartment, I must kill myself with a big bang! A public suicide may receive the necessary attention to bring my case to the forefront of the news-media. I must write a letter of explanation to a newspaper so that my suicide gets a full coverage."*

A few minutes later, clutching a pen and paper, he started scribbling a letter to a newspaper:

Dear editor,

Because I was seeking a spiritual meaning to my monotonous, boring life; I joined the Aum Shinrikyo organization led by Shoko Asahara. However, I have never condoned and never been a part of the violent, inhuman activities led by Asahara that killed many innocent bystanders in 1995. In fact, I stayed away from the organization's meetings after the murder of the lawyer Tsutsumi Sakamato and his family in late 1989. Even so, following the 1995 sarin gas attack, my loose connection to the organization cost me my engineering job, my wife, and all my friends. After being questioned repeatedly by the police, I was sure that I would be jailed. I felt the presence of a clear legal and social prejudice against me even though I was not a part of the heinous criminal activity of that reprehensible day. I felt the presence of an improper due process of law through which a prejudicial legal process declared me guilty without trial, forcing me into a life of a fugitive for so many years. This was an endless cruel punishment for an unproven guilt. By the time you receive this letter, I will be dead. My dying wish is to clear my name. I had nothing to do with the 1995 sarin gas attack.

Yosuke Oki

He slid the letter into an envelope and addressed it to the Editor of *Asahi Shimbun* in Tokyo. He then wrote a short note briefly stating his innocence and placed it in his jacket's side pocket for the police to discover. Reaching the bundle of money on the table, he removed a thousand-yen bill to pay for the postage and his last train ticket. He then placed the half-empty bottle of whiskey into a paper bag and reached for the pain pills spread across the table. After throwing a bunch of pills into the whiskey bag, he turned the lights off in the kitchen and walked out of the apartment without a backward glance.

...

It was eleven-thirty in the evening in downtown Osaka. At the Hankyu Railroad's Umeda terminal station, the train arriving from Takarazuka slowly approached the platform number four. Wearing a dark gray uniform, Driver Yorio Ishiro, a tall, slim man in his mid-sixties with full white hair and a confident demeanor, pulled the lever in the control room to completely to stop the train which allowed the train's conductor in the last wagon to open the compartments' exit doors. He then glanced out the side window at the passengers leaving the shiny maroon-colored wagons in a hurry. When the last person had departed, the conductor opened the doors facing the opposite platform to admit the new passengers into the compartments. Driver Ishiro, returning to his seat in front of the control panel, poured himself a cup of water and waited for the conductor's arrival to the front control compartment.

Saito Honda, a short and muscular conductor in his mid-thirties, left the train's rear control compartment and hurriedly walked toward the front of the train to change positions with Ishiro, train's driver. When Honda entered the front control room, Ishiro handed him a cup of water and asked, "What happened at the meeting with your wife's lawyer this morning?"

"Nothing good came out of it. The divorce proceedings will have to commence."

Ishiro remembered the conductor's wedding that he had attended hardly two years earlier. He advised Honda to be patient and understanding during his divorce proceedings and focus his attention to building a new life. As the driver stood to leave the control room, Honda, remembering that the coming train ride was to be Ishiro's last driving journey, looked at him and asked, "Boss, this is your last journey to Takarazuka. Are you prepared for the coming retirement?"

Staring at the almost empty terminal, Ishiro replied, "I believe that retirement is just another form of divorce. So, I guess I am prepared for my retirement as much as you are prepared for your coming divorce. The main difference between our two types of separations is that while you must create a peaceful but lonely existence for yourself, I must create a peaceful coexistence with my spouse who, I believe, will need a considerable adjustment to my continuous presence at home. I may have to find some extracurricular activities to join, such as playing mahjong or start playing tennis. Whatever! I am a bit too old to play tennis again, but you know I love singing old Japanese songs. Maybe I'll find a local choir to improve my singing."

Conductor Honda walked out of the control room to face Driver Ishiro. The young man bent his head respectfully and wished the retiring man a peaceful final journey to Takarazuka.

Strolling calmly toward the train's front control compartment, Driver Ishiro let his thoughts wander over his long career. He had started his first railroad job just over 35 years ago at a major subway company in Tokyo. Although satisfied with his work, he had been traumatized by the horrors of the 1995 sarin gas attack that targeted several subway trains. He had tried to help the suffering passengers, and his memories of them writhing in agony caused him many sleepless nights. A few months later, he resigned from the Tokyo Subway Company and transferred to Hankyu Railways in Osaka. Shortly thereafter, he settled in his birth place, Takarazuka. For the sake of the wonderful childhood memories, he bought a house in his old neighborhood near the rail station to raise his daughter who later married a fine local man and was about to give birth to his first grandchild. Furthermore, having been assigned five years ago to the Hankyu's Takarazuka line had made his life much easier; for the first time in his life, he could walk to work.

Driver Ishiro was suddenly awakened from his reverie when a young couple rushing toward the front of the train bumped into him from behind. Apologizing profusely, the young couple rushed into the compartment behind the control room. Ishiro shook his head and smiled. As he entered the control room, he murmured, "What a weird looking couple; the girl looks like a boy and the boy looks like a girl."

The young couple entered the compartment and quickly settled into two empty seats. As the doors closed, the skinny young man with a long, dyed blond ponytailed hair, secured his guitar between his legs and turned toward his companion sitting next to him.

"Noki-Chan, how wonderful to run into you as I was rushing to catch the last train to Takarazuka. I last saw you a few months ago at the *Takarazuka Theatre's* coffee shop. You were preparing for the *Otoko-yaku* male role in the Revue's next snow-troupe play. I want to hear how the play is progressing and how do you feel about playing a male role, but first tell me why are you in Umeda at this late hour?"

The tall, slender young woman with shiny dark, close-cropped short hair wrapped with a black bandana, was wearing a worn-out blue jean and a cream colored short-sleeved shirt. She smiled.

"It is good to see you Yoshi-chan. I am here because yesterday my grandfather Bunzaemon passed away suddenly from a massive heart attack. I joined my grandmother for the funeral preparations early this morning. I've never attended a funeral ceremony before. Seeing my grandfather dressed in traditional attire and being exquisitely prepared for the attendants' preview before he was placed into a furnace was something strangely bizarre to experience. The whole glittering ceremony before incinerating a dead body makes no sense to me at all."

Noki sighed and nervously clutched her handbag to her knees as her thoughts poured forth, "I have to put this affair out of my mind. I probably told you that my grandparents raised me. I was four years old when my parents got divorced. I haven't seen much of my father. After the divorce he moved out of Kyoto and my mother moved into my grandparents' house in Osaka. A few years later, she too moved away to Kobe with her new boyfriend and left me behind with my grandparents."

After a shuddering, heartfelt sigh, she continued with her story, "I really love my grandparents, particularly my grandfather. All his life, Grandfather Bunzaemon constantly reminded me how much I resembled his younger sister who had disappeared many years ago and later had been discovered that she had been abducted by foreign agents and taken to North Korea. Grandmother said that Grandfather Bunzaemon had hoped until his dying day that his sister would come back home one day, but she never did. Grandfather was a caring, sensible man who provided me with a stable home. Yet, a few years ago when I informed him that I was going to attend the training school for all-girl *Takarazuka Revue*, he reacted negatively because he considered it a weird, immoral and outright a lesbian conglomeration. When he later discovered that I had chosen the *Otoko-yaku* male role as my place in the all-girl revue, he completely rejected me. Two years ago, when we were together for the last time, I explained to him that the Takarazuka all-girls revue was established by the founder of Hankyu Railways, Ichizo Kobayashi nearly one hundred years earlier. I told him that it is a reputable performing arts institution. I asked him why he shows so much respect for all-male *Kabuki Theatre* actors acting as women but he completely rejects *Takarazuka Revue* women acting as men. He couldn't give me an answer, so he simply brushed me aside with a crude hand gesture. I haven't seen him since, and now he is gone forever without ever seeing me on stage."

Looking at Noki with an affectionate smile on his slender, handsome face, Yoshi whispered softly, "I am so sorry to hear that you had such a sorrowful day, dear friend. Though not as sad as yours, I too had somewhat a sad day. This afternoon before going to my band's performance at a downtown Osaka pub, I visited my dying father at the Osaka University Hospital. Even after he was diagnosed with serious heart problems nearly two years ago, he wouldn't stop smoking and drinking. I think he wanted to die. I told my mother that his choice to continue drinking and smoking is a painful, slow suicide. A few months ago, he suffered a major stroke. Much like your situation with your grandfather, my father has rejected me because of my lifestyle. Since he has been in a coma for the last two months, I visit him at least once a week to continue my one-way conversations with him. During these visits, I tell him my side of the story. In the past he refused to listen; but now, I know he cannot respond but hopefully he hears my words. When I went to the hospital this morning, I met my Uncle Yosuke for the first time in my life. He was visiting my father. In the past my father mentioned that his brother, who was a member of a religious cult, had suddenly disappeared."

Yoshi coughed awkwardly. "Let's change the subject! You know, whenever we got together in the past, there was a question that I couldn't bring myself to ask you."

Noki smiled coyly. "My dear friend, you can ask me anything you wish but I may not provide you an answer!"

"Fair enough! So… In your sex life, do you prefer girls over boys?"

Noki giggled, covering her mouth with one hand. "Since you've already told me, I don't have to ask you the same question. Right now, I don't have any particular sexual preference—I mean, I don't personally care for either sex. I know one thing for sure: that is, I don't like what a coercive male personality represents: crudeness and cruelty. The lack of kindness, gentleness and grace in male personality has made me realize that I simply don't want to share my body and emotions with such people. So, during my artistic performances, I embody a kind, genteel and graceful male character. Is that a good enough answer for you?"

"But you have so many female followers who wait at the theatre's exit doors after your performances. How do you explain that?"

"A few of them may be sexually attracted to me, but most just yearn for the truly romantic, graceful man I represent in my performances. They are there to congratulate me for embodying their dreams."

As the local train moved station by station toward Takarazuka, Noki told Yoshi about being selected to a lead male role in the forthcoming play in the revue's snow-troupe. After that, Yoshi told Noki what was happening in his music career, letting her know that he had assumed the lead guitarist role as well as singing a few songs during the band's past two performances. As the train moved through the evening gloom, they conversed freely about many emotionally sensitive issues related to their respective lifestyles.

...

Stopping at a convenience store, Kenji Zenda bought a stamp and then dropped the envelope into a nearby mailbox. At the Ikeda Station, he bought a train ticket and sat quietly on a bench, waiting for the station to empty. He then quietly walked to the end of the platform and climbed down the iron stairs to reach the tracks. He walked for a long while along the walkway, taking careful steps in the direction of Ishibashi station. A train barreled past noisily as he took cover in a dark, secluded area near the security wall. When the train had disappeared around the bend, he resumed walking until he felt that he was far enough from the Ikeda station. He then sat on the ground, took the pain pills out of the paper bag, and swallowed all of them with the rest of the whisky. He soon felt the combined effect of the pills and the alcohol pulling him down into unconsciousness, so he moved in between the rails and squatted down on the pebbles between two crossties. Lying on his back, he placed his neck on one side rail and his legs on the other, splaying his arms across the crossties. Gazing at the dark and starry sky above, he murmured, "What a gorgeous night to end a miserable life!"

After waiting for a while, he finally heard the rumbling sounds of an approaching train. He closed his eyes and emptied his mind; heart racing as the train neared and then sped by in an overwhelming cacophony. Sitting upright, he watched the train pass on the adjacent rail track.

With a bitter smile, he mumbled, "This is the divine comedy of my life; I can't do anything right!"

Placing his neck back on the rail, he tried to look at his watch, but it was obscured by the darkness. "If I'm lucky I will catch the last train to Takarazuka."

He was now waiting for the train that would soon leave Ishibashi Station. Heavily drugged and intoxicated, he soon had slipped into a deep euphoria before becoming unconscious.

After disembarking most of its passengers at Ishibashi Station, the train commenced its journey toward Ikeda. Looking around the nearly empty compartment, Yoshi smiled broadly and told Noki about his latest love affair with a former band member. Meanwhile, in the control room Driver Ishiro sat firmly at the helms of the train and stared blankly into the pitch darkness hardly ten meters ahead of the bright headlights. Watching the hypnotic swoop of the crossties disappearing beneath him, he eased the accelerator back as the train approached Ikeda Station. As he lowered his eyes to the speedometer to glance at the train's exact speed, he suddenly noticed a man lying flat on his back between the rails. He immediately reached for the brakes to stop the train, only to feel a soft bump beneath the train's front wheels.

The train came to a screeching halt, sending several passengers sprawling across the compartment floors. The train's driver Ishiro hurriedly ordered the conductor in the last wagon to check on the passengers. He then called the main dispatcher and reported the incident, requesting emergency assistance and police presence. As he waited for the emergency crew and the police to arrive, he calmly announced that due to an unexpected accident the train had to stop and the doors would remain closed until further notice.

At the first compartment, after helping Noki to her feet, Yoshi reached out to pluck his guitar off the floor and mumbled, "I think this was a suicide; we will be here for a long time."

As he sat next to Noki, he whispered, "Are you still a virgin?"

Noki, who was talking on her cellphone to inform her roommate at the *Takarazuka Revue* dormitory that she would be late, decided to ignore Yoshi's asinine question.

Thirty minutes later, led by the Ikeda station master, the orange-clad railroad emergency crew carrying boxes of materials needed for the cleanup process approached the train. Soon after their arrival, two police officers appeared and asked the train driver to explain what had happened.

After Ishiro finished his detailed explanation of the incident to police sergeant Ishihara, the chief of the emergency crew asked him to back up the train to allow access to the victim's body. Ishiro immediately put the train's gear in the reverse position and slowly started to move the train backward. A short while later, when the victim's body parts came into full view, the crew chief signaled the driver to stop. Ishiro, after stopping the train, ordered the conductor in the last wagon to wait for his instructions to lead the passengers to Ikeda Station. He then opened the door and climbed down onto the rail tracks. He walked toward the front of the train where several members of the emergency crew were collecting scattered body parts. He saw one worker with a face mask and gloves place the victim's bloody severed head into a thick, black nylon bag. He also saw the police sergeant on his knees between the rails searching the victim's torso, possibly looking for identity papers.

Breaking his gaze from the grisly scene, the chief of the emergency crew approached the driver.

"Once we remove the body parts, you can release your passengers. The station master will lead them to Ikeda Station and instruct them to wait there. It will take us a while to sweep the area, possibly around an hour or so."

Ishiro, still intensely staring at the bloody dismembered body, asked, "Who was he?"

Pointing at the police sergeant still near the victim's torso, the crew chief replied, "Ask the police sergeant, he may have an answer for you."

Sergeant Ishihara, flustered and somewhat nauseous, clutched the piece of paper he had just pulled from Kenji Zenda's tattered, bloody jacket. He grimaced as he mumbled, "This didn't turn out to be a peaceful night at all." Turning around, he ordered the emergency crew workers to remove the torso and walked toward the train's headlights. After skimming through the brief note he had found in the victim's jacket, he approached the crew chief and the train's driver.

Looking at the policeman, Ishiro solemnly asked, "Were you able to identify him?"

"Yes, I did. He was an un-apprehended member of the Aum Shinrikyo terror organization."

Hearing this reply, Ishiro was overwhelmed by this tremendously ominous incident that had happened during his last driving journey to Takarazuka. He quickly assumed that this suicide was a sign of divine justice; a delayed retribution for the innocent victims of the 1995 sarin gas attack.

Ishiro commented serenely, "He must have lived with so much guilt for such a long time that he finally decided to end it all tonight."

The contents of the suicide note, which appeared contrary to train driver's statement, still lingering in his mind, Sergeant Ishihara laconically replied, "It may be so! But then it may not be!"

Saddened that his last day at work ended with such a tragic event, Ishiro gazed solemnly at the police sergeant. After a moment, he lowered his head and murmured, "May Lord Buddha forgive his sins!"

Back in the control room, Ishiro poured himself a cup of water; as he took a sip, he watched the crew in front of the train carry the remains of the suicide victim inside thick black nylon bags and place them on the ground beside the tracks. When the emergency crew chief signaled him, Ishiro called Conductor Saito Honda, asking him and the station master to get the passengers off the train and guide them to the nearby station.

Saito Honda and the Ikeda Station manager, starting from the train's last wagon, asked the passengers to get off the train and follow them to the station hardly half-a-kilometer away. When the first Wagon behind the control room was reached by the crowd of people led by Saito Honda, everyone in the wagon, including Noki and Yoshi, lined up behind the passengers to get off the wagon. Holding tightly onto his guitar, Yoshi, helped Noki get off the wagon.

As they joined the passengers walking to the nearby station, Yoshi calmly commented, "Wow! No body part remaining around rails! Cleaning crew did a wonderful job!"

Noki, appearing disturbed by what had happened, briskly remarked, "I don't want to talk about the suicide. However, if you have to talk, then let's talk about something else."

Gleefully smiling, Yoshi quickly replied, "All right then! Tell me about what kinds of sex tools you use when you masturbate?"

"Yoshi, you're obviously a sex addict! Stop asking me stupid questions. You need to grow up."

For the rest of the walking journey to the station, they both remained quiet.

After arriving at the station platform, Noki, to break the silence, decided to start a conversation with Yoshi. She sweetly inquired, "I remember from our junior high school days that you had an older brother who wanted to become a sumo wrestler. Did he reach his goal?"

Now smiling, Yoshi replied, "Yes, he did. He now is wrestling in the Jurio division. He has gained a lot of weight; he is now over 130 kilos. He is hoping to advance to the most senior Makhinochi division by becoming a champion in the lower division."

"Do you attend any of his wrestling matches?"

"No, I don't. We do not communicate much anymore; like my father, he also does not accept my life style. If one day he decides to come to one of my music performances, then I might attend one of his wrestling matches. But I don't really expect that to happen."

Thirty minutes later, the chief of the emergency crew raised his arms, signaling the train's driver to move the train to Ikeda station to pick up the passengers.

Arriving at the Station, Driver Ishiro noticed, among the crowd of passengers waiting for the train, the weird-looking young couple who had earlier bumped into him at the Umeda Station. The young couple was staring at the slow-moving train while they conversed.

Without knowing that the victim was his Uncle Yosuke, Yoshi solemnly whispered, "I wonder who this person was and why did he decide to end his life tonight?"

Noki resolutely replied, "Don't worry! You'll hear all about it in tomorrow morning's news."

The young couple, now bearing forced sad smiles on their faces, noticed the train's driver staring at them from the control room's window. They respectfully bent their heads to salute the man who had gone through such a bloody horrible suicide turmoil.

Noticing the sincere salutes of the young couple, Ishiro mumbled, "It is good to see that the younger generations still retain the traditional values of respect."

Smiling broadly, he bent his head forward to salute the young couple and whispered, "Life goes on!"

Ishiro reached out to close the window pane and, as though in a dream, moved slowly to the front of the control panel. Now murmuring his favorite traditional song *Furusato— My Hometown*—he sat down on the driver's seat and eased the accelerator stick forward to resume his final journey to Takarazuka.

***

Hankyu Lines, Takarazuka Station, Osaka

Takarazuka Revue Productions

ANZACS IN GALLIPOLI

[AUSTRALIA]

[From: *A Prelude to Gallipoli, 2015*]

Gallipoli Landing 1915

ANZACS IN GALLIPOLI

It was rare luck that, after many attempts, I was finally granted an interview with Sir Ian Hamilton, the outgoing commander of the Allied forces at the Gallipoli Campaign. A few days earlier, while preparing for the interview with the commander, I was informed that Lord Kitchener, the Minister of War in London, hearing of the latest disasters at the Gallipoli Front, had relieved General Hamilton of his command. I arrived early for my interview with the commander. Browsing the deck of the cruiser Chatham, soon to take him back to England, I seriously wondered if the coming interview would yield anything concrete to write about. Probably not, as the general would likely not reveal the real reasons behind his dismissal. During the early part of October 1915, just a week before the general's release, there had been rumors that the Allied forces would withdraw completely from the Dardanelles and abandon the idea of reaching Constantinople. Actually, this possibly foregone idea was based on a bizarre Byzantine conspiracy to take over the capital city of the Ottoman Empire and turn it over to the tsar of Russia. I had also heard a rumor that the decision to destroy the Ottoman Empire had been made after all the efforts had failed to bring the Turks to the side of the British Empire. According to rumor, these efforts included a large bribe to Enver Pasha, the leader of the Young Turks, to lure him to join the British side. Contradicting this hearsay was an act by the Crown of England, which had refused before the beginning of the war to turn over two battleships paid for in advance by the Turks. That particular action had indicated that the British did not really want the Ottoman Empire, the sick man of Europe, on their side. Sitting on a bench in front of the general's cabin, I tried to imagine how Navy Minister Winston Churchill would welcome his protégé back to London. He must have realized by now that his military strategy of quickly ending the European War by eliminating the Turkish Empire had critically faltered at the shores of Gallipoli. I wondered what words would pass between the aspiring politician and the washed-up general, and what explanations and excuses they would give each other. I had prepared a set of questions for the General to clarify some of the issues related to this military failure.

As I waited, I became increasingly nervous and edgy; an interview with a disgraced and beaten military leader would not be easy. Given his situation, I was not sure the General would answer my inquiries honestly. After a long wait, a sailor informed me that my interview with General Hamilton had been cancelled because of a sudden military emergency. I was not surprised. I leaned against the railing and stared into the turquoise waters of the Aegean Sea. Then I slowly raised my eyes and looked at the sandy shore of the nearby island of Imbros. My mind was still busily composing my report on the meeting that had not taken place. To clear my head, I took a deep breath and felt the cold, moist sea air in my lungs; winter was approaching, and the island with leafless trees looked barren and brown. When I first arrived here six months ago in mid-March, the island had appeared as barren as it looked now. That was right before the Allied navy had unsuccessfully tried to pass through the Strait of Dardanelles to reach Constantinople. At the time, the weather had been much colder and windier around the strait where the greatest naval force on earth had faced a remarkable defeat at the hands of the unspeakable Turks. Oh, what a battle that had been! What an unexpected defeat for the Allied forces! Of the eighteen Allied battleships that entered the strait, three had been sunk, another three had been severely damaged, and, worst of all nearly one thousand sailors had been lost to the sea.

At the end of the following month, I returned to the Dardanelles with the ANZAC troops. Following a long period of intensive training at the British Army facilities in Egypt, the ANZAC troops were being transported to the Gallipoli Peninsula to begin the land invasion. I clearly remember our arrival in the quiet of night right before sunrise and dropping anchor near the shores of the island of Lemnos. I ran out of the sleeping quarters in a great hurry to reach the upper deck. I wanted a look at the island's famous Aegean sunrise in the spring. On the upper deck, crowded with sailors and soldiers, I felt the cool April air on my face. I pushed my way toward the railing to have a clearer view of the island. Our ship, the Minnewaska, had anchored in the wide harbor to join the many Allied naval vessels assembled for the upcoming land attack at Gallipoli. There it was! The island of Lemnos... It looked so beautiful and inviting that the neatly lined, whitewashed houses along the bay front surrounded by plush green hills made me wish it was a time of peace, not war. I suddenly noticed a familiar face to my immediate right. I recognized a young Australian soldier in a light-horseman uniform. He was hanging over the railing and shouting as loudly as he could to another Australian soldier on the deck below, "We will get those Turks and make them bleed!"

After that dreadful evening at a Mena nightclub two weeks before, I had not expected to see him again. It was in a smelly, noisy Egyptian nightclub that we had had a friendly chat over several mugs of warm English ale. But then, in the late evening hours when almost everyone was well intoxicated, he and a few of his   friends had tried to take on a large group of British Royal Navy officers, and been taken away by the military police. Resting against the iron railing, I calmly stared at the orange-colored early morning sun, shining upon the island and reflecting on the windows of her whitewashed homes. The island was slowly awakening to face a new day. As I contemplated our imminent landing on the rugged shores of Gallipoli, the horseman suddenly turned to me, and, with a surprised look on his face, said, "Good morning, sir. It is you Mister Keith: the newspaperman from Melbourne?"

"Yes, you're right! I am the war correspondent, and you're the rowdy light- horseman from a little town somewhere in New South Wales, right?"

"Yes, Broken Hill is the name of my town," he proudly replied. He then quickly inquired, "Will you join us for the coming landing?"

"I wouldn't miss it. But why do you look so pleased about going into a bloody battle? Being in a killing field may not be as exciting as you assume. Aren't you a little afraid?"

"A little bit, of course! But I am really excited about smashing a few Turks' heads before going to Constantinople for some fun."

"What do you have against the Turks?"

"I hate the terrorist bastards. I'd like to avenge what they did to my mate's fiancée."

Since recruitment of volunteers had begun in August of 1914, I had wondered what compelled these young chaps to enlist and travel to this faraway land to participate in a European war, which, at first, had not been of concern to Australia. It appeared that this young bloke had a story to tell. I asked him to sit down on the deck next to the railing and offered him a smoke.

After taking a few big puffs from the cigarette and exhaling the smoke forcefully, he started to talk. "It was a beautiful New Year's Day morning in Broken Hill, a perfect day for a picnic, warm and sunny..."

He suddenly became quiet; his light blue eyes downcast, as if reliving the incident, he was about to relate. He focused his attention on the glowing end of his cigarette. After several more, long puffs, he continued his story.

"You know," he said with a sudden bright smile on his face, "every New Year's Day, we have this community picnic that everyone attends. All local families get on the train to Silverton, a small town several miles southeast of Broken Hill. Everybody, particularly the young folks, looks forward to the New Year's Day picnic to have fun and enjoy good food."

I interrupted him, "It must have been a very long train to carry the whole town."

He replied with a glazed stare, as if he were seeing the train in front of him. "Yes, a very long train indeed, with more than forty open carriages full of wooden planks to sit on. This last New Year's Day, I was with my best friend and his fiancée in one of the wagons. While the train was whistling off to Silverton, a couple of bloody Turks attacked us with rifles. Many were killed, and my friend's fiancée, a beautiful seventeen-year-old girl, got her brains blown out. As she slumped forward, dying from her massive head wound, my friend tried to pack her brains back into her shattered skull. That was such a terrible scene. I hate the damned Turks for what they did that day, killing that beautiful young woman and other innocent people. Both my friend and I joined up and came here to teach them a lesson. We'll kill them and we'll take over their land."

He threw the cigarette butt into the sea and immediately asked for another. As I handed him the whole pack, I told him that last January I had read the news about the picnic train massacre in Broken Hill. As he lit his cigarette, I asked him, "What were the two Turks doing in the middle of Australia?"

"They were local Turks doing some menial jobs in the community."

"What happened to them?"

"They were caught and killed later that afternoon."

I looked at him and abruptly asked, "And how many Turks would you like to kill to avenge their attack on the picnic train?"

He got to his feet to join his company for the early morning exercises. As he walked away, he shouted, "As many as possible!"

I did not see the light-horseman again. After the disastrous landing at a shoreline near Gaba Tepe, I heard that he had been killed on the morning of April 25th, during the initial attempt to land at a rocky beach south of Arı Burnu. A few days later, one of his drinking buddies told me that the poor chap had not had the opportunity to kill a single Turk. His feet never touched the ground. A bullet ripped through his throat and he bled to death on the boat. It was indeed a sad ending for that light-horseman from the town of Broken Hill, but there were many more sad deaths of countless young men during the endless bloody months from April onwards. It seemed that the presence of these ANZAC troops in Gallipoli had no clear purpose or reason, save revenge. Five months later, when I was about to leave General Hamilton's battleship, it seemed obvious that the Gallipoli Campaign had been a strategic military disaster that cost three hundred thousand casualties and over sixty thousand deaths.

Since the morning of the first landing at the Gallipoli shore, I kept thinking about what I had been told by that horseman who died on a boat, and wondered why so many Australians and New Zealanders had come to this distant land to take revenge on the Turks. How many other young men had volunteered for military service because of the New Year's Day picnic train massacre in Broken Hill, where two Turks killed innocent people for no apparent reason? I wondered! Did this incident have anything to do with the ANZAC troops' overwhelming hatred of their Turkish foes? I had to know more about what happened that day, and why. I wanted to understand the reasons behind the sacrifices that were being made on the beaches and the hills of   Gallipoli by the many young men who had voluntarily enlisted to fight the unspeakable Turks. When the war finally ended in 1919, I left France for Australia. Landing at Melbourne, I felt lucky to be alive. I had seen so much death and destruction during the last four years that I needed some peace and tranquility to recover my lost sense of humanity. It took me more than two years to recall my promise to learn more about the Broken Hill picnic train massacre of New Year's Day, 1915. I had seen many young men die during the course of the war, but I had never forgotten the light-horseman from Broken Hill, ready to fight and die because he hated his enemy with such a passion.

I carefully looked into the matter. The newspapers of the day reported the headline: Turks Attack Australia; New Year's Day Massacre in Broken Hill; Picnic Train Attacked by Turks and

Many Killed, etc., etc. When I asked about the massacre, the attorney general's office said they had investigated the incident immediately after it happened, and the report that had been prepared by his office was now locked away for good. The court documents related to the criminal investigation were also not available for review. I was informed that during the picnic train attack and the ensuing bloody conflict at the white rocks, in total, six people had been killed and eight wounded. Of the six killed, one had been a Methodist preacher and one was the friend of the light-horseman I had met in Cairo. The attackers had not really been Turks, but local Afghans armed with rifles. They were killed that same day and buried before sunrise the next day in an unmarked grave in the basement of a municipal building no one was able or willing to identify. In the early evening hours before the burial of the perpetrators, a string of illogical and highly emotional outbursts had occurred. After setting fire to the German Club and attempting to storm the Afghan settlement, the members of the white community calmed down and buried the victims the next day. The matter was put to rest, but during the next few months, thousands of young men signed up for military duty to fight the terrorist Turks, apparently as a result of this massacre. During the rest of 1915, many of these young volunteers died on the shores of Gallipoli. Thinking of the poor bloke, the light-horseman from Broken Hill who died in a boat without avenging his friend, I felt overwhelming sadness, not only for him, but also for the thousands of young men who had died to avenge the victims of two deranged Afghans in Broken Hill. Was that all there was to it? Maybe, maybe not!

Someone in my office suggested that I speak with Frederick Wenzel, a local reporter who had covered the Broken Hill massacre. I thought it would be wise to meet with him and determine whether the incident had been caused by the two crazy Afghans without any connection to the Ottoman Empire, enemy of the British Empire at that time. If the two Afghans had acted alone, why then had the news been spun so as to stir up hatred toward the Turks? More importantly, why did an aura of secrecy continue to surround the matter? Was there more to this story then what met the eye? It seemed just a matter of time until the truth would be revealed. The train ride to Broken Hill was long and arduous, but worth the discomfort. I wanted to know more about this bizarre incident. My meeting with the local journalist, Frederick Wenzel, took place on a cool and windy afternoon in late March of 1921.

We met in the exquisitely decorated Palace Hotel on Argent Street. Sipping our morning coffee, we spoke extensively about the New Year's Day massacre in 1915. The discussion was as revealing as it was disturbing. Frederick Wenzel, a lanky reporter working for the local newspaper The Barrier Miner, confided that the attack on the picnic train, despite being clumsily planned and amateurishly set up, had resulted in substantial increases in enlistment for the Gallipoli and European Campaigns. With a know-it-all grin, he said, "I was there by the white rocks near the Cable Hotel. I saw the whole thing from its gory beginning to its bizarre end. What's more, this bloody incident made an unexpected recovery possible for the Broken Hill Proprietary Company, which by the end of the war had become a prosperous and diversified international firm - a pillar of the military industrial complex in Australia."

With glowing excitement, he concluded his revelations, "Let's also not forget that this affair marked the beginning of the end for Prime Minister Andrew Fisher's government. By the fall of 1915, Billy Hughes, deputy prime minister and attorney general in the Labor Party administration, took over the government through a cabinet-level internal coup."

Burning with curiosity, I asked, "Why do you call the bloody affair an amateurish set up?"

"My dear fellow," he replied calmly, "it would be hard to explain in exact terms, but I clearly remember that many things spun out of control. There were continuous efforts to cover up the mistakes made in planning the whole massacre. Topping it all were the phony suicide letters presumably written by the two assailants. Three days after the picnic train incident and the ensuing bloody conflict at the white rocks, these unauthenticated letters were discovered by James Lyons, a retired miner, under some rocks where the two Afghans had been killed. Suspicious, don't you agree?"

With a sudden realization that he had said more than he should have, he leaned toward me and growled in a whisper, "If you're thinking of writing about this matter, don't mention my name. Please remember that Billy Hughes is still in power, and Broken Hill is still a BHP territory. Say too much and they'll come after both of us."

I assured him not to worry and that I had no intention of exposing the matter. Then I told him about the light-horseman from Broken Hill. He listened attentively. Shaking his head, he said, "I know the bloke. What a sad ending!"

The next day, during the long train ride back to Melbourne, I thought over my meeting with Frederick Wenzel and wondered how he knew so much about the details of the picnic train massacre. As he watched the strange events of that tragic day in Broken Hill, he must have intently observed what was going on. Somehow, I knew he could tell me more if I gained his trust. In particular, I wanted to know more about something that he had only flippantly mentioned: shortly after the picnic train massacre, a militia lieutenant had changed his Germanic family name to an English one and joined the army to go to the European Front. Apparently, he had done that while some members of his family were being held in an internment camp in Melbourne. I decided that I should soon visit Frederick Wenzel again to learn more about this lieutenant and the others that were part of the 'amateurish set up' he mentioned. While the rough and noisy train monotonously ground its way toward the next stop at Adelaide, I formulated a new set of questions for Frederick Wenzel. This effort stretched my imagination, forcing me to use what I had discovered so far to reconstruct the strange affairs leading up to the New Year's Day massacre in Broken Hill. It was a scary mental trip into the inhumane intricacies of wartime politics.

I was woken up by the gentle touch of the conductor. With a smile on his face, he reminded me that the train was about to arrive in Melbourne. The last thing I remembered before falling asleep was that the train had stopped for a short while at Adelaide Station, where I had gone out onto the platform to buy some biscuits and water. I do not usually remember my dreams, but this one remained vividly in my memory for years. I am sure my visit to Broken Hill and long-winded discussions with local reporter Frederick Wenzel had set the stage for this dreadful dream. My mind was subconsciously trying to recreate some rational explanations for what had happened during that sorrowful event. Did it really happen the way I dreamed? It does seem that what actually happened was not what was presented in the national media. Was it a conspiracy of the worst kind, in which innocent lives were deliberately destroyed for political expediency and where the actual perpetrators and true murderers were intentionally left unidentified, unprosecuted and unpunished? My nightmare seemed to reflect something of the nature of injustice and immorality inherent to wartime politics. Just thinking of it made me furious to the depths of my soul, especially when I remember the light-horseman who died on a boat along the shorelines of Gallipoli. Thinking of the thousands of young men killed for nothing, I become disenchanted and resentful of the system that justified and condoned this horrible massacre for reasons of national glory. Wiping sweat from my forehead, I stared out the window. We were on the outskirts of Melbourne and about to arrive at the central station. To soothe my anger and emotional confusion, I asked myself, "Could this dream just be a mental trick or an elaborate piece of casuistry, making me believe what I want to believe?" I was confident that my nightmare had almost a rational and logical basis. There were many inexplicable circumstances and obvious irregularities about the dreadful event in Broken Hill, which my mind had reconstructed the bloody affair within a more realistic framework. A suicide mission of two simple-minded camel-men seemed farfetched, but it had suited the expectations of the unscrupulous perpetrators as well as the war-hyped mass media. Given that the only proof of such a suicide mission was the after-the-fact discovery of a couple of phony suicide letters, one would naturally question the motives of all parties who had been involved in the framing and ensuing cover-up of the incident. At that juncture, a prevailing sense of morality brings forward the ultimate question: why would a man of religious affiliation and a man who sold ice cream to children shoot and kill innocent people? Even if one assumed that the Afghans' hatred toward the white community, who had mistreated them for such a long time, were sufficient motive for committing a bloody attack on the picnic train, camouflaging such a massacre under a Turkish flag introduced an added level of sophistication, which called for a proper investigation and in-depth analysis of the events preceding the incident. Obviously, the authorities handling the case had not wanted to   pursue the matter to that extent. In fact, they had done just the opposite: destroying or sealing all the documentary evidence and ha be as corpus that might have proved the existence of a broader conspiracy at the national level, led by perpetrators in public and private sectors to remold public opinion in support of the ongoing war. The actual occurrences of events and the personalities that were part of my dream might not be an exact mirror of what really had happened. The true events may have followed different patterns and sequences, and the individual actors may not have been the ones who actually planned and committed these dreadful crimes. Still, I am certain that my dream was closer to reality than what was reported by a war-hyped media. Neither the Afghans nor the Turks had anything to do with the massacre in Broken Hill. Perhaps one day, the truth may be revealed and the matter put to rest.

The train slowly came to a full stop at the central platform. I was the last person to disembark. On the platform, as I walked toward the main exit, a newspaper boy approached me shouting loudly: "A MEMBER OF PARLIAMENT FROM BROKEN HILL IS ASSASSINATED IN A TRAIN STATION. READ ALL ABOUT IT!"

I reached out and grabbed a newspaper, and for the longest time I stared at the headline: another bloody day in

Australian politics. I quickly read the shocking details. A well-known member of parliament and respected national labor leader, Percy Brookfield, had been killed in a train station south of Broken Hill. At least for the time being, this morbid news forced my mind away from my wretched nightmare about the picnic train massacre.

On the way home, I stopped by the newspaper office to catch up with ongoing global events. On my desk I found a long-awaited telegram - my application for a journalist's dream job at a major newspaper in New York City had been accepted; I was on my way to the United States of America.

Broken Hill Picnic Train, January 1, 1915

SUNSET IN MAHDIYA

[THE SUDAN]

[From: *Bones in the Nile, 2016*]

SUNSET IN MAHDIYA

At the British Landing Site

In the vast desert surrounding the convergence of the Blue and White Niles, the windless and fervently hot first day of September in 1898 was about to end. The orange-hued sun was slowly disappearing behind the rolling sandy hills overlooking the flatlands around the small fishing village of Kerrari. The British and Anglo-Egyptian army units and river-based Royal Navy, under the command of General Herbert Horatio Kitchener, vigorously prepared to confront the immense army of the Mahdiya, camped behind hills overlooking the fields of Kerrari, approximately twenty kilometers northwest of Omdurman.

Having crossed the Sudanese border in March of 1896, the Anglo-Egyptian army of twenty-five thousand men had since steadily advanced on Omdurman. Upon arriving at the banks of the Nile near the village of El Egeiga, British gunboats, unaware that the sixty-thousand-strong Sudanese Mahdiya army had vacated the city days earlier, began bombarding the fortifications at Omdurman. The army of Khalifa Abdullah was now camped behind a large rocky hill named Jebel Surgham that faced the fields of Kerrari.

The Nile was high and rough, flowing strongly past the Anglo-Egyptian personnel carriers and heavily armored river vessels. The gunboats fell silent with the arrival of sunset. The soldiers, the British in handsome khaki uniforms and white helmets and the Egyptian fellahin and black Sudanese in dull-gray uniforms and crimson-red fezzes, prepared to settle in for their evening meals. Several senior British officers converged around the mess tents near General Kitchener's headquarters, smoking nervously and discussing the impending battle, particularly focusing on the following question: Would the enemy attack the British positions or defend Omdurman, their capital? A few officers expressed hope that the army of the Khalifa would retreat into the desert and escape to El Obeid, the provincial capital of Kordofan.

As the restless officers argued about the coming battle, a fair-skinned, blue-eyed, diminutive British military reporter with light-brown hair fiddled agitatedly with his notebook. He had lost patience with the nonsense spoken by those around him. He slowly rose to his feet, and before stepping out, sternly addressed a nearby group of frustrated junior officers: "Gentlemen, there is no need to speculate. Tomorrow morning, we shall all learn our fates."

As he left the mess tent, two smartly-uniformed senior officers greeted the lieutenant.

"Lieutenant Churchill," one of the officers asked, "have you decided to which regiment you will be attached during the battle?"

"Yes, Colonel," Winston Churchill replied. "I would like to be attached to the Twenty-First Lancer Regiment."

Smiling broadly, Colonel Francis Reginald Wingate enthusiastically replied, "Lieutenant, I am impressed with your bravery. It seems you expect the lancers to encounter an exciting battle. Tell me, what is your assessment of our situation?"

After remaining quiet for a moment, the young lieutenant asked, "Permission to speak freely, sir?"

Puzzled, the colonel murmured, "Proceed, Lieutenant."

"I've just noticed that Commander Kitchener is taking a nap in his tent. I presume he anticipates a peaceful night and, if it remains so, then tomorrow we could be victorious by the day's end. On the other hand, if the Khalifa's immense army decides to attack our positions during the night, we will be in serious trouble. Many regiments are spread too thinly along the riverbank. If the enemy decides to attack us during complete darkness of the night, our superior firepower may prove insufficient to halt the onslaught of a vicious crowd of dervishes. I don't think General Kitchener seriously has considered the possibility of a night attack. I think we should reposition night camp area into a compact quadrilateral arrangement for better defense. Colonel, if you get the chance, please mention this strategic oversight to the Commander."

In a somber tone that bespoke both irritation and concern, Colonel Wingate replied, "I understand your concern, Lieutenant, but I assure you that General Kitchener has considered all possible strategic circumstances before deciding tonight's camp arrangements."

Before walking away, Lieutenant Churchill calmly saluted both officers and remarked, "I hope that you're correct, Colonel. Gentlemen, I wish you both a pleasant evening."

After the departure of the *Morning Post* war correspondent, Colonel Wingate turned toward his companion. Using Rudolf von Slatin's nickname, he asked, "Rowdy, I presume you've met Lieutenant Churchill before?"

As he removed his crimson fez and tucked it under his right arm, Colonel Slatin, also a *pasha* in the service of the

Egyptian Khedive, replied nonchalantly, "I've seen him around since our departure from Cairo, but I hadn't had the opportunity to meet him. He seems to be a bright young fellow, if a bit overconfident and conceited."

"You are quite right," Wingate said blandly. "He is intelligent and charming but overly opinionated and assertive at times. He comes from a prominent and wealthy English family. He could have a promising military career if only General Kitchener liked him."

Colonel Slatin replied with a sly smile, "Herbert doesn't like me either, but thanks to your influence, my military career has flourished since my escape from Omdurman."

"Indeed, it has! Within four years you became a British Colonel and also a pasha in the Egyptian Khedive's service. Please don't take it personally that you weren't invited to the senior staff meeting this evening."

"I am certainly insulted, but I will gracefully accept it. Truth be told, I don't fully understand why Herbert constantly refuses to seek my advice. It seems he does not want to utilize my years of experience with the Mahdist military elite."

Wingate laid his hand on his friend's arm.

"Rest assured that at this evening's meeting I will relay your views on Khalifa Abdullah and his scheming brother Yakub. I completely understand your concerns about our vulnerable positions along the riverbank—the same concerns, in fact, just expressed by Lieutenant Churchill. I will introduce this issue during the meeting. I cannot guess how Kitchener will respond. Frankly I am concerned that he is still undecided about tomorrow's plans. He could decide to attack the Mahdist army by dawn or choose to remain on the defensive and wait for the enemy to engage us."

At the Mahdiya Army Camp

Twenty kilometers from the British encampment, an important gathering was taking place in the Ansar army camp behind the rocky hills of Kerrari. The *amirs-al-umara* convened in the massive tent of Khalifa Abdullah, the absolute ruler of the Sudanese Mahdiya. Abdullah ibn Muhammed al Ta'ishi, known as the Khalifat-*ul-Mahdi* to his subjects, sat atop an elevated, well-cushioned, leather-spun wooden *angareb*. He gazed with gloomy intensity at the congregated ruling elite of the Mahdiya. To his right, at the front of the gathering, were his two heirs to the Mahdiya throne: the Khalifa's eldest son, Amir Osman Sheikh ed-Din, and older half-brother, Amir Yakub ibn Muhammed al Ta'ishi. They were both speaking excitedly with their cousin Osman al Azrak. To Khalifa Abdullah's left stood a group of senior *amirs* around Osman Digna and Ibrahim Khalil, arguing heatedly over the military strategies slated for discussion.

Wearing a silken white *jubbeh* and a cotton Mecca-*takia* over which a cream-colored silk *turban* was loosely wrapped, Khalifa Abdullah, who was bothered by the humming conversations of the congregated amirs, suddenly raised his right hand and growled loudly, "Be quiet!"

As the room fell silent, the strong baritone voice of the Mahdiya's absolute ruler erupted over the gathering.

"A day of discernment is upon us. We owe it to most generous and gracious Allah to defend our land, our homes, and our dignity. Our beloved departed leader Muhammed Ahmed Al Mahdi would have reminded us that now is the time to pay our dues to the Almighty. The infidels are camped at the banks of the Nile River and spend the day bombarding our beloved city

147

Omdurman. During the rainstorm two nights ago, I slipped out into the desert and watched them land at the riverbanks near El Egeiga village. Their army is large and full of British, Egyptian, and black Sudanese soldiers."

A nervous murmur arose throughout the assembled amirs, which the Khalifa silenced it with a stern wave of hand.

"Some of you are concerned about our chances of defeating this intimidating infidel army. Need I remind you that our Ansar army is much larger than theirs, or that our warriors are more daring and courageous than the infidels could ever be?"

The Khalifa's voice rose as he vented his vexation at the invaders.

"This malicious Christian army is here to destroy our homes, our faith, and our very way of life. As we did before under the unfailing guidance of our beloved leader Al Mahdi, we shall prevail and remove the infidel from our homeland once and for all."

The Khalifa, shaking from the force of his own oration, stiffened his back. After clearing his throat and gently running a hand over his scraggly white beard, he resumed his speech, "I know that some of you have strategic suggestions, which is why I have called this meeting. You may speak now."

His son, Osman Sheikh ed-Din, took the floor.

"We face a small army with its back to the Nile. As dawn breaks, we should block their flanks and launch a strong frontal assault. If it is the will of Allah, we shall push them into the river by noon."

Amidst cheers and shouts in support of Osman Sheikh ed-Din's strategy, Amir Osman Digna raised his right hand and asked permission to respond. Seeing Khalifa Abdullah's affirmative nod, Osman Digna stood. Gently bowing his head toward his sovereign, he spoke confidently.

"Amir Sheikh ed-Din, I admire your courage and the trust you have in our brave warriors, and I fully agree that we should attack the enemy with all of our might. I must, however, respectfully disagree with your suggestion to attack in the broad morning daylight. We have spent the last two years resisting repeated British invasions of our land and losing every battle. We must not repeat our mistakes. The enemy is well-armed and well-supplied with improved machine-guns and heavy artillery. It would be wise for us to fight under the cover of darkness, when our warriors won't become easy targets. Your cousin, Amir Osman al Azrak, recently scouted the British army camp. He supports my recommendation. I firmly believe that if we attack before dawn, we shall take them by surprise. In the cover of darkness, we will reach the enemy camps and kill many in close hand-to-hand combat. The enemy won't be able to leverage their superior firepower, leaving us with fewer casualties. I am convinced that only with a night attack can we hope to seize victory."

Turning toward Khalifa Abdullah, Amir Osman Digna concluded with an appeal. "My respected Khalifat-ul-Mahdi, I beg you to give serious consideration to my proposal for a nighttime attack on the enemy positions spread thinly along the riverbank."

Many long and arduous hours of argument later, Khalifa Abdullah decided in favor of the strategy proposed by his son and supported by his brother, Amir Yakub ibn Muhammed. The Khalifa then adjourned the meeting, instructing all of the senior amirs to prepare for a full-frontal attack at dawn.

The Black Flag

The night was undisturbed and silent. The battle of Kerrari was to be fought in broad daylight. Fifteen minutes before the sun shone its bright orange face over the shimmering waters of the Nile, a crowd of twelve thousand Ansar soldiers appeared behind the steep and rocky Surgham Hills facing the sandy plains of Kerrari. Under the dark-green banner of Amir Osman Sheikh ed-Din, and with a concerted roar of "Allah is great!" thousands of patched jubbeh-clad Ansar warriors led by Amir Osman al Azrak rushed the Anglo-Egyptian army positions covering the riverbank. In less than half an hour, Maxim machine guns and well-aimed gunboat barrages mowed down thousands who approached on horseback, on camels, and on foot. Not a single Ansar warrior reached the Anglo-Egyptian front lines. Amir Osman al Azrak, dressed in a colorfully patched Ansar jubbeh, lay lifeless among the thousands of dead and dying. Realizing the hopelessness of the situation, Amir Sheikh ed-Din, commander of the Ansar regiment carrying the dark-green banner, withdrew with his remaining forces to the security of the hills and ridges above the flat fields of Kerrari.

Around the upstream edge of the Anglo-Egyptian defense line, a small battalion of Egyptian cavalry and a few camel-mounted Sudanese riflemen waited to move into the battle. A European in a dull-gray Egyptian army uniform and crimson fez stood next to a British colonel. They were both staring intensely at the horizon through their telescopes.

"Rex," said the officer in Egyptian uniform, "this battle is going much better than expected. That foolish Khalifa pushed his army straight into the hellfire of our Maxim guns and artillery."

Colonel Reginald Wingate's pudgy round face was red with excitement.

"Rowdy!" he shouted back. "This is your chance for revenge against Khalifa Abdullah and his brother Yakub! General Kitchener expects you to capture the crafty old Khalifa before he disappears into Omdurman. When the opportunity presents itself, seize the bloody old bastard."

For the next two hours, Rudolf von Slatin, known to the Mahdists as Mulazimin Abdulkadir Saladin, observed the battle unfolding across the vast fields of Kerrari. He saw that the army of the Mahdiya was in serious trouble and might withdraw to Omdurman. Then he suddenly noticed over the horizon a large column of Ansar cavalry and foot soldiers under the black banner of the khalifa. The column, led by Yakub ibn Muhammed al Ta'ishi, moved toward the left flank of the battlefield, opening a renewed attack on the Anglo-Egyptian forces as they pushed towards Omdurman. Mounting his horse, Rudolf von Slatin Pasha ordered his battalion to move out.

...

Yakub ibn Muhammed al Ta'ishi nudged his horse and galloped toward his younger half-brother, the Khalifa, who sat astride his favorite gray donkey surrounded by bodyguards on horseback.

As they drew near the entourage, Khalifa Abdullah yelled, "Yakub, attack the enemy regiments moving toward Omdurman. As you stall their advance, the fighters of Osman Sheikh ed-Din will support your left flank. I've ordered Ali Wad Helu to advance his mounted Degheim fighters from your far-left flank toward the British cavalry; that will separate the enemy from their main support column. Move against them as swiftly as possible. If for any reason you do not succeed, withdraw to Omdurman. I've sent Ibrahim Khalil with five hundred men to support Osman Digna's Hadendowa warriors, who are defending the lines of retreat. May Allah protect all of you and grant us victory soon."

This was the last time Khalifa Abdullah ibn Muhammed al Ta'ishi saw his brother. When the Mahdiya forces under the black flag attacked the Anglo-Egyptian columns, neither the Ansars of Amir Osman Sheikh ed-Din nor the cavalry of Ali Wad Helu were positioned to support the faltering left flank of the Mahdist frontal offensive. Before they could execute an attack on the Anglo-Egyptian positions, the British cavalry pinned them down. At the same time, the Twenty-First British Lancer Regiment attacked the forces of Osman Digna and Ibrahim Khalil on their right flank, blocking the retreat to Omdurman. Without cavalry, artillery support, or a well-defended retreat route, Khalifa Abdullah realized too late the disastrous consequences of his decision to charge the advancing British columns. The Ansar soldiers—mostly armed with rifles, swords, and spears—had no chance against the Maxim machine guns and the pinpoint artillery fire of the well-positioned British gunboats.

In less than an hour, thirteen thousand warriors perished on the southwestern flank of the Kerrari fields. Yakub ibn Muhammed al Ta'ishi, commanding Amir of the Mahdiya, watched helplessly as the incessant barrage tore his forces apart. As warriors dropped dead around him, the tragedy crystallized into a moment of brutal clarity: his past accomplishments were now futile and his dreams for the future dead.

As he tried to dodge bullets buzzing past his head, a sharp pain tore through his chest. Spitting blood, he fell to his knees. Leaning on the sword in his right hand, he glanced at the distant enemy lines and took a painful breath.

"Saladin had warned me," he whispered, "that one day, the British would find a way to avenge the killing of Gordon Pasha in Khartoum."

He blinked rapidly to clear his vision. *Before I starved him to death in the prison,* he mused, *Fadl al Maula warned me about the fate of Muhammed Ahmed...*

A bullet pierced his forehead, ending the amir's musings. He fell backward on the blood-soaked ground among the lifeless bodies of the Baggara guards, who had fallen defending the black flag of the Khalifat-ul-Mahdi that stood erect and fluttered gently over the killing fields of Kerrari.

As the battle came to its tragic end, two camps—one at the south end of the Ansar lines and the other at the northern flank of the British defense lines—watched the battle dramatically unfold.

In the southern camp, Khalifa Abdullah cursed the enemy loudly. Tears poured down his wrinkled, sunburned cheeks into his scraggly white beard.

As he put down his telescope, he murmured, "Oh my poor brother Yakub, now you're in the realm of our creator. Your sufferings are no more. May Allah forgive all your sins and grant you a place in heaven."

He turned abruptly toward the horizon, where he expected large columns of warriors and horsemen under the command of his son Osman Sheikh ed-Din to appear.

"For Allah's sake!" he shouted. "Osman, my son, where are you? Where are you, Ali Wad Helu? You have both disappeared at the moment you are most needed. Because of your inactions, we are now defeated and completely ruined."

Meanwhile, on a ridge at the northern flank of the British defense lines, Rudolf von Slatin hurriedly put down his telescope and remarked, "Good Lord! The bloody Khalifa is getting on his donkey to run away to Omdurman. Your time is up, Abdullah. I will catch you and cut your throat, you scoundrel!"

The Khalifa on His Donkey

Khalifa Abdullah ibn Muhammed al Ta'ishi, the battered and beaten ruler of the Sudanese Mahdiya, returned to his besieged capital on the back of his favorite gray donkey. His bodyguards followed on horses and camels. Before entering his house, he rushed into the mausoleum of Muhammed Ahmed Al Mahdi, which had received a direct hit from the morning's bombardment that partially collapsed its dome. The Khalifa ordered the bodyguards to leave him alone in the shrine and then cautiously walked among the shattered stones and brick rubble. When he reached the tomb of Al Mahdi, he approached the soiled black satin cloth covering the wooden catacomb. Then he fell to his knees and loudly recited prayers.

Completing his prayers, he murmured, "You have forsaken me, my master! What wrong have I done to deserve this defeat at the hands of the damned infidels? Almighty Allah, why am I being punished for serving my country and my people? What should I do now? Where do I go? How do I recover from such a defeat? Oh Allah, most gracious and generous creator of all things on Earth, forgive my faults and mistakes and guide me along a righteous path so I can lead my people to recover our national dignity. Oh Allah...give us another chance."

Khalifa Abdullah spent a long time in prayer. Then he rose and walked to his home across the mausoleum. He ordered that all the *noggaras* be beaten loudly and the *ombayas* blown strongly, signaling that the Ansar warriors should return to Omdurman. He then sent his remaining bodyguards to the outskirts of Omdurman to tell the surviving warriors to assemble for a final defense.

As he sat down for a short meal prepared by his principal wife, he was informed that the house's rear section had received a direct hit in the morning. Several people, including his young wife Jamilla, had been killed. Before Khalifa Abdullah could respond, a wounded Ansar warrior from Ibrahim Khalil's regiment apprehensively entered the room.

"My respected Khalifa," the soldier mumbled loudly, "you should leave Omdurman quickly. Mulazimin Abdulkadir Saladin and his soldiers are approaching."

Khalifa Abdullah thanked the man and ordered him to receive treatment for his wound. After the soldier's departure, Abdullah's principal wife of entered the room in a rush.

"My honored husband," she said in a panic, "to stay alive, we must leave Omdurman and escape to El Obeid immediately."

Abdullah stood and loudly uttered what had been on his mind ever since the wounded warrior's announcement, "The biggest mistake of my life was to trust Saladin and make him an officer of my court. The day after he escaped Omdurman four years ago, I should have listened to Yakub's advice and sent soldiers to catch and hang him. I allowed that miserable two-faced European traitor to escape, hoping he would return to his country and stay there. Now that filthy dog is at my doorstep. I won't give him the satisfaction of finding me."

It was nearly noon. After barely five hours, the battle of Kerrari had ended with the two-mile-long British and Egyptian infantry line advancing westward, chasing the remnants of the Mahdist army away from Omdurman and into the vast, barren landscape that led to Kordofan.

A British lieutenant, commanding a group of Egyptian infantry soldiers, led a mop-up operation on the battlefield. He found the sacred black banner of the Mahdiya still erect and fluttering, propped up by its fallen defenders. The lieutenant reached over the pile of bloody corpses and retrieved the Mahdist flag. He rushed it to his regimental commander, who in turn ordered a cavalry officer to deliver it to General Kitchener's headquarters before the general ordered the march on Omdurman.

By late afternoon; with the perimeters of Omdurman secured, General Sir Herbert Horatio Kitchener decided to lead his victorious army into Omdurman. Before the procession commenced, a cavalry captain approached the commander's entourage and handed the folded flag to an aide-de-camp. When the matter was brought to his attention, General Kitchener ordered the flag unfolded and raised alongside the British and the Egyptian flags during the march into Omdurman.

As the Anglo-Egyptian army moved across the wide and flat Kerrari plain, they passed over thousands of dead and dying Sudanese warriors. Several British soldiers succumbed to unexpected attacks from wounded Ansar soldiers feigning death. When this was reported to General Kitchener, he casually ordered that wounded enemy soldiers be shot on sight.

The advancing Anglo-Egyptian army quickly reached the crest of a flat-topped ridge overlooking the broad panorama of Omdurman. They saw the battered dome of Al Mahdi's tomb and the minarets of the great mosque. Surrounding the mosque, a multitude of mud-walled huts were interwoven erratically into a cobweb of sandy pathways approaching the glittering confluence of the two Niles.

After a few minor skirmishes, the victorious British general entered Omdurman. He rode without glancing at the muddy streets, which were littered with the lifeless bodies of old men, women, and children.

Riding high and proud at the head of his sizable entourage, Kitchener glared bitterly at the destroyed tomb of Al Mahdi. Across from the tomb, in front of the modest palace, he gracefully dismounted and asked the whereabouts of Khalifa Abdullah. He was told that the Mahdist ruler was not in his palace. As he walked toward the palace entry, two British artillery shells exploded nearby. The shrapnel missed the general but mortally wounded Lieutenant Hubert Howard, a British war correspondent standing nearby. General Kitchener calmly ordered his aide-de-camp, Major James Watson, to send a messenger to the British gunboats to cease fire.

After Major Watson's departure, an officer fully dressed in an Egyptian uniform and wearing a crimson fez approached the general. After saluting the general, the officer loudly reported, "General Kitchener, sir, I am sorry to report that a short while ago, Khalifa Abdullah escaped Omdurman on the back of a donkey."

Without emotion, the tall and husky British general stared down at the small and wiry Austrian officer in Egyptian uniform.

"Slatin Pasha," Kitchener said coarsely, "get back on your horse. If you ride fast enough, you will catch up with your nemesis on a jackass. Bring him back here alive."

Bones in the Nile

On the second of September 1898, the Anglo-Egyptian armed forces soundly defeated the huge army of Khalifa

Abdullah, last sovereign of the Sudanese theocratic realm called the Mahdiya. The day after the fall of Omdurman, General Sir Herbert Horatio Kitchener summoned Major W. S. Gordon, nephew of the famed General Charles George Gordon, who was martyred defending Khartoum thirteen years earlier. General Kitchener ordered Major Gordon to completely destroy the mausoleum of Muhammed Ahmed Al Mahdi, founder of the independent state of Mahdiya in the Sudan. Al Mahdi had died mysteriously and unexpectedly in June 1885, less than five months after liberating his country from the British colonial domination.

Two days after the battle of Kerrari, a special flag-raising ceremony was conducted at the ruins of the Saraya, the governor's palace in Khartoum. The ritual took place during the early morning hours of September 4, 1898, in memory of Charles George Gordon, renowned British army general and last Anglo-Egyptian governor of the Sudan. Thirteen years earlier, during the final push to occupy Khartoum on January 26, 1885, a small group of Sudanese Ansar soldiers had slaughtered the British general against the explicit orders of Al Mahdi to retrieve Gordon alive. The Sudanese leader had intended to exchange the British General for two Ottoman pashas: an Egyptian army officer named Ahmed Arabi, exiled to the British colony of Ceylon since 1883 and a Sudanese Ja'aliyin Arab named Zubeir Rahmat Mansur, the conqueror of vast provinces of Bahr el Ghazal and Darfur, who had been under house arrest in Cairo for almost a decade.

Following the memorial ceremony in the ruins of the governmental palace in Khartoum, the triumphant General Sir Herbert Horatio Kitchener, accompanied by Colonel Francis

Reginald Wingate, Major W. S. Gordon, Rudolf von Slatin Pasha, and Lieutenant Winston Churchill, proceeded to the partially destroyed mausoleum of Al Mahdi in Omdurman.

At the devastated mausoleum, the vengeful British General instructed his aide-de-camp Major James Watson to exhume the bones of Muhammed Ahmed Al Mahdi. British soldiers removed the iron railing surrounding the wooden catacomb. After breaking the wooden encasing, they opened the grave and unearthed the skeletal remains of Al Mahdi. His skull was unceremoniously severed and the decomposing bones of the revered leader of Sudanese independence were crushed to pieces. Then a soldier stuffed the skull into a burlap bag and carried it to Major Watson.

As he held the bag under his left arm, the aide-de-camp saluted the disdainful general and asked what should be done with the skull and the crushed bones of Al Mahdi.

General Herbert Horatio Kitchener, his face stoic, remained motionless and upright on his horse. After a lengthy pause, the general callously instructed Major Watson to deliver the bag with the skull to his quarters. Then, deliberately stretching his left arm to point in the direction of the River Nile, Kitchener answered the rest of the question: "Bones ... in the Nile!"

November 1899: The Battle at Umm Dibeikarat

Since Omdurman's fall in September 1898, Khalifa Abdullah had become a fugitive in his own land; he had been constantly on the run for the last fourteen months. He had escaped from Omdurman on a donkey following the loss of most of his glorious Ansar army in an ill-advised morning attack against the invading British army. He had since been trying to gather his dispersed warriors to face the enemy for a conclusive battle. Finally, the Khalifa, the surviving elite of the Mahdiya, and a considerable number of followers were gathered in the northwestern part of Kordofan to organize resistance against the occupying enemy army. They had already won a few skirmishes against the Anglo-Egyptian forces searching for Khalifa Abdullah and the remnants of his army in the vast territories of Kordofan and southern Darfur.

As the Mahdist resistance army grew, their need for food and water increased accordingly. Their diminishing supplies made the khalifa decide to move closer to Umm Dibeikarat, a sparsely wooded area near the fertile lands of the Nile. With his new army properly fed and watered in and around Umm Dibeikarat, Khalifa Abdullah intended to cross the Nile and push into the agricultural lands of El Jezira. This would give him the opportunity to reach Omdurman and challenge the enemy that had pushed him out of his capital more than a year earlier. Through this strategy, he hoped to outmaneuver the enemy forces that had been chasing him all over the flatlands of Kordofan for the past six months.

Immediately after reaching the secluded woods of Umm Dibeikarat, Khalifa Abdullah called an urgent meeting of his elite commanders.

"Once we cross the Nile and move into El Jezira," he announced resolutely, "the infidel army, which has been unaware of our movement, will continue searching fruitlessly in the boundless territories of Kordofan. A few regiments will stay behind to keep the enemy busy. Soon after our arrival in Messalamia, we'll attack and destroy the enemy's main forces near Khartoum before they have a chance to react. We'll definitely surprise them, and, if it's the will of Allah, kick them out of our land."

Wingate, the Hunter

After the Arab informant left his tent, Colonel Reginald Wingate sat on the edge of his cot and thanked his lucky stars. A month earlier, Herbert Kitchener—the Governor General of the Sudan—had ordered the Colonel to hunt down and eliminate the elusive Khalifa and his large Mahdist entourage. An Arab informant had just confirmed a tip that Wingate had earlier received from an unreliable source.

He summoned his aide-de-camp and ordered him to prepare the regiment for a quick move into the wooded fields of Umm Dibeikarat, where the Ansar forces were camped. Within a few hours, the Anglo-Egyptian regiment was ready to advance. Before commencing the march, Colonel Wingate called his commanding officers for a review meeting.

"We must move swiftly," he instructed the officers firmly. "Even if it takes all day and night, we must reach Umm Dibeikarat before the Khalifa's army moves on. If we surprise them, we can finally stamp out the remnants of the Mahdist elite and their unruly fol

s regiment out, he packed his personal lowers."

Before leading hipapers into a bag that contained confidential information. Sealing the bag, he wished Rudolf van Slatin, who had been unexpectedly summoned to Cairo on General Kitchener's orders, was with him now so that he would finally catch up with the elusive Khalifa.

"Dear friend," he whispered, "you should be here for revenge against your former tormentor.

Walking out the tent, he mused, *If all goes well tomorrow, we will surround and eliminate the Ansar army. I'll see to it that all traces of the Mahdist movement are fully eradicated.*

The Night of the Harbinger

Late that evening, one of the scouts who had been placed on the outskirts of the Ansar camp in Umm Dibeikarat rushed into Amir Muhammed al Nur Angara's tent.

"A large enemy force has just appeared on the northern horizon!" the scout hollered. "Enemy soldiers are rapidly advancing and will soon surround us."

Amir Muhammed al Nur Angara rushed to Khalifa Abdullah's zariba. The Baggara guard went into the Khalifa's tent to awaken Abdullah. After a short wait, the guard holding a lit candle led the Khalifa out of the tent. Several servants hurriedly laid a large fleece carpet on the ground and set down a huge pillow for the Khalifa to lean on.

Sitting upon the carpet and leaning back on the pillow, Khalifa Abdullah spoke in a deep, sleepy voice, "Sit down, Muhammed al Nur. I am sure you have awoken me for a good reason."

"My respected Khalifat-ul-Mahdi," meekly whispered the Amir, "there are enemy soldiers in the vicinity. They are about to surround our camp."

"Where did you get that information?" asked the Khalifa sullenly.

"Before sunset, I placed scouts around the periphery of the camp to observe the horizon."

"That was smart," said the Khalifa. "I wonder how the enemy discovered our location. Only a handful people know my decisions on matters of movement and logistics. Someone must have informed the enemy before we came here. How sad that I am surrounded by liars, cheaters, and traitors. It seems some of my senior commanders will sell me out to the enemy for a few measly gold coins. I have lost all reason and purpose to continue with this struggle. I cannot win battles without reliable, trustworthy fighters who are devoted to our cause to regain our country. Do you remember how it was at the beginning of our struggle almost two decades ago? We were all obedient servants of our beloved leader Muhammed Ahmed, who promised victory and freedom. We followed him with complete devotion."

"Of course, I remember those times, my respected Khalifa," Amir Angara said softly. "We have to get you to a safe location before the enemy surrounds us."

As Muhammed al Nur Angara completed his last words, a scout emerged from some dried mimosa bushes and rapidly approached the Amir. Not noticing Khalifa Abdullah's presence, the scout agitatedly shouted, "The enemy soldiers are about to reach the camp periphery! We will soon be completely surrounded."

Khalifa Abdullah quickly asked a few questions and then dismissed the scout.

"It is too late to escape, and there is no longer any reason to run away. Even if I do, the enemy will soon discover my new whereabouts because we have obviously been fully infiltrated. If it is the will of Allah, we will win this coming confrontation; if not, we die with dignity."

Bending forward toward Khalifa Abdullah, Muhammed al Nur Angara meekly whispered, "My respected Khalifat-ul-

Mahdi, may I reveal a secret that I have kept locked in my heart for the past seven years?"

"Of course, Muhammed al Nur," replied the Khalifa coarsely. "But why now, and why have you waited so long?"

"I have kept this incriminating secret hidden for my own survival, but I wish to reveal it now because I may not have another chance."

Pushing the candle in front of him aside for a clear look at the Amir's face, Khalifa Abdullah complacently said, "Tell me your secret."

Muhammed al Nur Angara then told the Khalifa what he had heard from Fadl al Maula before he died of starvation seven years earlier in Omdurman's infamous prison.

"With his last breath," Amir Angara said resolutely, "Fadl told me that his brother Hamdan and your brother Yakub poisoned our great leader, Muhammed Ahmed Al Mahdi. They planned this horrendous crime so that you would become absolute ruler of the Mahdiya."

Upon hearing these last words of Fadl al Maula from Muhammed al Nur Angara, Khalifa Abdullah, now deeply grief-stricken, stared at the flickering candles to his left and remained silent for a long while. Then, with a sudden wave of his right hand, he tersely dismissed Amir al Nur Angara.

Standing to take his leave, the Amir sheepishly inquired, "My respected Khalifa, should I awaken the camp and tell them to prepare for battle?"

Remaining seated, the Khalifa replied, "Listen carefully. You know where my family and the Ashraf are located. Before the fighting starts, take a few soldiers and discreetly smuggle my infant son Daoud and Al Mahdi's two young sons, Ali and Abdullah, to distant locations where they will be raised safely.

This is my last request of you Muhammed al Nur. Go now, and may most compassionate and generous Allah protect you and our progeny, who are now in your custody."

Now alone on the thick fleece carpet, Khalifa Abdullah blew the candles out one by one, letting darkness set in. As he shook his head back and forth, he begged Allah's forgiveness for his brother's grand sin and for his own failure to prevent such a monstrous act against his mentor and revered leader, Muhammed Ahmed.

He suddenly remembered what a sage had told him many moons ago: "Only Abu Anga knows."

Abdullah put his large hands at the sides of his head and mused, *Hamdan Abu Anga—that half-breed Ta'ishi—did not survive to tell me what he knew. Yakub said that he died from taking one of his own concoctions. Was that also Yakub's doing? As for Hamdan's brother Fadl, I remember that Yakub imprisoned him until he starved. Did Yakub killed them because they knew too much?*

As tears rolled down his wrinkled cheeks into his scraggly white beard, Abdullah closed his eyes and tilted his head forward toward the ground. He prayed for a long time, begging Allah again and again to absolve him for not preventing the horrendous crime his brother had committed against Muhammed Ahmed. For a long time, he swayed back and forth and repeatedly asked forgiveness for the death of his beloved leader.

Before dawn, Khalifa Abdullah called on the Baggara guards and ordered them to summon all of his senior associates.

"Tell them to bring their prayer rugs!" he shouted after the guards.

One by one, all of the senior commanders arrived. Khalifa Abdullah then calmly told them to place their rugs around him and get ready to conduct morning prayers. After the prayers were completed, he turned around and faced his flock.

"I will fight no more!" he announced resolutely. "This is a good day to die; it is time to depart with honor and dignity. Let us pray and ask most compassionate and generous Allah to forgive our sins and open the doors of heaven for us."

He turned to face the direction of Mecca. As whispered prayer filled the cool morning air and the sunlight illuminated Khalifa Abdullah and his entire entourage, everyone remained motionless on their lambskin prayer rugs, heads bowed in complete submission to the will of Allah.

When Colonel Wingate issued the order to attack, the British soldiers, clueless about what was going on, opened fire on the Ansar camp. With little or no resistance, Khalifa Abdullah ibn Muhammed al Ta'ishi, the last ruler of the Mahdiya; Ali Wad Helu, the Khalifa-in-waiting; and most of the senior Ansar commanders were quickly killed by a barrage of British bullets. The last remaining Khalifa, Muhammed al Sharif, together with Khalifa Abdullah's two brothers and Muhammed Ahmed's eldest son, Sadik al Mahdi, as they tried to escape the battlefield, were arrested and promptly executed. The surviving Mahdist elite were quickly rounded up and shipped off to various prison facilities in Egypt. The wounded Amir Osman Sheikh ed-Din, the eldest son of Khalifa Abdullah, was not identified and thereby escaped execution. He was sent to Egypt with the prisoners.

The battle at Umm Dibeikarat ended Khalifa Abdullah's life and his quest to recover Mahdiya. The battle lasted less than an hour with only three deaths and twenty-three wounded among the Colonel Wingate's Anglo-Egyptian regiment.

Only two high-ranking Mahdiya commanders survived the British slaughter in Umm Dibeikarat: Amir Osman Digna, who knew when to escape a losing battle as he had done many times before, and Amir Muhammed al Nur Angara, who absconded with Muhammed Ahmed Al Mahdi's two young sons, Ali and Abdullah, and Khalifa Abdullah's infant son, Daoud.

Months later, Amir Osman Digna was arrested in a cave near his hometown in the Red Sea Province and imprisoned in Egypt, where he died many years later. Muhammed al Nur Angara was the only senior Mahdist Amir left at large. He spent rest of his life in disguise in a small village at the outskirts of Omdurman.

Death of Mahdist Khalifa Abdullah Al Taishi
Umm Dibeikarat, November 1899

***

THE MITROVICA AFFAIR

[KOSOVO]

[From: *Farewell to Kosovo, 2012*]

Source: Reuters, Association of Serb Municipalities.

THE MITROVICA AFFAIR

Before the Balkan Conflicts: 1910

Just as the sun was about to set behind a bend in the river, Burhan, a Kosovar renegade in the Serbian army, reached the outskirts of Mitrovica. He noticed a group of Serbian nationalist soldiers approaching him. One of the soldiers shouted at Burhan to stop. Immediately he stopped walking and waited for the soldiers to reach him. One of the soldiers, apparently the head of the group, ordered Burhan to raise his hands. The soldier searched Burhan's body for weapons. Finding none, he asked for identification papers. Burhan told the soldier that he had no papers because he was returning from a special mission to Pristina. The soldier stared at Burhan for a long moment before suddenly kicking him in the groin. Coldly watching Burhan curl into a fetal position on the ground, he ordered another soldier to tie Burhan's hands behind his back.

A few minutes later, Burhan was dragged into the Mitrovica militia headquarters for interrogation and placed in a sparsely furnished room. Looking out the window into the courtyard below, he felt cold, humid air blowing through the broken windowpane. It was a very chilly and wet evening. Shivering, he wondered how to make his interrogators believe him. Eventually, a young militia officer entered the room and ordered Burhan to sit on the other side of the desk.

The officer asked him where he had been going when he was arrested. Burhan explained that he had been returning from a special mission to Pristina.

"Under whose authority was this special mission?" the officer asked Burhan.

"I've received my orders directly from Commander Karaevitch," replied Burhan. He then asked the officer to summon Lieutenant Michailovitch to confirm his story. The request was ignored; it was obvious to Burhan that the officer did not believe him.

Over the following long hours, Burhan was questioned by several other officers. Finally, the last officer ordered the guards to take him to jail. At the entry to the large prison cell, Burhan hesitated and was kicked in the rear by the guard so forcefully that he sprawled onto his face on the crowded chamber's dirt floor. He slowly rose to his feet, wiping dirt from his face.

A young man came up to Burhan and asked, in Serbo-Croatian, who he was. Before answering, Burhan glanced quickly around the cell. He saw many men of various ages crowded into the cold, damp room. To Burhan, most of the jailed men looked like Turkish-Albanian thugs. His intuition told him that if they knew who he really was, they would kill him immediately. He decided to pretend he was an Albanian villager. He told the young man that when the nationalists had attacked his village south of Mitrovica, he had been taken hostage. In order to prevent further inquiry, Burhan quickly asked him why he was in prison.

The young man first introduced himself, and then asked Burhan his name. Burhan shook the hand of this new acquaintance, who was named Memodagic, and asked him where he was from.

"In this cell all of us are from Sanjak and other southern Serbian provinces," Memodagic replied. "We are Slavic Muslims.

There are eighteen of us here in this cell. For many weeks we've been under interrogation. In Serbia, many of us fought on the side of the Serbian nationalists. After many battles, most of the Slavic Muslims were arrested as traitors."

Burhan coldly responded, "You must have done something to be identified as a traitor."

"Most of us are being punished for not agreeing to kill defenseless civilians," answered Memodagic. "Some will be executed for refusing to murder Muslim prisoners."

"What do you mean by murder of Muslim prisoners? I thought nationalists never took prisoners."

"Not true. The nationalist army occasionally makes prisoners of soldiers who surrender or who are slightly wounded. First, the prisoners are tortured until they give information. Then they're executed in the cruelest way. If you're interested, you're welcome to watch the bloody executions from the cell window tomorrow morning."

After a long pause, the young prisoner, who had been staring intently into Burhan's face, loudly remarked, "It's very strange that they put you, an Albanian villager, in this cell with us. I don't think you are telling us the truth."

Burhan suddenly felt panicky; how could he have known that the guards would throw him into a cell full of Slavic Muslims?

He quickly responded to Memodagic's inquiry. "I thought you were a group of Albanian prisoners. To protect myself, I told you that I'm an Albanian. Actually, I'm a Montenegrin Muslim. Like you, I'm under suspicion for being a traitor."

Memodagic, now joined by two other young men, continued to stare intently into Burhan's eyes. "I don't think you are either an Albanian or a Muslim Montenegrin. I think you are a Serbian or a Croat. Take down your trousers; we'll see if you are really a Muslim."

Burhan knew he had no choice but to expose his penis to prove that he was circumcised. He quickly lowered his trousers and underwear, exposing himself to the scrutiny of the three young prisoners. Memodagic loudly declared to the other prisoners that the newcomer's circumcised penis had spoken; it had revealed the truth.

As the inmates roared with laughter, Memodagic turned to Burhan and explained, "There are no shared jail cells with Albanian or Ottoman prisoners. After an Ottoman or Albanian soldier is caught, he is usually interrogated, tortured, and then placed in a wretched isolation cell. A day or two later, the prisoner is executed in the courtyard. As I said before, you can watch tomorrow morning. I think several Ottoman soldiers, a few local Turks, and some Albanian thugs are scheduled for execution."

Bayonet Training

The remainder of the night was quiet but uncomfortable for Burhan. He could not sleep, thinking constantly about his father and Ismet.

When the first rays of sun illuminated the dark, smelly cell, Memodagic walked toward the window. He pointed to the center of the courtyard where a dozen thick, wooden poles had been buried in the ground approximately one meter apart. "That is where the prisoners are executed," he said. "It's a training ground for new recruits." With a humorless smile on his face, he continued, "Here they are. Go ahead and watch; I've seen it several times already."

Burhan moved closer to the window to see what was happening in the courtyard. Twelve men of various ages were waiting to be lashed to the poles. A few of the prisoners wore Ottoman uniforms, but most were in civilian clothes. Two military guards brought a tall, slender Ottoman soldier next to the pole. They pressed his back straight against the pole and tied his hands at the back. They then pulled his legs apart and tied them tightly to the pole. One by one, all the prisoners were tied to the poles in the same manner. Burhan noticed that the courtyard was now full of nationalist soldiers. He counted: there were exactly forty-eight. He wondered why so many would be needed for a firing squad.

The commanding officer ordered the soldiers into formations of twelve lines with four soldiers in each line. The officer then asked the soldiers to prepare their bayonets and line up approximately ten meters across from each pole. When the soldiers were ready, the officer raised his hand and, after a long pause, bellowed, "Charge!" Twelve newly recruited soldiers with fixed bayonets charged toward the twelve doomed prisoners tied to the poles. Burhan could detect shades of fear and horror on the faces of the prisoners whose eyes were not covered. Upon reaching the body of the prisoners, each soldier forcefully thrust his bayonet into the midsection of the prisoner he was facing. As they twisted their rifles to cause maximal damage to the internal organs, the soldiers pulled their bayonets out of the screaming prisoners. Then they moved behind the poles to allow the second column of soldiers to charge against the already mauled and bleeding bodies of the doomed prisoners.

Sickened by the cruelty of the execution, Burhan lowered his head to look at Memodagic, who was sitting on the floor right below him. "But why?" he asked.

Memodagic coldly answered, "It saves bullets and gets the new recruits ready for battle."

Burhan, shaken and nauseated by what he had witnessed, slowly slid down to the floor next to Memodagic.

"What ails you, my friend?" Memodagic asked. Without waiting for Burhan's answer, he continued, "This is nothing compared to what I, or most of us in this cell, have been exposed to during the past few months. At the beginning, our nonparticipation during the deadly attacks on unarmed Muslim civilians was ignored. But later, we were ordered to participate in acts of violence against the Muslim civilians, mostly Turks and Albanians. When we refused, the officer-in-charge explained to us that these violent attacks were part of a strategy to scare the Muslims into leaving. He said that if these attacks on Muslim communities resulted in voluntary evacuations, there would be no need for further violence or killing. Based on this warped rationale, almost all the Serbian officers ignored the cruel and inhuman activities of their troops. This resulted in most soldiers raping and killing many young Muslim girls. As part of the ploy, a few of the Turkish men and the raped young girls were allowed to escape so they could spread fear in the hearts of Muslims in areas still under Ottoman control."

Burhan, staring blankly ahead, told Memodagic of the similar situations he had witnessed during several battles.

"But I never thought that it was a strategic plan to force local Muslims to move away and vacate their towns and villages. Using human beings for bayonet practice is an outrageously inhumane thing to do."

Memodagic calmly responded, "To the nationalists, these targets are not human beings; they are just enemies to be destroyed. It's a common military conditioning tactic to desensitize the newly recruited troops."

A few hours later, Lieutenant Michailovitch, entering the jail-room stood outside the communal cell door and identified Burhan to the guard. As he heard the door open, Burhan looked up and saw the lieutenant. The husky prison guard rudely ordered Burhan to get up and follow him. Burhan turned to Memodagic and wished him good luck. The young Slavic Muslim, appearing sad, told Burhan that it would soon be over and that he would meet his maker. Realizing that Memodagic assumed him to be on his way to execution, Burhan gave Memodagic a hug. As he turned around to leave the smelly, cold prison cell, Burhan replied, "Sooner or later we all meet our maker."

Staring coldly at Burhan, Lieutenant Michailovitch's first comment was that he looked sick and smelled like rotting meat. Burhan responded, "I feel worse than I look. It's been a tough ordeal indeed. What happened? Why didn't the special unit meet me at the rendezvous point?"

Michailovitch answered stoically, "The special unit was attacked by an Ottoman infantry group and was delayed in arriving at the meeting point. When they finally arrived, the soldiers found the mutilated body of an Ottoman military police sergeant. They assumed that you had been killed by the Ottoman soldiers. When I received a note from the officer who interrogated you about your story of being on a special mission ordered by Commander Karaevitch, I decided to come here and check the prison to see if you were here. Aren't you glad to see me? Tomorrow you'll meet Karaevitch and brief him on your important discoveries. You smell terrible. Please, take a bath and get a new uniform."

Burhan replied without hesitation, "I don't care how bad I smell! I'm starving. First, take me to the kitchen."

The next morning Burhan and Lieutenant Michalovitch joined the Serbian special army units camped at the northern part of Mitrovica.

A Village Marked for Destruction

A few weeks later, toward the end of a rainy, cold afternoon, fifty well-armed members of the nationalist special attack unit entered the outskirts of northern Kosovo village. The unit's commander, Lieutenant Michailovitch, selected two groups of ten men to attack the local police office and the gendarme station, which were near each other. He told the other soldiers to spread out in groups of three and attack local residences. He ordered that all males, regardless of age, be killed.

A leering grin distorting his face, Michailovitch commanded, "Do not take any action against residents until attacks on the police and the gendarmes have begun. Give us a fifteen-minute lead before you make your move. What you do with the females is entirely up to you. Take your pick for the night's entertainment."

Burhan kept a low profile and was not selected to be in the primary attack units. He wanted to stay behind to provide some protection to Ismet's family. As he prepared to lead the main attack group down the hilly road, Michailovitch turned to Burhan and ordered him to take charge of all the units that would attack residential areas. He instructed Burhan to ensure that all units inflicted maximum damage on the civilians and their properties.

"Remember, have no mercy!" Michailovitch shouted. "Eliminate them all! Take no prisoners, except a few women for tonight's entertainment. Burn the houses down. Leave the village before sunset and go to the area where we set up camp this morning."

Feeling blessed by this sudden stroke of good luck, Burhan saluted Michailovitch. With a mischievous grin, he replied, "Yes, Lieutenant. What needs to be done will be done."

As the group leaders circled around him, he assigned them to approach in small groups to various parts of the village except the area where village-head's house was located. He saved that area for himself. He selected two men with some degree of intelligence and maturity to join him. After everyone had dispersed in various directions, Burhan and the two soldiers created mayhem in that neighborhood. They entered houses and shot at anything that moved.

As always, Burhan refrained from killing women and children and made sure that the two Serbian soldiers also refrained from shooting them. One exception to this rule occurred unexpectedly. As they entered a house one block up the hill from Ismet's residence, they were fired on by a young boy. The soldier next to Burhan took a bullet in his chest. The other Serbian soldier fired his gun at the young boy, killing him instantly. The soldier then entered the main room and chased after several screaming women and young children trying to escape through the window. Distraught by the loss of his comrade, he brutally fired upon them.

Storming into the room, Burhan grabbed the Serbian soldier by the shoulder and loudly ordered him to stop. The soldier turned his gun on him and snarled, "You goddamn Muslim shit, don't ever touch me." Burhan, holding his revolver at hip level, fired immediately. The soldier hit the floor with a fatal wound to his abdomen.

Burhan, as he removed the rifle from the dying soldier's hand, peeked into the room. He saw bloody bodies of women and children tangled and motionless on the floor. He entered the room to check if anyone had survived. Suddenly, one of the motionless bodies on the floor leapt to her feet. Screaming and slashing with a long butcher knife, she viciously attacked Burhan. Quickly grabbing her wrist, Burhan struck her head with the butt of his revolver, knocking her back to the floor. She fell unconscious on the dead bodies of two children spread-eagled on the wooden floor.

Burhan sat next to her and tied her hands and feet. His attacker was a pretty, young girl, tall and strong in appearance. A few minutes later, as she slowly regained consciousness, she tried to spit in his face. Burhan shouted at her in Turkish to stop and behave. "That is, if you would like to stay alive," he said abruptly.

She did not reply; she just turned her head away to hide her tears.

"I'm leaving now," Burhan said. "You must stay put. If you start screaming, soldiers will find you. If anyone comes into this room, pretend you're dead. I'll come back for you later."

Burhan got up, slung the rifle over his left shoulder and walked out of the house. He ran down the street toward the village-head's residence. He heard gunshots nearby and saw women and children running every which way. Within a few minutes he reached the house. He kicked the door open, entered the house and carefully checked every room. Suddenly, as he entered the kitchen, he came face-to-face with a young man, who was pointing an old revolver ready to fire. After a short stare at Burhan's face, the young man pulled the trigger and the gun's cock snapped into firing position. Fortunately for Burhan, the old gun failed to ignite.

Burhan then slowly raised his rifle, pointing it at young man's chest, got ready to fire. Before he pulled the trigger, however, Burhan noticed in the corner of the room a woman holding an infant baby in her arms. Upon seeing them, he refrained from firing the gun.

Realizing that he was about to be killed, the young Albanian cursed loudly. "You're a filthy Serbian! Go ahead! Shoot me!"

Keeping his gun still pointed at him, Burhan yelled back, "I didn't come here to harm you or anyone in your family."

He ordered the young man to turn around and lie face down on the floor next to his family. He informed the family that the nationalist soldiers were here to destroy the village. He then asked him where the rest of his family were.

"When we heard the gunshots," The Albanian replied, "my great uncle and my aunt left the house with the younger women and children. They went to hide in the woods."

Burhan was perplexed. "Why didn't you go with them?" he asked.

After throwing a hefty spit on the floor, young Albanian answered, "I felt that going into the woods was not a smart thing to do. I told them not to go into the forest. But they wouldn't listen to me."

Burhan continued questioning him: "Is there a cellar in this house?" After his affirmation, Burhan told him to hide in the cellar with his family and leave the house in the morning before sunrise.

"Go to Skopje to save yourself and your family," Burhan said. "Do not go through Pristina; go around the city by circling its southwestern periphery. Don't use the main roads. Travel toward Skopje through secluded, wooded areas."

Getting to his feet, The Albanian limped to the middle of the kitchen. He pulled on the handle of a wooden hatch on the floor. After guiding his family into the cellar's wooden staircase, which led down to the storage area under the house, he stood on the stairway and turned around. "Why are you doing this?" he asked.

"I'm paying off my debt to a few Albanian, who helped me in the past," replied Burhan.

Burhan, as he held the wooden hatch open for the family to descend, asked the Albanian man, "I'm going to ask you a favor. I found a young Turkish girl four houses up the hill on the other side of the street. All her family members are dead. I'm going to bring her here in a short while. She is your neighbor; I'm sure you know her. Please, help her get away with you to Skopje."

"Yes, I know the house," said the Albanian. "She must be one of the daughters of Hasan Efendi, the owner of the coffee shop in the village square. I'll help her to safety."

Before closing the cellar hatch, Burhan handed him his revolver.

"Thank God, your antique gun didn't fire, otherwise I'd be dead. Use this one to protect your family. Good luck!"

He closed the hatch and placed an old kilim over it.

The street outside village-head's house was now strangely quiet. Many dead bodies were strewn about the wide dirt road. Several houses in the street below were on fire. It appeared that nationalist soldiers were about to move into village-head's neighborhood to burn the houses down. Burhan realized that he should get the young Turkish girl out of harm's way before the soldiers with torches reached the houses on the street. He rushed into the house where she had been left tied on the floor. In the hallway, he stopped to take the revolver from the dead Serbian soldier and put it in his holster. He stepped into the room to find the young girl. She was sitting on the floor, looking at him with wide eyes full of fear.

Burhan sat on the floor next to her. "Young lady," he said, "what's your name?"

Without looking at him, she answered, "My name is Nurjahan."

"Listen to me very carefully, Nurjahan. I'll take you to another house where an Albanian family is hiding in the cellar. You just follow him to safety. Please remember, when we're out on the street, you must behave. Don't do anything crazy, just be calm and control yourself. When you see the Serbian soldiers, don't panic, don't look at them, keep your head down, and follow my instructions."

Burhan walked out of the house with the young Turkish girl whose hands still were loosely tied behind her back. She followed Burhan closely. Suddenly, two nationalist soldiers ran toward Burhan. One stopped in front of him to stare at the pretty young girl. With a sneer on his face, he hollered, "Sergeant, you've discovered a treasure for the night!"

The other soldier, torch in hand, first saluted and then reported, "The lieutenant is looking for you, Sergeant."

Burhan quickly turned toward the soldier who had made the crude comment earlier and ordered him to throw the torch in his hand onto the ground. He then asked the other soldier, "Where's the lieutenant?"

"He is with several women prisoners in a house a few blocks down the street. I think he's selecting a few female companions for the night."

Pulling the young girl along by her arm, Burhan ordered both soldiers to stop burning houses and gather everyone at the entrance to the forest immediately. He then started to walk downhill toward village-head's house. As he approached it, another soldier with a torch ran past him to set fire to the house. He stopped the soldier, asked him to hand over the torch, and ordered him to go up the hill to the rendezvous point.

As the soldier ran up the hill, Burhan threw away the torch. He then turned toward the young girl and said, "I have to make sure this house is not burned down." Opening the door, Burhan ordered Nurjahan: "Go ahead walk into the house. Inside, find a safe corner to hide and keep quiet until everyone has gone. Then go to the kitchen and look for a cellar door on the floor under an old kilim. Before you open it, announce yourself. Otherwise, you might get shot."

When Burhan turned around to guide the young girl into the house, he came face-to-face with Lieutenant Michailovitch.

"Burhan, you are a lucky bastard!" Michailovitch loudly hollered, "You found yourself a beauty. Come on; let's go back to the camp! We are running late."

Burhan realized that he had no choice but to follow Lieutenant Michailovitch's entourage of a few soldiers and several young women who were being herded toward a terrible fate. Still gripping Nurjahan's arm, Burhan whispered to her in Turkish to be calm and quiet. As they walked up the hill, he saw that tears were pouring down her rosy cheeks. He reassured Nurjahan that no one would harm her.

A Camp of Cruelty

When they reached the designated camping area in a secluded corner of the forest, Lieutenant Michailovitch told everyone to settle down and rest. Burhan held Nurjahan by the arm and discreetly pulled her away from the center of the camp. He intended to let Nurjahan escape during the night to find the village-head's house and join the young Albanian and his family.

After finding a secluded area at the far edge of the camp, he placed the camping gear near a tree trunk and then untied Nurjahan's hands. "Please, relax and remain quiet," he said firmly. "Before we settle in this spot, we should wait for others to pitch their tents. I want to make sure no one is too close to us."

The young girl was shivering. Burhan removed a blanket from his camping bag and draped it over her shoulders. Nurjahan, eyes downcast, thanked him. "You haven't told me your name," she whispered. "But I've heard the Serbian officer call you Burhan. You are a Muslim, aren't you?"

"Yes, I'm a Muslim," Burhan said. Unwilling to say anything more, he changed the subject. "Would you like to help me pitch the tent? It's a small tent for one person. You'll have to share it with me. We must pretend that you are my ..." He stopped talking. He simply couldn't bring himself to say the word 'woman'.

Noticing Burhan's sudden confusion, Nurjahan looked up at him. "I understand, Sergeant. I'll play the part. What will happen to the other girls?"

Burhan, searching for the right words, remained silent for a while. He then spoke: "They will be raped tonight and possibly murdered in the morning."

The young girl began sobbing. "But why?" she asked. "What have they done to deserve such cruelty?"

"Nurjahan, I don't know why some men behave the way they do during war. Maybe it happens because of the complete breakdown of human reasoning and compassion. But one thing I know for sure is that both sides of this conflict conduct similar atrocities, particularly against young women."

Nurjahan, childishly, asked, "Can't you do anything to help them?"

"Myself? Alone?" Burhan responded briskly, "That would be suicide, but I hope I can at least save you."

Nurjahan turned her head away abruptly.

"But you didn't prevent the murder of my brother."

Remembering every detail of the incident, Burhan answered, "Your brother shot one of our soldiers before he was killed. If we hadn't killed him, he would have killed more of us."

He then asked her to get up and help him unfold the tent. After the tent was set up, he told Nurjahan that he would leave her alone for a short while to get something to eat. Earlier, during the raid, soldiers had looted some food items from the village houses before burning them to the ground. After he lit a couple of candles, he gave Nurjahan a canteen full of water and cautioned, "If anyone comes by the tent, just keep quiet. If they come into the tent, tell them that you're my woman. Do you speak enough Serbo-Croatian to say that?" After she nodded,

Burhan continued, "Just try keeping them away from you by talking to them. Do not fight or scream. I'll be back as quickly as I can."

In the pitch darkness, Burhan rushed toward the large bonfire in the middle of the camp-ground where most of the tents had been set up. While he looked for the pile of food that had been brought from the village, he saw several young women being dragged into tents. Despite the violence going on all around, the camp was strangely quiet. He kept walking around until he located the makeshift kitchen where several soldiers were preparing meals. He picked up some loaves of bread, chunks of cheese, and boiled potatoes. Arms loaded with food, he turned to leave the kitchen.

He stopped abruptly when one of the soldiers shouted, "Sergeant, a short while ago the lieutenant was asking about your tent's whereabouts."

In response, Burhan asked the soldier where the lieutenant's tent was. The soldier pointed to a large, double-sized tent next to the flaming bonfire. Burhan then ordered the soldier to tell the lieutenant that he would be there in ten minutes.

Burhan ran back to his tent and handed the armload of food to Nurjahan. "I've got to leave again," he said hurriedly. "It may be a while before I return. Feed yourself."

As he was leaving, he reminded her, "If anyone comes, you should do everything possible to keep yourself alive." Without waiting for a response, he disappeared into the darkness.

Lieutenant Michailovitch warmly welcomed Burhan to his tent. The spacious canvas tent was remarkably warm and reeked of body odor. The source of heat was the red-hot charcoal container placed near the entry. The strong body odor had been generated by heavy sweating. Hearing a deep moan coming from the rear of the tent, Burhan realized that the lieutenant had just completed his entertainment for the night.

As he straightened his trousers with one hand, Michailovitch clung to the wooden post in the center of the tent with the other. He was highly intoxicated. "Are you enjoying yourself with your young Turkish woman?" he mumbled.

Burhan forced a smile and said, "Yes, very much so Lieutenant. I was told that you wanted to see me."

"We lost five men this afternoon; two from your company. Tell me what happened."

During the next few minutes, Burhan explained how and where he had lost the two men. For obvious reasons, he did not admit shooting one of them. He invented a heroic story about the death of that particular soldier.

Michailovitch, still leaning on the tent's center post, listened closely to every word with great intensity and then brusquely told Burhan to be more careful with the men under his command. "I'll be watching you during the coming battles," he hissed.

After a few more words of advice, Michailovitch told Burhan to walk with him to the end of the tent. A young woman was lying atop several layers of thick woolen blankets spread on the ground. Her body was covered with a large army overcoat.

Bending forward, the lieutenant held a candle closer to the moaning figure shivering under the coat, and sneered, "Look at this gorgeous woman! Isn't she beautiful?"

He reached down and jerked the army coat off the young woman, uncovering her completely naked body. She was bound and gagged; her eyes were red and badly swollen. Her elbows were tied to her ankles behind her body, forcing her legs to bend outward at the knees. Her breasts and genitals were completely exposed. She was clearly in great pain and shock from this cruel treatment.

The horrendous sight made Burhan feel that he was about to gag. He turned around to avoid looking at such extreme cruelty. "But why, Lieutenant?" he plaintively asked.

Michailovitch answered, "Earlier this evening, one of the Albanian girls almost gouged out the eye of a soldier as he was raping her. So, at the suggestion of the sergeant, we have decided to take necessary precautions by roping their hands and feet. It's much safer this way."

"What happened to the girl who resisted the rape?"

"She was cut to pieces by the soldier. By the way, how are you handling your Turkish delight?"

Burhan lied, "She's roped up as well, but just her hands."

"Doesn't she kick your ass?" asked Michailovitch mockingly.

Sick and tired of this conversation, Burhan replied, "I like it that way!" Then he quickly asked, "What's going to happen to these women, Lieutenant?"

"We'll let them go back to their village in the morning," Michailovitch replied casually. "They can tell all the Muslim villagers in southern Kosovo that we intend to get rid of them once and for all."

Enraged, Burhan left Michailovitch's tent in a hurry.

As he hurriedly walked toward his tent, he silently cursed the Serbian officer. Muttering in Albanian, "I would love to put a bullet in his brain."

Approaching his tent, he heard noises coming from inside. He unsheathed his knife, placed it between his jaws, threw himself on the ground, and crawled toward the entrance to the tent. He pushed aside the canvas flap, and saw the silhouette of a soldier on top of Nurjahan. She was loudly begging the soldier to stop in Serbo-Croatian. Burhan very cautiously and quietly slipped into the tent, grabbed the man by the hair, and laid the razor-sharp blade on his throat. "If you make a move or a sound, I'll cut your throat," he whispered into the soldier's ear. He then forcefully jerked the soldier out of the tent and rammed him down on the ground on his belly. With his knee planted firmly on the soldier's back and the knife still at the soldier's throat, he asked Nurjahan if she was all right.

As she peered through the open canvas flap, Nurjahan replied in a voice trembling with fear and relief, "I'm glad you've returned in time. I'm not hurt. What will you do with him?"

Burhan did not answer. Instead, he yanked the soldier to his feet and turned him toward the camp fire in the distance.

He hoarsely hollered, "Stay away from my woman. If I see you near my tent again, I'll kill you. Now get lost!"

He watched the young soldier stumble away toward the camp fire. Sheathing his knife, he entered the tent and lit a candle.

Nurjahan, fumbling in haste to put her clothes back on, loudly called his name.

"If you had arrived one minute later, that animal would have raped me."

Burhan replied, "I am glad I came back on time. Are you feeling well?"

"Yes and no!"

He knew what she meant.

"Try to get some sleep. You'll have another tough day tomorrow. You should be rested for your escape in the morning."

Nurjahan lay down and pulled the blanket over her head. Burhan, sitting on the ground, retrieved the piece of bread and cheese that had been thrown to the back of the tent during the struggle with the intruder. Hungrily, he bit into a large piece of bread. As he felt and tasted gritty dirt in his mouth, he quickly spat it out and searched for his canteen. He pulled out the cork to take a drink of water and, subconsciously, began to do something he had not done for a long time: he started to pray.

A few hours later, Burhan awoke and gently touched Nurjahan's shoulder, urging her to wake up. After telling her to get ready quickly, he left the tent to check on the night guards positioned at camp's periphery. After surveying the grounds for a short while, he decided to lead Nurjahan on a path between two snoring guards. He retrieved her from the tent and told her to follow him quietly.

In the middle of the night, they walked side by side in silence like two friendly ghosts moving through the darkness of the forest. As soon as they had reached the edge of the woods, Burhan stopped and turned toward her. "This is where we separate," he whispered. "Do you remember the house I told you about yesterday?"

"Yes, I remember. It's the house of the village headman."

"You're a smart girl. Be very careful going down the hill in the dark. When you reach the house, find the entrance to the cellar in the kitchen. Before opening the cellar hatch, announce yourself loudly; otherwise, you will face a loaded pistol. In the cellar, you will find a young Albanian and his family. You should all leave immediately for Skopje. May the Lord protect all of you!"

Burhan hunkered down against a large tree trunk, watching her walk down the hill. When she disappeared into the darkness, he whispered, "I'd like to see her again."

As if in a dream, he slowly walked back to the camp. Inside his tent, he laid flat on his back. Smelling the sweet scent of Nurjahan on the blanket, he quickly fell asleep.

$$* * *$$

A FLOUNDERING FRIGATE

[TÜRKİYE]

©Omer Ertur
[From: *The Sirens of Funagora, 2014*]

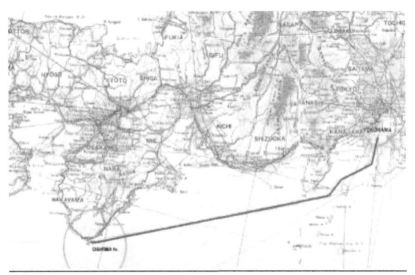

Frigate Ertugrul's Last journey from Yokohama to Oshima, September 16, 1890

Ottoman Frigate Ertugrul

A FLOUNDERING FRIGATE

On the ominous evening of September 16, 1890, one day after it had begun its return journey to Constantinople from the quarantined seaport of Nagaura near Yokohama, the frigate Ertugrul, an elderly but well-endowed wooden Ottoman warship with sails and a steam engine, rushed straight into the peripheral storms of a full-blown typhoon in the Sea of Kumanonada. She carried Rear Admiral Osman Emin Pasha, the Ottoman Empire's first diplomatic emissary to Japan, and four-hundred-and-ninety-six Ottoman navy personnel. Unable to use its sails safely and properly due to the multidirectional and gusty winds, the floundering vessel struggled to advance through the threatening, white-foamed waves of the Kumanonada Sea with its single propeller steam engine. It appeared for a while that the struggling frigate would reach the relatively calm waters of Osaka Bay, hardly sixty-five nautical miles away. But, fueled by low-quality, wet coal, her two boilers suddenly lost the needed steam pressure to run the engine efficiently and could no longer push the frigate forward through the formidable rainstorm, ceaseless giant waves, and a high tide coupled with a strong coastal crosscurrent that were all incessantly pushing her toward the deadly shoreline. For hours, the frigate had been stranded without the use of sails and the engine power necessary to move her away from the approaching coastline and take her into the safety of Osaka Bay.

The ship's captain, Commodore Tekirdagli Ali Mehmet, in an oversized rubber raincoat thrown over his naval uniform, wiped raindrops off his forehead and looked anxiously into the stormy darkness to search for the beacon of the lighthouse. Not detecting any noticeable light-beam ahead, he then glanced at the smokestack in front him, hoping to detect grey smoke coming out of its funnel. Not seeing the desired fumes, he abruptly ordered a junior bridge officer to summon Major Hasan Tahsin, the ship's chief navigator. The officer rushed down to the deck below, where the ship's chief navigator was desperately holding onto a clump of maps and charts on a secured table that was lit by an oil lamp hanging above. The young officer positioned himself near the chief navigator, who intently stared into a large compass in his hand. Grabbing tightly onto the wooden railing near the table, the deck officer informed Tahsin Bey that the commodore had asked him to come to the upper deck immediately. Arriving at the canvas-covered upper bridge deck, the chief navigator slowly and cautiously approached the steering compartment. A strong gale pushed him back to the steep staircase. Clutching tightly onto the side railings, he finally reached the steering area, where Commodore Ali, hanging forward on the front railings, shouted orders at the helmsman. Commodore Ali, the ship's skipper, abruptly turned around and faced the chief navigator.

"Tahsin Bey," he bellowed, "the sun has already set and the grayish twilight will soon disappear. We will be in complete darkness. It'll be impossible for us to detect the threatening shoreline on our starboard horizon. Do you remember those frightening rock formations that looked like the jaws of a dragon? We saw them between the two lighthouses that we passed on our way to Yokohama three months ago."

Chief navigation officer Tahsin, looking confused, unconvincingly replied, "I vaguely remember them, sir."

"How far do you think we are from the lighthouse furthest north?" asked Commodore Ali.

As he blankly stared at the gray horizon to his right, Tahsin Bey replied, "I cannot give you a reliable answer, sir, because over the past two hours we have been moving towards constantly changing directions due to highly irregular wind patterns. Under such circumstances, where the wind's direction and velocity is constantly changing, it is impossible for me to determine exactly where we are, but I am somewhat certain that we have been moving toward southwest over the past several hours. Since I cannot pinpoint our location, it is impossible for me to determine accurately where we are headed. We may be headed toward the safe waters of Osaka Bay, approximately sixty-five nautical miles southwest of the nearest lighthouse, or we may be heading straight into the rocky shoreline surrounding the cape in front of the lighthouse. There is no way of knowing our precise location except by the sight of the lighthouse beacon. Given the poor visibility, we might detect the beacon only when it is too late."

Before the commodore could respond to the comments of the chief navigator, Deputy Captain Lieutenant Colonel Jemil appeared on the bridge deck and rushed toward Commodore Ali.

"Sir!" the second officer shouted excitedly. "We have located and temporarily plugged all water seepages around the engine compartment. We've also substantially slowed down the seepage that was flooding the coal storage area. However, a considerable amount of seawater accumulated on the floor base near the boilers. There are still some piles of dry coal remaining at the front end of the stowage, so loads of dry coal from the upper bins are now being brought to the furnaces. Chief Engineer Ibrahim Bey is working closely with the boiler crew on possibly re-igniting the furnaces. If he is successful in his efforts, we might soon have enough steam pressure to run the engine. However, unless we find a way to drain the accumulated water from the coal storage area and the floor-base near the boilers, we won't have enough dry coal to continuously feed the furnaces. We urgently need lots of manpower to remove seawater from the coal storage area and prevent the water level from reaching the furnaces."

Rear Admiral Osman Emin Pasha, the commanding officer of the frigate and chief of the Ottoman delegation to Japan, wearing a thick rubber raincoat over his uniform, had been silently standing near the railing in the far port-side corner of the upper deck. He moved swiftly toward the captain and hollered, "Ali Bey, I will go down to the engine room to see what is going on. I'll assess the situation and have a talk with the chief engineer. As soon as possible, he must find a way to reignite the furnaces and establish sufficient steam pressure in both boilers. In the meantime, we have to remove the accumulated water in the coal storage areas and around the boilers. Immediately send as many men with buckets as you can muster down to the engine compartment."

Osman Pasha turned around and promptly asked Lieutenant Colonel Jemil, the deputy captain of the ship, to follow him. They rushed to the stairs and climbed down the swaying bridge's starboard side to the front of the lower bridge deck. Watching them disappear below, the captain immediately ordered a junior officer standing by to summon Lieutenant Ismail, the leader of the ship's marching band. Then he turned around to search for Major Nuri Huseyin, the third officer in charge of the sailing crew, who was supposed to be in the steering area waiting for orders to raise the sails when needed.

A deck officer located Major Nuri, who, ignoring the howling rainstorm and the threateningly high waves, was hanging out over the upper deck's railings to have a closer look at the ship's immediate surroundings on the starboard horizon. Hearing his name called by the junior deck officer, Major Nuri pulled away from the railings, wiped the rainwater off his face, and walked swiftly toward the captain.

"Ali Bey, if we cannot make the boilers provide the necessary steam power to engage the engine, we will soon be at the mercy of this damned storm," he yelled. "Without the power of the propeller or the power of the sails, the gusty southeasterly wind and the high seas will definitely force us ashore. Furthermore, since we are constantly moving toward the shoreline, I am sure that we are now within a coastal stream that is also pushing us toward the shore. I strongly suggest that you turn this ship around at once and get the southeasterly wind behind the sails to move us away from the approaching shore."

Irritated with his underling's comments, the captain sharply replied, "Nuri Bey, don't repeat things that I am already aware of and don't tell me what to do. If you have any practical suggestions on how we can utilize the sails to move forward under these drastic weather conditions, just spit it out."

"Commander Ali," Major Nuri shouted, "it is obvious that you are not hearing me. Please remember, when we were on our way to Hong Kong, you correctly decided to maneuver away from the coming storm and return to port in Saigon. Why don't you consider doing the same now to get the ship away from a clearly dangerous storm that is pushing her toward the shore?"

Glaring at the Major, Commodore Ali replied, "Nuri Bey, listen to me carefully. The circumstances we were facing in the middle of the South China Sea were very different from what we are facing today. I am confident that before this storm gets any worse, we will reach the safety of Osaka Bay. Get your men to raise the mainmast course and middle sails immediately. In case we cannot reignite the boilers, the use of sails is our only chance to get us out of trouble."

"I am not sure we'll be able to put up the sails while facing such gusty and multidirectional winds, sir," Major Nuri replied sternly. "Even if we were able to raise some of the sails, we wouldn't be able to control them to move the ship in the southwesterly direction that would take us out to safety. Furthermore, the sails and the spars might not be able to stand the extraordinary strains put on them by such horrendous gales. I repeat, sir, we should do what you suggest after you turn the ship around to get the wind behind the sails and take us away from the approaching shoreline."

"Nuri Bey, don't argue with me; do as I tell you." snapped the captain. "We will have to do what we can to take the ship into the port of Kobe in the calm waters of Osaka Bay."

Major Nuri moved closer to Commodore Ali and loudly hissed, "Excuse me for saying this, Captain, but rather than charging into it, we should have turned our back on this ghastly storm six hours ago and returned to Yokohama. We would now be in the unruffled waters of Yokohama Bay."

"This is not a good time to discuss what we decided six hours ago," the captain somberly replied. "Now, you have to listen to me carefully; set your best men aloft to raising the mainmast course and middle sails. If the engine does not start soon, we'll have to use the sails to guide us away from the approaching shoreline."

Realizing that the captain was not about to change his mind, Major Nuri turned around and rushed out of the bridge.

Soon after the third officer's departure from the upper deck, Lieutenant Ismail entered the bridge from the starboard stairs and rapidly approached the captain. Saluting as he tried to hold onto the railing, he shouted, "Yes, sir!"

"Lieutenant, a lot of seawater has accumulated in the coal storage area and it is approaching the furnaces. The sump pumps are not working at the moment. Therefore, the accumulated water has to be dumped out manually. Take all the men in your band and others you find on the main deck and mess hall down into the engine compartment to help the crew remove the seawater that has accumulated around the boilers. You should take with you as many buckets you can find and organize your men to haul the accumulated water out of the coal storage area and the floor base near the furnaces as quickly and efficiently as possible."

Lieutenant Ismail, rushing down the stairway, ran into the ship's imam, Hafiz Ali Efendi; the ship's photographer, Ensign Haydar and the head cook, Sergeant Hilmi, who were standing near the main deck's landing. All three men hung tightly to the deck's central railings surrounding the stairs that led to below deck. They were intensely observing Major Nuri and several sailors on the main deck as they ran around the flying sail lines and shouted at each other while trying hard to raise the mainmast's course sails.

Wiping raindrops off his face, Ismail hollered, "Hafiz Efendi, Ensign Haydar, Sergeant Hilmi, please come with me. We have to haul seawater out of the coal storage area."

Together they rushed down the stairs to the lower deck's open central area near the gunnery station to summon the rest of the band members and anyone still around the mess hall or the sleeping quarters. Within a few minutes, Lieutenant Ismail had lined up all the band members, cooks, cleaners, and gunnery sailors he could find in rows stretching from the coal storage area at the bottom level to the stairs' outlet at the main deck. As the buckets full of water were being passed from one man to another to be dumped into the sea, Ismail ordered Sergeant Rashid, the band's base drummer, to oversee the crew carrying the empty buckets back down to the coal storage area. At that moment, Lieutenant Ismail heard a loud cracking sound and looked up towards the mainmast where dozens of sailors were attempting to raise the topsails. Under the strain of the strong cross winds, the long middle yard with half-raised topsails swung wildly toward the port side of the ship and splintered away from the mainmast's rigging with a big crashing sound. Before falling on the upper deck, the broken yard temporarily rested on the lower spar of the mainmast, its swirling half-open bottom sails and lines dangling at the bottom of the mast. As he ran toward his men, who were still busily emptying buckets of seawater, Ismail shouted a warning for them to get away from the falling broken yard. The topsail of the mainmast swung sideways toward port and crashed on the main deck with sailors still hanging onto its yard, crushing several of the sailors, holding buckets of seawater. Luckily for Ismail, it missed him completely but landed on the band's young trumpet player, Corporal Musa. As he thanked Allah for his luck, Ismail together with Haydar and a few others carried Corporal Musa and other badly hurt sailors down to the sickbay for medical attention. The entrance to the sickbay was overcrowded with many maimed and bloodied sailors, most of whom remained motionless on the hallway floor. Inside the doctor's office, two medical assistants were helping Colonel Husnu, the ship's doctor. They carried a severely injured and unconscious sailor onto an examination table lit by a dim oil lamp that an orderly was holding. As the ship shifted side to side and up and down with loud squealing sounds emanating from the lower belly of the elderly frigate, Colonel Husnu asked his medical assistant, Cerrah Shevket Mehmet Efendi, to keep a tight grip on the patient. He steadied himself and tried to check the pulse of the wounded sailor.

Noticing no heartbeat, he quickly ordered, "This one is dead, take him away. Bring in only the ones that appear to be alive." He then turned toward the ship's pharmacist, Captain Yasef Jak Efendi, who was helping a medical assistant carry a wounded sailor out of the overcrowded entry hallway and into the treatment room. "Yasef Efendi, Yasef Efendi!" hollered Colonel Husnu. "Immediately bring all the pain-relieving herbal concoctions that you can find in the medicine cupboard."

Hearing the loud crashing sound from above, Osman Pasha decided to return to the bridge to find out what had happened. Before departing, he abruptly ordered the chief engineer to reignite the stalled furnaces as soon as possible.

"It won't be easy, sir," replied the frustrated chief engineer. "In addition to its sogginess, the low quality of the Japanese coal is preventing us from igniting it quickly."

Irritated with the chief engineer's response, Osman Pasha curtly replied, "As ordered, you should have purchased the best quality coal. You obviously did not do that, and now you have no choice but to reignite the furnaces with the coal you have."

Without waiting for the chief engineer's response to his command, Osman Pasha ordered Lieutenant Colonel Jemil to stay behind and see to it that the furnaces soon be reignited to build up steam pressure in the boilers and power the engine. He turned around and hurriedly climbed the stairs leading to the upper deck. From the direction and extent of the crashing sound, he guessed that the sails and parts of the mainmast that had been recently repaired in Singapore had not held together in the face of the devastating windstorm. As he pushed his way up the crowded stairway, he prayed for a miracle that would restore steam power to run the stalled engine. "Otherwise," he murmured, "we are doomed."

When he was about to reach the upper deck, his way to the captain's quarters was blocked by an officer who, after recognizing Osman Pasha, abruptly stopped and saluted. Acknowledging the officer standing in his way, Osman Pasha hollered, "Tahsin Bey, where are you rushing to?"

"Sir," the chief navigation officer nervously answered, "Commodore Ali has ordered me to get ready to drop both anchors."

Holding the officer's arm to stop him from going down the stairs, Osman Pasha hollered, "For God's sake, what good will that do in deep water?"

"Commodore Ali has seen the lighthouse's beacon and he thinks we are too close to the rocky coastline."

"You are the navigation officer of this ship. Now, tell me: are we or are we not too close to the shoreline?"

"I don't know the exact answer, sir! But if Commodore Ali saw the lighthouse beam, we could be approaching the coast." Osman Pasha impatiently replied, "If the commodore asked you to be ready to drop anchors, we are obviously too close to the shore."

Releasing his arm, Osman Pasha let the navigation officer hurriedly go down the stairs. Then he rushed back up to the upper bridge deck. In the noisy and wet commotion of the ongoing storm, he staggered toward the steering wheel to find Commodore Ali.

When Rear Admiral Osman Pasha appeared on the upper bridge, leaning into the rain and saltwater-splattering eastern wind blowing vigorously from the portside direction, he could barely advance forward enough to reach the steering area. Tightly clinging to the railings on the starboard side of the bridge, he slowly approached the bridge and called for Commodore Ali. His calls, unheard by anyone on the bridge, were carried away by the strong wind. He let go of the railing and leaped forward toward the bridge, where he found Commodore Ali firmly holding the wooden post near the steering wheel and shouting at the helmsman to steer the ship portside. The helmsman shouted back that the steering was now fully turned toward the portside, but it still would not respond properly. Osman Pasha grabbed Commodore Ali's arm to get his attention. Ignoring the helmsman's final words, Ali turned around to see who was clutching to his arm. When he recognized his commanding officer, he reached out and pulled him into the steering area.

"Osman Pasha, I presume all is well in the engine room," he said hurriedly.

"The flooding is under control," replied the admiral. "And the furnaces are now being fed dry coal. As soon as the necessary steam pressure has built up in the boilers, Ibrahim Bey will be able to restart the engine. By the way, when I was down in the engine room, I heard a crash on the main deck. Did something go wrong with the mainmast sails?"

"A fore-and-aft rig and boom broke away from the mainmast and caused the beam to crash onto the main deck. Unfortunately, several course and mid-level sails were also damaged in the process. Nuri Bey's sailors are still struggling to repair a few of the remaining sails to open. If he is successful, that might give us a chance to open the repaired course and topgallant sails on the mainmast."

"Ali Bey," Osman Pasha loudly asked, "any casualties?"

"I don't know the exact number, but I presume several sailors were hurt. I saw a few people being carried down to the sickbay. Sir, I should also inform you that in order to successfully move the ship away from the approaching coastline, we will have to raise the sails on the foremast and mizzenmast as well. Unfortunately, at this moment I don't think we can raise any of the sails on the foremast because it is highly unstable. There is a carpenter crew under the command of Captain Tevfik working to stabilize the wobbly foremast. I will order Nuri Bey to open the course sails of the mizzenmast."

"Ali Bey," Osman Pasha shouted, "let me remind you that there is no possible way the sails on any mast will open properly while such strong gales are blowing from the port side. Under such drastic wind conditions, the sails won't be able to assist you in changing the ship's present starboard direction to portside, and they might actually result in the opposite, pushing you further toward the coastline. Such horrendous winds, giant waves, and a strong crosscurrent are forcing us closer and closer to the shore. Also, Tahsin Bey just informed me that you asked him to get ready to drop anchor. Ali Bey, you should know better: under these kinds of circumstances, dropping anchor could not possibly stop us from crashing into the rocky coastline. By the way, how did you determine that we are too close to the shore?"

"A short while ago, I happened to detect on our starboard side a reflection on the thick clouds above. I think it was the lighthouse beam at approximately the two o'clock position. I've estimated that we are roughly two nautical miles away from the first lighthouse. Due to a sudden and drastic change in wind's direction, we are now being continuously pushed toward the shoreline by the storm."

"Are you sure that it is the first lighthouse, not the second one that would guide us into Osaka Bay?"

"I am afraid we are near the first lighthouse, which indicates that we have many miles of rocky shoreline in front of us before we reach the second lighthouse."

"If that is the case," replied Osman Pasha, "the only thing that might let us escape the approaching coastline is the engine power. Let's hope that Ibrahim Bey will get the engine running soon."

Glancing at the low-rise smokestack behind the mainmast, Ali Bey noticed a puff of dark gray fumes coming out of the funnel. Gleefully, he yelled, "It seems Ibrahim Bey will soon have enough steam pressure to engage the engine."

Down in the engine room, the chief engineer and his crew were doing everything they could to restart the stalled engine. A dozen half-naked men, sweating profusely, threw into the furnaces shovels of dry coal that had been hauled in from the upper parts of the partially flooded coal storage bins. After successfully reigniting a strong coal fire that burned fiercely, the chief engineer was able to bring up the steam pressure in both boilers to a respectable level. He felt optimistic that soon he would be ready to engage the engine. The chief engineer nervously grabbed the main lever that connected the spinning engine transmission to the propeller, and waved at the second officer, who was standing next to the portside steam boiler.

"Jemil Bey, run up to the bridge," the chief engineer shouted. "Inform Osman Pasha and Ali Bey that we are about to have full steam power and the ability to move forward. I will soon push the control box indicator into the ready position and wait for the captain's order to move forward."

Lieutenant Colonel Jemil climbed the stairs in such a hurry that he stumbled twice, scraping his arms on the rough wooden railings. Above deck, he blindly forced himself against the torrential wind. When he reached the bridge, he jumped into the steering compartment where he found Osman Pasha and Commodore Ali celebrating the appearance of dark gray fumes on the tip of the smokestack. Grabbing the railing around the steering area, Lieutenant Colonel Jemil faced both officers and shouted, "The engine will soon be ready to engage transmission. Ibrahim Bey is waiting for your instruction to move forward."

Ali Bey looked at the control box and noticed that the indicator was in the ready position. As he pushed the control box's lever to the full-forward position, he cried, "Thanks are due to Allah that we are now able to pull away from the deadly coastline."

"Jemil Bey," Commodore Ali yelled, "go down to the main deck and inform Major Nuri that we now have full engine power. No need to raise the sails. But he should remain ready to open the mainmast and mizzenmast course sails on short notice. Then find Major Tahsin near the starboard anchor station. He should remain ready to drop both anchors in case we come too close to the shoreline."

Osman Pasha abruptly interrupted, "Ali Bey, as I've already told you, dropping the anchors will do us no good."

"Sir, if I notice at the last moment that we are dangerously close to the coast, it is worth dropping anchor to try and stop the ship from grounding."

As he wiped the rainwater off his face, Osman Pasha calmly replied, "I sincerely hope we won't be in a situation where you drop anchor as a last resort. The engine is now running and soon, Allah willing, we will move away from the shoreline."

Down in the engine room, Lieutenant Colonel Ibrahim, still holding onto the control lever and smiling, mumbled, "Thanks are due to almighty Allah; the engine is humming and we are moving forward." Glancing at the steam indicator, he whispered, "The steam power indicator is well above fourteen. Soon we will have full steam pressure to move us swiftly away from the shoreline."

He immediately ordered the hauling crew to bring in more loads of dry coal from the upper part of the storage bins. He then commanded the men shoveling coal into the furnaces to be steadfast. He shouted, "Move faster, faster! We have to reach a maximum feasible steam power to push the ship out to the open seas and away from the dangerous shoreline."

At the bridge, Lieutenant Colonel Jemil rushed down to the main deck to carry Commodore Ali's instructions to Major Nuri. As he stepped onto the landing, he was approached by Lieutenant Ismail.

"Sir," Ismail shouted, "With the resumption of electric power, the sump pumps should be working by now. Should we stop hauling water out of the engine room?"

Without pausing, Lieutenant Colonel Jemil hollered back, "Continue with the manual hauling of water. Do not stop what you are doing until Ibrahim Bey orders you to do otherwise."

After acknowledging the order given by Lieutenant Colonel Jemil, Lieutenant Ismail hurled himself toward the starboard railings immediately in front of the bridge deck,

Ensign Haydar following closely behind. Holding firmly onto the railing with his right hand, Ismail cupped his left hand over his left ear and leaned on the balustrade. Hearing the splashing sounds of waves on the approaching rocks, he murmured, "Oh my God, I can hear the songs of the damned sirens luring us into the jaws of destruction. We are doomed."

Ismail grabbed Ensign Haydar's arm to show him the slowly moving light beam above their head. As he pointed at the beam gradually moving away, he shouted into Haydar's ear, "It feels like we are right under the lighthouse."

Wiping the rainwater off his face, Ensign Haydar fearfully replied, "You're right; we are too damn close to the coastline."

Walking cautiously amidst the debris of broken wood pieces and torn sails spread across the main deck, Lieutenant Colonel Jemil reached Major Nuri, who was shouting loud instructions to a couple of sailors who were getting ready to climb the mainmast.

"Nuri Bey," Lieutenant Colonel Jemil shouted, "The engine is now running. We will soon move forward and get away from the approaching shoreline. Ali Bey orders you and your crew to remain ready to raise the mainmast and mizzenmast course sails."

Major Nuri, holding tightly to a line wrapped around the mainmast, called back, "Thank God that the engine is repaired. But for God's sake, why does Ali Bey still insist on using the sails in this stormy weather?" Without waiting for Lieutenant Colonel Jemil's reply, he turned around and ordered the few sailors hanging around the mainmast to inform the others up on the mainmast to refrain from opening any sails but to stay put where they were. Then, suddenly, he froze as if he had seen the devil himself.

He looked up to his left and screamed, "Jemil Bey, look at the moving beam of light above your head! We are right in front of the lighthouse. Oh my God, we are too close to the shore. This area is full of monstrous rocks. We are definitely doomed."

The second person spotting the lighthouse beam was the chief navigator, Major Tahsin, who stood next to the four-man crew above the starboard side of the anchor chain storage bulkhead at the front end of the frigate. Not only did he see the bright beam passing by over his head but also, he noticed the rocky shoreline to his immediate left. He hurriedly ordered the crew to drop both anchors. As the anchor chains noisily brushed against the ship's hull and fell into the choppy sea, Major Tahsin prayed for a miracle that the anchors would catch on to something at the seafloor to prevent the ship moving toward the rocky coastline. Unfortunately, his prayers, which were tangled with the deadly siren songs issuing from the rocks of calamity, were not answered. With a big thud, both anchor chains snapped from their housing and disappeared into the foamy darkness. Tahsin, realizing the gravity of the situation, glanced over the bowsprit at his immediate left and saw the dark and threatening silhouette of a large boulder that rose several meters above the violently choppy sea. He quickly turned toward the bridge. Both arms high in the air, he pointed to his left to warn Commodore Ali of the fast-approaching boulder.

On the upper bridge, though the captain had not yet noticed either Major Tahsin or his deputies jumping up and down on the main deck to warn him, he spotted within seconds the approaching massive boulder at approximately two o'clock on the starboard side. "We are too damn close to the shoreline!"

he shrieked. The engine's power is insufficient to drive us away from the shore,"

Ali Bey quickly realized. The wind and waves are pushing us into the spikes of doom in front of the lighthouse. Hoping for a quick response from the chief engineer, he immediately pulled the lever to the reverse position and ordered the helmsman to turn the steering to the forward position. Removing the hood of his rubber cloak, he stared in terror at the fast- approaching boulder. Biting his lips, he murmured, "We are about to be destroyed."

In the engine room, receiving the captain's unexpected order to put the transmission into reverse position, Ibrahim Bey pushed the lever first into neutral, then swiftly switched gear into reverse and engaged it. As he held the lever in position, he wondered why the captain had suddenly ordered him to reverse power. Feeling that the propeller was now in full reverse position, he let go of the lever, took a large handkerchief out of his pocket and wiped the sweat off his balding forehead. He was completely drained of energy.

"I need fresh air and some food," he mumbled, taking a deep breath and closing his eyes momentarily to relax. Suddenly, hearing an enormous thud and cracking sound coming from the ship's starboard side immediately behind the steam boilers, he quickly turned around to see what was happening. What he saw was the inward creasing of the ship's starboard side timber planks. All of a sudden, with a thunderous fracturing sound, the planks broke open and a gush of foaming seawater poured over the red-hot boiler tank immediately below. He realized with dread that this sudden contact with cold seawater could cause the boiler to explode within seconds. He then felt the ship jerking away from the impact spot, causing more water to pour in from the large crack in the starboard side of the ship. He understood then what had happened: the ship had run into a rock.

"Before the boiler explodes, we should vacate the engine room." he thought.

This was the chief engineer's last thought. As he had expected, the starboard side boiler exploded with such ferocity that it caused the ship's mid-section to rip open completely. Immediately after that, the doomed frigate crashed again, straight into Funagora, the largest and most prominent boulder of the rocks that span the Cape of Kashinozaki's coastline around the lighthouse. When the frigate's starboard midsection crashed into Funagora for the third time, the impact broke her main beam, almost splitting the ship in two. For a short while, two loosely connected midsections of the frigate floated away from Funagora before crashing into the boulder for a fourth time. Almost all of the deckhands around the mainmast were sucked into the collapsed midsection of the ship and crushed to death. The sailors who remained on the upper levels of the mainmast were thrown violently toward the jaws of Funagora and the surrounding boulders.

A few sailors, Lieutenant Colonel Jemil, and Major Nuri were flung into the dark, rough waters alongside the carnage. Landing in front of Nuri in the water, Jemil made a loud gurgling sound and slowly disappeared into the water. Nuri, badly maimed but still conscious, tried to stay afloat in the choppy sea. Glimpsing the sinking frigate and hearing the desperate screams, he realized that he was dying. Murmuring his last rites, he closed his eyes and let himself sink into the abyss.

As the mainmast broke away from the main beam and was about to collapse on the bridge, Commodore Ali, seeing his ship about to split in two, leaned over the railing and shouted as loudly as he could, "Abandon ship!" These were the commodore's last words. After the doomed frigate crashed into the Funagora for the last time, the mainmast suddenly collapsed onto the bridge, completely destroying the steering area and instantly killing most of the crew and the commodore. After the main beam was broken in two, the fore half of the frigate started to sink, and within a few minutes, it had completely disappeared under water. As it sank, it gradually pulled the rear section of the ship down into the chaotic abyss beneath the dark and turbulent waters surrounding the Cape of Kashinozaki.

It was almost nine o'clock on September sixteenth when the unfortunate frigate was hurled toward the rugged coastline of the Cape of Kashinozaki by the gusty winds and high waves of the typhoon. After crashing several times into the massive boulder named Funagora, the frigate Ertugrul completely fell apart and quickly disappeared into the depths around the colossal rock.

Of the four-hundred-and-ninety-seven souls that had been on the frigate, the ones who had been stationed in positions below deck in the front and back halves of the ship had practically no chance of survival. The explosion of the boilers and the gushing seawater immediately killed most of them. A few sailors who could have rushed to the stairs leading up to the main deck were thrown back by the rushing seawater pouring into the lower levels. Due to the sudden rupture of the frigate and the haste with which the front end of the ship was submerged, only a few of the people who were on the front part of the upper deck had a chance of survival. Major Tahsin and most of the sailors around him in the anchor station might have had sufficient time to jump out of the sinking ship's front section, but would have fallen into a destructive cavity of high waves carrying large chunks of the ship's debris. The only people who had chances of survival were the ones at the rearmost deck of the sinking frigate. Those who remained on the rear main deck and on the partially destroyed lower and upper bridges had a small chance for survival by staying put on the sinking ship until it had disappeared under their feet. Of the nearly one hundred and fifty souls who fearfully but patiently waited for the ship's deck to submerge, fewer than half of them had the chance to survive.

The sirens of Funagora played dice with the lives of the ones who struggled to swim away from sunken ship's debris and turbulence in complete darkness in a violently choppy sea with torrential winds and a rainstorm over their heads. Most of them tried unsuccessfully to avoid the swift large debris trail behind their heads and the sharp edges of the colossal rocks that surrounded them. The strong ebbs and flows of the waves that the deadly storm carried in threw the struggling sailors back and forth, over and over again, toward the rocks and large chunks of timber.

The only ones who could survive this turmoil were the young, strong sailors who were also good swimmers. Rear Admiral Osman Pasha, Imam Hafiz Ali Efendi, Lieutenant Ismail, and Ensign Haydar were among the men who had waited at the starboard edge of the collapsed upper bridge until the seawater was up to their knees and then pushed themselves into the choppy waters before the next big wave could plunge the sunken rear section of the frigate onto the submerged rocks surrounding Funagora, causing it to completely fall apart.

Many, including Osman Pasha, desperately tried to float by hanging onto large pieces of broken lumber. Captain Tevfik broke his leg during the fall into the deadly havoc and was about to lose consciousness. He screamed for help. Osman Pasha, who was stationed securely on a large portion of the broken mainmast, reached out into the dark void, catching Tevfik by the collar of his jacket and pulling him next to the floating mast right before a giant wave landed a big broken piece of debris on Osman Pasha's neck, knocking him back into the turbulent water. Osman Pasha was pulled under water and killed by the blows of the debris that ferociously moved back and forth among the boulders. Many others who successfully avoided the threatening debris were thrown so violently against the partially submerged rocks that they ended up being towed under the sea and drowned.

Several survivors, including Captain Tevfik, Lieutenant Ismail, Ensign Haydar, Imam Ali Efendi, head cook Sergeant Hilmi, gunnery sergeant Arap Hayri, junior clerk Mustafa Efendi, Corporal Veli, and a young deckhand named Ali clung desperately to nearby boulders, which were as slimy as the shells of a sea turtle. The strong ones who could climb onto the large boulders had the opportunity to rest and search for the safest possible way to reach the shoreline, hardly one hundred meters away. The swirling beam of the lighthouse that constantly reappeared above their heads gave them hope that, upon reaching the beach, they could search for help.

***

The Cape of Kashinozaki, Oshima, Japan

Sinking of Frigate Ertugrul, September 16, 1890

HANNAH FOR FUN AND PLEASURE

[THE USA]

©Omer Ertur
[From: Hannah's Colored Paradise, 2022]

Slave Trade in Senegambia, c.1850

HANNAH FOR FUN AND PLEASURE

New Orleans 1856

After counting the ship's slaves in shackles and checking each and every one of them for good health and proper appearance, the slave merchant walked up to the upper deck and handed the captain a pouch full of bank notes and gold coins. Walking out of the slave ship *Clotilda* that had travelled from West Africa across the Atlantic Ocean and recently anchored at the port of New Orleans, Louisiana, the slave merchant ordered his assistants to take all the Africans out of the ship and deliver them to the main slave market near the port facility.

At the slave market, newly arrived Africans were first assigned numbers for identification and then separated into gender and age categories. Following that process, the required legal forms were filled for each African who would soon become a slave.

As this was going on, a tall and shapely young adolescent girl from an Igbo speaking tribe of the Senegambia region of West Africa, noticed her father at the far end of the large field standing among a group of African men in chains. She hollered to get his attention. When he turned his head and looked at her, she raised her arms high up in the air with a forced big smile on her face to let him know she was all right.

She shouted, "I am fine, Father!"

221

When she could not hear his reply, holding her tears, she waved her arms as she realized that she might not ever see him again.

After inspecting and assigning them into various sale categories and determining appropriate prices for all the African males, the slave merchant started to inspect the female Africans. He suddenly stopped in front of a tall, well-built, good looking young African girl with the number 14 hanging over her neck. As he glanced at the half naked girl, he loudly growled, "This is excellent merchandise. Let's put a high price on this one: say $900 and mark the sign as *'For Fun and Pleasure'*."

"What name should I assign her and how old do you think she is?" asked the assistant.

Staring at her gleefully, the slave merchant replied, "She looks like a Hannah to me! I think she is a thirteen-years-old young virgin chick."

Kangela, an adolescent girl from an Igbo speaking tribe living in Senegambia region of West Africa, now renamed and registered as Hannah on the slave roster by a slave merchant, was one of the last African slaves on an old copper-sheathed schooner named *Clotilda* that had arrived at the North America's only remaining active slave port New Orleans in 1856. These coffin shaped slave ships have been transporting millions of black Africans to Europe's and North America's ports since 1619. Regardless of the anti-slavery legislations enacted in many of the European countries since the end of 18th Century and also the US Federal Government's ban of international slave trade at the beginning of 19th Century, the port of New Orleans had remained active to meet the demands of the North American slave markets and had continued to flourish until the beginning of the United States Civil War in 1861.

It was a well-known fact that nearly one-third of the kidnapped Africans perished at sea due to unsafe and unhealthy seafaring circumstances and harsh treatments they received from the slave-ship's personnel during the months long Atlantic Ocean crossings. Even before boarding a slave ship for the deadly seafaring journey, some of the kidnapped African tribesmen, women and children died on their way to the slave port facilities along the West African shoreline. Upon arrival at a slave port facility, slaves were delivered to the slave-ships. After being separated into gender and various age groups, kidnapped Africans were tightly stored in the lower decks of the wooden sailing ships. Under such inhuman and unhealthy conditions, many slaves died and were thrown overboard to the sharks that followed the ships.

Upon reaching the Port of New Orleans, the final destination to disembark the cargo of surviving Africans, the captain of the ship, upon receiving a payment in cash, allowed the slave market representative to take over the valuable human cargo. This human property now owned by slave market operators would soon be marketed at various slave distribution centers in New Orleans for further sale to various customers coming from wealthy households with vested interests in commercial, agricultural and industrial estates that had prevailed in the American society. The representatives of these households at the slave markets shopped for African slaves to be used as household servants, farm hands and at times as factory workers.

Young African girl Kangela was then and there named and registered as "Hannah" into the slave registry books and was now ready to be auctioned at the New Orleans slave market.

A few hours later, after being groomed and dressed in presentable clothes, she was forced up to a sales platform. Kangela now wore a large sign around her neck that read *'HANNAH FOR FUN & PLEASURE'*.

Later that afternoon, with an asking price of $900, she was sold for $600 to a New Orleans slave dealer, who was specialized in providing women slaves to the houses of ill-repute in and around the downtown of New Orleans.

The following day, Kangela and a few other female Africans were taken to the lobby of a major New Orleans hotel, where they were displayed for further sale to interested entities, mostly well-known prostitution houses in downtown.

A well-dressed madame of a bordello named *Paradise,* serving high-paying customers around New Orleans, bought Kangela for a hefty $800 and took the young African girl to her establishment located near the major hotels and businesses in downtown. Upon arriving at the house of pleasures, the madame ordered a middle-aged black servant to take good care of the newly purchased young African virgin called Hannah.

"She should rest at least for a few days. Make sure she is well fed. When she appears healthy and ready for action, let me know. Before offering her to our customers, we will dress her up in an attractive outfit and put makeup on her face."

As she was walking out of the room, the madame was calculating in her head how much profit this good-looking black virgin would bring in after only a few tricks. As she closed the door behind her, she murmured, "I am glad I went to the slave market this morning. This was a lucky catch!"

After a few days of rest and good food placed Hannah, whose true African name was Kangela, in relatively better physical health but her confused state of mind with anxiety and depression had only worsened. She had no idea where she was, who these people were and what they wanted from her. Staring out of the room's large window, she curiously watched the busy downtown street full of people and fast-running phaetons. She muttered to herself in Igbo, "Where am I? This is a very different world, full of strangely dressed white people."

Turning her attention back to the room, she sat on the bed, closing her eyes, she tried to remember all that had happened during the past several months.

One warm, sunny morning, together with my parents, I was in the fields checking on the conditions of our cassava and sweet potato crops. A small group of men wearing strange outfits and carrying rifles in their hands suddenly appeared in front of us. After tying our hands, they forced us to walk toward the nearby forest where a large group of previously kidnapped villagers, mostly young adults, were gathered.

Then, they forced us walk for many days to the nearby shoreline. Upon reaching the seashore, we were put on small boats and taken to a large wooden sailing ship. On the ship, mean-looking sailors separated the men and women. Then forced us to move into the ship's lower deck and installed chains on our arms and legs. During the miserable, horrible long night,

I hung onto my mother's arms. The next day early in the morning the ship sailed away.

A few days later, my mother became ill and fainted. She was caried away by two sailors. I tried talking to the women around me who spoke Igbo, but they had no idea where my mother was and what had happened to her. Standing up, I tried to locate my father. Far ahead toward the front end of the lower deck I could see him in chains among the male captives. He was too far away from me to get his attention. Later that day, I was able to see him when all of us were taken to the upper deck for forced exercises. I shouted at him that mother was taken ill but I was all right. I am not sure he heard me.

When I returned below deck, the woman chained next to me told me that one of the captive African boys helping the sailors above deck informed her that my mother had recovered from her illness in the ship's infirmary. When I asked her why she wasn't back here with us, she told me that the captain of the ship had decided to keep her in his cabin to enjoy her company. A few days later, she also told me that, the night before, my mother had jumped overboard into the dark sea and had probably been eaten by sharks that followed the ship. The next day, I was taken up to the main deck for forced exercises. As I pretended to exercise, I stared out at the sea and noticed a few sharks still following the ship. I started to cry and wondered why my mother killed herself.

Opening her eyes in New Orleans, she realized that she was now in an unfamiliar room in a strange land. Tears running down her cheeks, she mumbled, "Why was I kidnapped from my village and brought to this strange faraway land?"

Suddenly, her caretaker entered the room and asked, "How are you doing Miss Hannah?"

By now, able to recognize the slave-name she had been assigned, Kangela hollered back in her native tongue, "Stop calling me Miss Hannah. My name is Kangela."

A few days later, the madame of the brothel had decided that the young African girl Hannah was now ready to be displayed for business. She was hoping for a rich customer who would be willing to pay a lot of money to have sex with a beautiful young African virgin.

In preparations to display to prospective customers, Kangela was made to dress in a colorful cotton dress that showed her curvy futures. Then, the madame herself put make up on her face and sprayed her body with perfumes to make her sexually more desirable. During the early hours of the evening, she was taken to the well-lit entry hall to welcome the incoming customers. She and several other ladies of the night were lined up next to the wall, waiting for the arrival of men with deep pockets.

Kangela had no idea about what was going on around her. She stared at the girl next to her with a questioning look on her face. There was no reaction. Even if the girl next to her would attempt to tell Kangela what was about to happen, highly confused African girl would not understand a word of English. Kangela slowly moved away from the girls and went into a far corner of the room where she nervously and shyly watched the whole thing almost like a curious but scared spectator until one middle aged, chubby, short white man came near her and asked her name. The madame who was nearby rushed toward the customer and told him she was a virgin African girl named Hannah and told him what her price was. When the man made a counter offer, the madame refused and told him if he wanted to have sex with a young virgin, that is what he would have to pay. After a few moments of indecision, the man, now smiling broadly, agreed to the asking price and paid immediately in cash.

The customer was then ushered into a gaudy room with a large bed. He got undressed quickly and sat on the edge of the bed in his underwear. He impatiently waited for the young virgin African girl's entry.

The madame brought Kangela into the room. With a serious demeanor, she told the half-naked man to be gentle with her. Without waiting for his reply, she turned around and left the room.

At that point, Kangela figured out what was about to happen. After the madame's departure, she quickly withdrew to the far corner of the room. The half-naked man slowly approached her with the intent to take her clothes off. Like a cornered cat, Kangela smacked the man on the groin with a tight fist, then hit him hard on the side of his face, knocking him flat on his back. As the man tried to pull himself up, Kangela gave his head a hefty kick. She then ran out of the room. Before she could get near the main entrance door, she was caught by the house-guards. The two heavyset rough-looking men grabbed her and dragged her into the backyard. After throwing the young African girl on the ground, they wildly kicked her.

Hearing the commotion, the madame rushed into the backyard. As she shouted that they were damaging her property, she ordered the guards to stop. At that precise moment,

Kangela's would be customer with a bloodied face came out to the backyard, carrying a long heavy metal rod with a serious intent to punish the African girl. The madame quickly got in front of the angry man and told him that she would give his money back plus another lady would be providing him with free services. Getting his money back, the man threw the metal rod on the ground and returned to the house.

Afterwards, Kangela was carried back to her room. Looking at her bloodied face, the madame asked her assistant to clean up her wounds.

The next day, realizing that the young African girl with an attitude problem would not be any use in this kind of business, the madame ordered her assistant to take Kangela back to the main slave market to be resold.

A few days later, Kangela was put back on the sale roster of the auction block with several other black women with identification tags that read, "GOOD FOR HOUSE SERVICE AND FARMWORK".

As she was pushed again on the slave sale platform with several African women, Kangela took a look at the tag that was placed around her neck. She recognized her recently assigned slave-name 'Hannah' but could not understand the rest of the sentence that read, "*Experienced Household Servant and Strong Farm Hand*". Given her past family farming experience, most of the sentence, unknown to Kangela, was true.

That day in early February 1856, Kangela, as identified on her slave records as 'Hannah', was purchased by a slave merchant from Natchez, Mississippi, a small port-city on the

Grand Old River. Her new owner would take Kangela and all other newly purchased slaves to Natchez, located around 400 miles north of New Orleans, to be resold to many slave-masters that came regularly from the large cotton plantations nearby.

The next day, all of the recently purchased slaves and many large crates containing various farm supplies were placed unto a big steam-propelled barge to travel north toward the port of Natchez on the Mississippi River. All of the black slaves sat shoulder-to-shoulder on the wet floor backs against large wooden crates that were securely placed in the middle of the deck.

As the slow-moving barge traveled against the river's strong current, Kangela, wondering where she was being taken to, curiously watched the everchanging landscape and the scraggy shoreline full of overgrown vegetation fed by the muddy waters of the Grand Old River. When the barge passed towns and villages near the shoreline, Kangela raised her head to glance at the white and few black folks sullenly walking around the pedestrian walkways.

Twice a day, two armed guards served the slaves large, over-cooked cathead corn biscuits and drinking water in metal cups. If anyone of the slaves needed to respond to nature's call, there was a large bucket at the backend of the barge to be used in the open. When the bucket was full, the last slave using it would empty the bucket into the muddy waters of the river.

As she sat shyly and uncomfortably on the bucket in front of other slaves and several guards, Kangela thought, *"This is a little better than the situation I faced on that horrible slave ship that brought me to this strange land full of white people."*

On the slave ship, she recalled, she had to call the guard to unshackle her, allowing her to reach the bucket that was in the midsection of the lower deck area that was surrounded by sailors and a large crowd of shackled slaves. Sometimes, when her request to access the bucket was completely ignored by the guards, she would end up defecating on the floor she was sitting on. She was not the only one who ended up doing that; many slaves who were tightly confined in this stinky, foul-aired hell-hole had to relieve themselves on the floor in their chained positions. By the late afternoon, they had to breath the stinky foul air as they sat in their own excretes until the next morning's forced exercise session that would remove all of them up to the main deck. During the slaves' forced exercise session, ship's crew would wash the soiled floors below deck with buckets of sea water.

After two nights stop overs at local port facilities, the barge traveling on the Mississippi River reached the port of Natchez late afternoon of the third day. The slaves were taken out to a grassy open field and placed in a large canvass tent. The next morning, with their identification tags around their necks, they were again put on a high platform to be sold.

A few days later, Kangela and two young male African slaves were bought by a white slave-master of a large cotton plantation located near the Mississippi River town of Greenville, right across from the state of Arkansas.

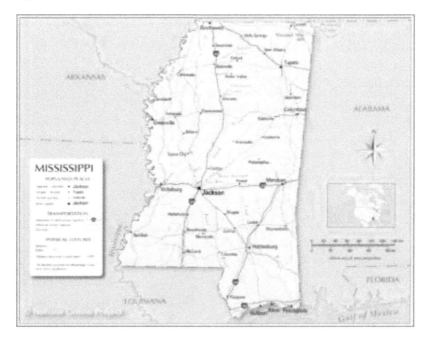

At the Mississippi Cotton Plantation

After nearly all-day ride on a long and wide four horse wooden cart that was loaded with large bags of supplies and three African slaves in shackles, including Kangela, entered through the main gate of a 3000-acre cotton plantation that was located nearly twenty miles of north of the town of Greenville and 150 miles south of the city of Memphis, Tennessee. This immense plantation was owned for nearly three generations by a wealthy southern family: David and Dorothy Franklin and their four children.

The Franklin plantation, an agricultural production entity considered economically self-sufficient, grew cotton for profit and also planted several types of grains, vegetables and fruit trees and maintained large number of animals for consumption and transportation use.

The plantation had ninety black slaves, one third of which were females, mostly used in household services such as cleaning, cooking, washing and ironing. Most of the male and a few of the female slaves, under the guidance of a white slave-master named Steve and his two assistants efficiently but at times rudely managed the slave workers in the cotton fields, guided the wheat and oats planting and maintained various vegetable gardens and fruit trees. They also took care of farm animals such as horses and mules and managed the care and slaughter of cows, pigs and chickens that were raised in the plantation.

In 1856, the State of Mississippi, like most of the southern and a few of the northern states, legally allowed slavery to remain a part of the local economic framework. Slaves were treated as property with practically no rights or freedoms. They were bought and sold in various slave markets all over the state. If any of the slaves, misbehaved, acted disrespectfully or did not work hard, the punishment would be anything from a heavy scolding to a bloody whipping. If they escaped, they would be pursued by slave-catchers or law enforcement. When caught they were severely punished by the slavers with whippings and imprisonment.

...

Stepping off of the horse-cart in front of a large wooden storage shack where carts and phaetons were kept, Kangela, standing erect, intensely browsed her immediate environment. Everything that surrounded her appeared strangely different than what she was used to seeing around her father's farm in

West Africa. In her village her family lived in a large thatched-roof hut that was surrounded by numerous chicken coups and large cultivated fields of sweet potatoes and cassava. Now in this new landscape, she glanced intensely at the tall trees, plush greenery and vegetation that surrounded her. She realized that she was in an entirely different world. Also, looking at the buildings around her, she noticed how different and colossal these wooden and brick structures appeared compared to the thatched-roof huts she lived in her African village.

As she sullenly stood in front of the wooden cart, she suddenly remembered all that had happened since she was kidnapped from her village. She recalled the scarry faces of the black kidnappers who were clad in strange-looking outfits and spoke a tongue she did not understand. On the big wooden boat, the sulky, bearded faces of mean-looking white sailors carrying long sticks was permanently etched in her memory. Everyone on that miserable ship looked, dressed and talked so differently and acted so violently that she could not make any sense of what was going on. The only thing she was able to grasp that she was being forcefully taken to a very far away land. Not yet aware of the reason behind her forced relocation, Kangela was completely lost. All these traumatic and sorrowful memories made her extremely sad. Feeling dizzy, she crouched on the ground.

Steve, the slave-master, approached her and ordered her to stand up and follow him. When Kangela did not respond, he grabbed her arm; forcing her to stand. He dragged her by her arm to a large wooden building that was the plantation's kitchen facility located near the two-floor white plastered large colonial style house of the plantation owner.

Entering the immense food preparation facility that fed nearly one hundred people three times a day, Steve brought her in front of an overweight middle-aged black woman.

Releasing Kangela's arm, Steve, with an obvious sneer on his face, glanced at the plantation's senior cook.

"Mama Rose! Here is the kitchen help you've been asking for."

Looking intensely at the young slave woman, Mama Rose inquired, "What is your name, girl?"

When there was no reply, Steve, looking at the papers in his hand, replied, "The document says her name is Hannah. I leave her in your good hands Mama. I have to hand these papers to Master David."

After Steve's departure, Mama Rose summoned the kitchen help nearby and asked the black woman to take the newcomer to the slave quarters behind the kitchen facility. She ordered her to show the new slave girl her bed, assist her to take a bath and give her a clean set of underwear and a uniform worn by the plantation slaves.

"Before we eat our meals this evening, bring her to the dining area. Tomorrow morning I'll decide what kind of work she'll be doing in the kitchen."

This was the beginning of Kangela's new life as a slave in a cotton plantation in Greenville, Mississippi. During the next few months, she grew to accept her new name Hannah. Also, during that time she fully grasped the meaning of being a slave. After making a few mistakes, she realized that to survive as a slave she had to accept her fate and do properly and efficiently what was expected of her. She became a quick learner as she carefully followed Mama Rose's work-related instructions.

***

Stories from an Unsettling World

THE LITTLE BOY

AND

THE FAT MAN

[JAPAN]

Nagasaki

THE LITTLE BOY AND THE FAT MAN

A Little Boy's Nightmare

Many little boys upon waking up from a horrible nightmare would soon put it out of their minds. In many occasions I was able to do exactly that except when I had a nightmare during which, as a result of a powerful nuclear bomb blast, I was completely burned and died in pain. Upon waking up and sweating profusely, I sat in my bed and asked myself, "Why did I experience such a painful death in my dream?"

Nearly half a century later when I was visiting the atomic bomb museum in Nagasaki, Japan I discovered the answer to my childhood nightmare question. As I was walking through the photos of the Nagasaki nuclear bombing, I came upon a photo of a dead young boy's charcoaled body lying behind recognition on a school playground. I suddenly recalled my dream and discovered the answer to my age-old question, "Why me?" Upon understanding the true meaning of the answer that I realized in the museum that day, I decided that such premonition should guide me to write that little boy's sad story.

The First-born Little Boy Named Taro

Late in July of 1945, Lieutenant Kendo Nomura, the chief training officer of the mini-submarine unit at the Yokosuka Naval Base near Yokohama, receiving the approval of his rest and relaxation leave to visit his family, barely caught his three-hour naval air flight to Nagasaki on time. During the late hours of the evening, he reached his home at the military personnel living quarters in the Nagasaki Naval Base. His wife Kuniko, a

food shortages, how did you manage to feed yourselves during the past three months?"

"We make do with what is available in the military base's grocery store. Fortunately, I was able to get some extra rice and a small amount of sugar to prepare Taro his favorite sweet rice cakes. It is so wonderful that you are here for his birthday tomorrow."

"It wasn't easy to get a three days family furlough. Given our recent military situation, I was surprised that my leave request was approved."

Hearing the doorbell rang, Kendo went to the entry hall. A few minutes later, he returned back to the living room with Captain Takahiro Akashi, a maritime engineer at the naval base's ship maintenance unit, also a resident with his family at the same military residential complex. After properly saluting the Captain, Kuniko excused herself to let the two men carry on with their conversations.

Kendo brought out the bottle of sake he had in the cupboard. Together with two small sake glasses, he placed the bottle on the small table in front of Takahiro. Kendo couched down and, after crossing his legs, sat erectly across his friend. He then poured generous amounts of sake into the glasses.

After he handed his friend a glassful of sake, they raised their glasses. After saluting loudly, they quickly gobbled down their first shots.

With a broad smile on his face, Takahiro commented, "Thank you for letting me know that you were coming home. How is your kamikaze mini-submarine program doing?"

"Not so well. So far, only a few men we sent out to the ocean to encounter some enemy naval ships were successful in their attempts."

"Why do you think such a drastic failure is happening?"

"I think there is one basic problem: not having enough depth is causing the mini-submarines to be noticed by the enemy air recognizance missions before they were able to attack the enemy's ships. By being too close to the ocean's surface they were noticed by the enemy airplanes, resulting in many of them being destroyed before they can complete their missions."

"I think such problem could be corrected by some basic design improvements."

"To dive deeper requires a larger mini-submarine which becomes harder to be managed by one man. Furthermore, it becomes too costly to be feasible."

"What are you going to do?"

"The only thing I can do is to improve training of the men in correctly handling their mini-submarines and effectively manage their timeframe during their final suicide attack. In the meantime, I will fully retrain them in a few below-surface maneuver techniques to become less noticeable."

"How do you personally feel when the chosen young warriors get into their mini-submarines for their suicidal missions to sink enemy ships?"

"I try not to think about it. I know for a fact that they are volunteers and that they are fully aware of their sacrifice. Obviously, they are willing to die to protect their country. I think we both would do the same, don't you think so?"

After remaining silent a few seconds, Takahiro replied, "Specially, under the given military circumstances that we are about to lose this war against America, I think we have to do all we can to protect our homeland. Are you aware that government recently formed a commission to study the possible options for an armistice?"

"No, I haven't heard about it. What are the possible options?"

"We either ask for peace with our archenemy America or with our most recent enemy, the Soviet Union that has recently occupied Manchuria."

"Would it make any difference which one we choose to have a ceasefire?"

"That is the important question the emperor's special commission is searching for an answer. Which one would you choose?"

Kendo quickly replied, "I rather die fighting than to give up to any one of our enemies."

To change the subject, he then quickly asked Takahiro, "What happened with your request to transfer to active naval duty?"

"I withdrew my request. Given the increased level of repairs on the war damaged ships, I realized that my request would not be approved anyway. So, I will remain Nagasaki and stay busy in repairing damaged ships."

As they sipped their sake, they kept on talking until the late hours of the night. Before departing from Kendo's apartment, Takahiro commented, "Do you think Kuniko soon would agree to move to Yokosuka Naval Base?"

"During this trip, I will try again to convince her that she and Taro should move to Yokosuka to be with me. You know she loves her students and enjoys teaching at the neighborhood primary school. May be if I am lucky, I'll be able to convince her this time around."

The next morning, Taro was up before his parents. He kept himself occupied with his toys. When he heard his parents waking up, he rushed into their bedroom.

Kuniko, smiling at her first born, loudly asked, "Are you ready for your birthday?"

Hand in hand, mother and son went to the kitchen. Seeing his plateful of sweet rice cakes on the kitchen table, Taro excitedly shouted, "My sweet rice cakes looks really delicious Mama!"

A few minutes later, Kendo also joined the family for the breakfast to celebrate their son's 8th birthday. A few days earlier, Kuniko was able to find a wooden toy soldier and a small porcelain horse statue at the local farmer's market. She bought both items for Taro. After they finished eating most of the sweet rice cakes, Kuniko presented the toy soldier and the horse to Taro, who jumped up and down with joy with his new toys.

After the birthday breakfast, Kuniko informed Kendo that she has to attend a civil defense group meeting that would take place at the nearby elementary school building. Most of the school teachers were required to work for the civil defense force during the summer breaks. After the breakfast, she left her husband and son alone to have a quality time together at home.

This was a great opportunity for Kendo just to be with his first born. When he was transferred from the submarine maintenance unit in Nagasaki to Yokosuka's mini-submarine operation's site two years earlier, he wanted to take the whole family to the Yokosuka Naval Base but his wife Kuniko, who was in her first-year assignment as an elementary teacher, wanted to remain in Nagasaki. Hoping that his assignment in the Yokosuka submarine base would be a short one, he agreed to leave the family back in Nagasaki. As he played with his son out in the front yard, he made up his mind first to convince his wife to move to Yokosuka and then, before departing Nagasaki, he would officially request his family's transfer to Yokosuka Naval Base.

Two days later, early in the morning, Kendo entered his son's bedroom and said goodbye to his firstborn. Afterwards, he sat around the dinner table with Kuniko to discuss the matter of transfer to Yokosuka Naval Base. He was surprised to hear that his wife finally agreed to move to Yokosuka. With a happy grin on his face, Kendo said, "Don't worry, you will soon find a good teaching job near the Yokosuka Base."

After bidding his farewell to Kuniko, he walked to the main naval office building to have a meeting with the senior relocation officer to request his family's transfer to Yokosuka. After completing all the necessary paperwork, he was told that the final approval would take two weeks' time. Receiving that information, made him feel good about being together again with his family in the near future. He then hopped into a jeep that would take him to the military airbase to fly to Yokohama.

Kuniko was sad to see her husband leave home. She told him that morning that she was now willing to leave Nagasaki so that the family would be together in Yokosuka. After her husband's departure, Kuniko got ready to go to the civil defense group's meeting at the nearby primary school facility. Mother and son gently walked side by side toward the school ground. Upon arrival, she left Taro in care of a playground caretaker who would watch over several children of the teachers and public officials who were attending the civil defense group meeting.

During the coming many days, even though there were a few sirens warning about possible enemy air attacks, Kuniko and Taro lived their days happily and in good health. Kuniko almost every day slowly packed their household stuff to get ready to move to Yokosuka. Hopefully by mid-August she would receive the official approval to move the family to near her husband's base. In the meantime, she helped Taro improve his reading and writing to make his second-grade classes a bit easier when the school would be resumed at end of August. At least three times a week, the mother and son would walk together to the nearby primary school ground. As Kuniko attended the civil defense group meetings, Taro happily played with his friends at the playground.

As this was going on in Nagasaki, Lieutenant Nomura worked hard in Yokosuka Naval Base near Yokohama to retrain his kamikaze volunteers to become more effective in their attempts to sink enemy warships. He also put pressure on the mini-submarine program managers to come up with a better design so that the mini-submarines would not be so easily noticed by the enemy airplanes.

Early August he received the official approval of his family to move to Yokosuka Naval Base. He was able to make a short phone call to his neighbor Captain Takahiro Akashi, asking him to inform his wife Kuniko about the decision. The following day, Captain called him back with information that his family relocation to Yokosuka was now scheduled to take place latest on the 10th of August.

The Fat Man

The Fat Man is the name assigned to an implosion-type nuclear weapon with solid plutonium core. It came into existence at the times of the Manhattan Nuclear Research project's Los Alamos laboratory in New Mexico during the early part of summer in 1945 under the overall guidance of Robert

Oppenheimer, who after the explosion of atomic bombs on two Japanese cities accepted the impact of his personal role in the creation of the nuclear bombs by stating that he now was an agent of death. However, in this case, the true agent of death was Harry Truman, the President of the United States, who authorized the dropping of the nuclear bombs on two well-populated urban areas of Japan that was about to capitulate.

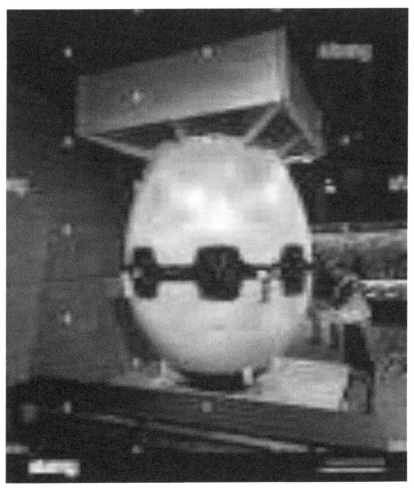

Nagasaki Atomic Bomb [The Fat Man]

After completing several testing stages, together with his compatriot nuclear bomb *The Little Boy*, The Fat Man was loaded into heavy cruiser *Indianapolis* at a west coast naval facility to be shipped to the Tinian Island in the Pacific Ocean, nearly one thousand miles south of Nagasaki. Luckily, the Fat Man and his compatriot the Little Boy survived the long maritime journey and were delivered to the Port of Tinian Island early July, 1945. After completing its delivery of the extremely valuable cargo to Tinian Naval Base, the cruiser USS Indianapolis unexpectedly was sunk by a Japanese submarine hardly two weeks later. If the Japanese submarine that sunk the heavy cruiser Indianapolis would have struck and sunk it with the Fat Man and Little Boy inside the warship before she reached Tinian, that would have become a game-changing event that would have ruined President Truman's wish to end the Japanese war a bit earlier.

Actually, as the two nuclear bombs were getting ready to be dropped on two Japanese cities, President Truman was having his final meetings with his cabinet and military leaders to finally authorize the dropping of the nuclear bombs on an enemy that appeared ready to capitulate. When some of his top military leaders, including General Eisenhower, and a few of his cabinet members clearly stood against dropping nuclear bombs on a clearly defeated enemy, President Truman justified his decision to drop them on Japan to save lives of many American soldiers who would possibly become casualties during the occupation of Japan. But the truth of the matter was that as much as saving American soldiers' lives, Truman wanted to scare the new enemy number one of the United States – the Soviet

Union. Unfortunately, the President, during his decision-making process, obviously gave no consideration to the long-term effects of nuclear bombs that would be dropped on two Japanese cities with civilian populations without paying any attention to the fact that during the Pearl Harbor attack, the Japanese military purposely focused on attacking the naval and air-force facilities and avoided bombing the civilian parts of Honolulu. Clearly, a strong presence of revenge, which was not justified at all, was strongly present in the mind of the American President, who, at the end of his deliberations, convinced himself to destroy, unnecessarily and unjustifiably, many innocent civilian lives.

Both nuclear bombs safely made it to Tinian Island and they were made ready to be airdropped on Hiroshima on August 6 and on Kokura City on August 9, 1945. Hiroshima was successfully nuclear bombed as planned on August 6, causing unimaginable immediate and long-term physical damage and massive human casualties. However, the planned mission to drop the nuclear bomb, the Fat Man, on Kokura City on August 9 became impossible due to weather conditions. It was decided, while in the air, by the pilot of the B-29 airplane *Bock's Car*, Major Charles Sweeney, who was gleefully hoped that the weather conditions would allow him to drop the nuclear bomb that he was carrying on Nagasaki to destroy the military hardware producing Mitsubishi Factory located right in the middle of a heavily populated urban area of Nagasaki.

On August 6, 1945, an American Air Force plane dropped first ever nuclear bomb on Hiroshima, causing unimaginable physical damage to the infrastructure of the city and killing and wounding hundreds of thousands of civilians, mostly women, children and the elderly. For national security reasons, Japanese government did not publicly announce the results of the atomic bomb destruction of Hiroshima. So, the people of Nagasaki were not aware of what had happened to the people of Hiroshima. Even if they were aware of the utter destructive power of a nuclear bomb, there wasn't much of anything anyone could do to prevent it from reoccurring in another city. No civil defense preparations would have made the people of Nagasaki to properly prepare for a nuclear bomb that would soon be dropped on their city. Actually, not even the American military was fully aware of the atomic bomb's destructive power and its long-term effects on the immediate human environment.

Doomsday for the people of Nagasaki: August 9, 1945

Major Charles Sweeney, the pilot of the B-29 military plane that carrying 'The Fat Man' on board, was indecisive about where to drop the nuclear bomb. After flying for many hours away from Tinian Island towards Japan, he discovered that the intended target location of Kokura City was under heavy clouds making it impossible for him to drop the bomb. He flew to Nagasaki to try his luck there. Noticing that his intended secondary target was also under heavy clouds, he seriously considered flying back to Tinian Island. However, given the explosive nature of the plutonium-based nuclear bomb 'Fat Man', such an option was implausible because a possible accidental detonation at the Tinian Island would destroy the whole American airbase.

Worriedly shaking his head, he mumbled, "I may have to drop the damn thing into the Pacific Ocean."

As he was making a maneuver to leave Nagasaki airspace, one of his co-pilots, Captain Kermit Beahan hollered that he could now see the red roofs of the Mitsubishi factory buildings. Hearing that comment, Major Sweeney quickly decided to drop the bomb on Nagasaki. A few minutes later the Fat Man, a 3.3 meters tall nuclear bomb with a wide 1.5 meters girth, weighing nearly five thousand kilograms left the airplane and started its doomsday journey toward the center of Nagasaki. After a freefall lasting 43 seconds, the Fat Man detonated at an altitude of 500 meters exactly on 11:02 am.

...

Early in the morning of that ominous day, Kuniko got up before sunrise to finalize her packing. She was informed that the following morning she and Taro would be flown to Yokohama and be transferred to the Yokosuka Naval Base's residential complex. She planned to inform the civil defense meeting organizers that today's meeting would be her last attendance.

By nine o'clock, Kuniko, holding Taro's hand, reached the school playground where nearly a dozen children, under the guidance of an elderly women caretaker, were playing games and noisily enjoying each other's company. As she bowed to the caretaker, Kuniko informed the caretaker that the meeting she was attending would end by noon. Then, looking at her son affectionately, she told him to be respectful toward the caretaker and if the sirens come on before an enemy air attack, she reminded him to follow the caretaker to the underground bunker near the school building. Before entering the building, she turned around and glanced at his son one more time as if she would never see him again. Brushing the negative thoughts of a possible enemy air raid off her mind, she rushed into her meeting taking place at the main auditorium.

Watching his mother disappear into the building, Taro searched the playground for his best friend Haruto. Finding him on the swing set, he waited patiently for him to stop swinging. Then he asked him if he would like to play football. After placing four large stones to mark the goal posts, they started to chase after an old, warn out, airless football. Soon they were joined by several other boys to have rough football game that lasted more than an hour. At the end of the game, all the boys sat next to the small gymnasium building's outer wall to have a rest.

Suddenly when it was 10:58 am in the morning, air-attack sirens came on to warn the people of Nagasaki about a possible enemy air-attack. The caretaker in the playground shouted to remind the children to run to the nearby underground bunker. At that precise moment, Taro who was in the gymnasium's toilet facility, heard the sirens. He hurriedly departed from the toilet and rushed out of the gymnasium. Outside the building, he saw the caretaker at the entry of the underground bunker; she was loudly calling him to hurry up. Taro, now facing the bunker, started to run toward the bunker to join his friends.

After he had taken hardly a few steps toward the bunker, all of a sudden, a very strong bright light flashed in front of Taro's eyes almost completely blinding him. Now in a complete shock, he tried to take a deep breath, but he couldn't. He felt his lungs and throat burn. As he coughed loudly, his hands reached toward his mouth. Suddenly, a strong wave of burning hot air knocked him off his feet. He fell flat on his back. Feeling the excruciatingly painful sense of being burned alive, he tried to reach toward his face to cover his eyes. Hardly within a few seconds, Taro, an innocent little boy died in a first ever nuclear hell, without ever understanding the magnitude of the immense power that destroyed his young life. He definitely paid the ultimate price for the mistakes of his forefathers and for an obvious callousness of the enemy that completely lacked any sense of humanity.

An innocent Child's Agonizing Death in Nagasaki [Yosuke Yamahata]

The net immediate result of a nuclear bomb explosion over Nagasaki was that nearly twenty thousand buildings were completely destroyed and over one hundred thousand people were killed or wounded. None of the people who were in the elementary school building survived including Taro's mother Kuniko and Taro himself, whose charred body on the destroyed playground was later photographed by a well-known Japanese newspaper photographer Yosuke Yamahata.

The innocent young life of Taro was terminated by a nuclear bomb crudely named the Fat Man, dropped on Nagasaki by an American warplane. A person only has to just glance at the photo taken a few hours after the explosion of the nuclear bomb to feel the agony of a painful death young boy Taro had faced that morning as he played with his friends in the elementary school playground.

The aftermath

Late afternoon of August 9, the news that American Airforce has dropped a nuclear bomb on Nagasaki has reached the Naval Base in Yokosuka. Lieutenant Kendo Nomura was busy in getting a small group of mini-submarines that was scheduled to attack the following day the American naval ships, particularly the aircraft carriers that might soon dare to get too close to the main island Honshu. When he heard the news about the bombing of Nagasaki, he rushed into the communications room to contact Nagasaki Naval Base to learn about his family's situation. No one had answered all his calls. As a last resort, he sent a telegram to his neighbor Captain Takahiro Akashi who was a maintenance engineer at the naval base. The reply he received from the naval base indicated that his telegram due to circumstances could not be delivered. He then rushed into the office of the most senior administrative officer. He was not able to reach the senior officer who apparently was attending a meeting. An administrative assistant to the colonel in charge of communication volunteered to help Lieutenant Nomura by calling the main naval office in Nagasaki. After several calls, he finally got an answer that would further frustrate Lieutenant Nomura. The administrative assistant basically told the Lieutenant that, similar to Hiroshima, the powerful bomb that was dropped on Nagasaki had completely destroyed most of the buildings and possibly killed thousands of people.

Kendo Nomura was not able to sleep that night. Up until the early hours of the morning; he kept on calling the Nagasaki Naval Base. Finally, during the late hours of the following morning, he received a very disturbing telegram message from Captain Takahiro Akashi stating that while he was out on the sea to test a recently repaired warship, the whole naval base including the Mitsubishi factories were completely destroyed by a powerful bomb.

"If I was on the base, you would not receive this message." He wrote. *"I would also be dead. Unfortunately, nobody in the family residential units has survived. The primary school facility that in close proximity to the naval base was also completely destroyed. It is very sad for me to inform you that both our families are no longer with us on this earth. May God give us both the strength to survive such bad news of losing our wives and children."*

As he folded the message, Lieutenant Nomura whispered, "I was supposed to welcome them home this afternoon. Now, my family is dead."

Trying not to cry publicly, he rushed into his office. Locking the door to his office, he silently let the tears of deep sorrow pour out of his eyes.

The following morning, Lieutenant Nomura after giving his final instructions to six young suicide mission naval soldiers, went to the office of his immediate superior officer and asked his permission to join the suicide mission on a seventh mini-submarine. When his request was turned down, he simply saluted his superior and walked out of his room. Without a proper authorization, he knew well that he could not get a seventh mini-submarine prepared to join the approved suicide mission.

He went into the main preparations center and summoned six young soldiers who volunteered for the suicide mission. He slowly walked toward the youngest soldier, an 18-year-old volunteer, and told him that he now was rescheduled for the next mission. He ordered him to go back to his unit and wait for further instructions.

After young man's departure, Lieutenant Nomura led his suicide team to the six mini-submarines that were ready for action. Within an hour, they would all be ready move into the depths of the Pacific Ocean to search for American warships that were approaching the Japanese shores.

Kamikaze mini-submarines in Yokosuke Naval Base

Lieutenant Nomura, before getting into his mini-submarine, closed his eyes and stood still silently to peacefully accept his upcoming fate. With a sad smile slowly appearing on his sanguine face, he whispered, "I no longer have a family and a country to live in; it is now a good time to join my ancestors."

Before opening his eyes, he made his last wish, "I hope, I will be lucky enough to sink an American warship before I meet my ancestors." He firmly gripped the railing to get himself into the tiny submarine.

Twenty minutes later, six kamikaze mini-submarines moved out to the open seas to search for enemy warships to sink.

None of the six mini-submarines ever returned to the naval base and it is not known that if they were ever able to sink any enemy warships during that particular day.

The following day, Japanese military received a direct order from the emperor's office to cease all hostilities against the enemy forces.

...

After the destruction of Hiroshima on August 6 by the first ever nuclear bomb, Emperor Showa had a period of self-reflection about the war against United States of America. He recalled that when the military cadre of 1941 approved the attack Pearl Harbor, he warned the military leaders that such a decision was extremely dangerous and might cause a drastic military response from the United States. When the military leaders argued that the imperialistic intensions of both, the Americans and the Europeans, could only be eliminated by strong military actions, he agreed to the attack on Pearl Harbor to destroy America's major Pacific naval base. In retrospect, he felt that while they were fighting to clear Asia from its long time European colonial occupiers, he should not have agreed to open a new front against the Americans.

Furthermore, during the past six months Emperor Showa felt that the war was already lost. Soon after becoming aware of the genuine military threat of Soviet Union against Japan, he formed a committee that would study possible options for a ceasefire and if surrender was imminent, with which enemy should Japan sue for peace: USA or USSR. Committee's decision was in favor of a ceasefire with the Americans. It was the feeling of the committee members that while the Americans would be more amenable to an armistice with conditions that would protect the Emperor, the Soviets would not accept such conditionality that would protect the Japanese throne.

A few days before nuclear bombs were dropped on Hiroshima and Nagasaki, the Emperor, based on the armistice commission's suggestion, instructed his government to ask Americans for a conditional ceasefire. No response was received from the American government.

On August 9th, Emperor Showa was promptly informed that a second powerful bomb was dropped on Nagasaki, destroying the town almost completely. On August 10, Emperor Showa called his government cabinet and the military leaders to discuss the matter of surrendering to Americans with conditions that would protect the people of Japan and the imperial throne. Military leadership was against surrendering and strongly insisted on the continuation of the war. However, the cabinet members fully agreed with the Emperor that Japan should sue for a conditional ceasefire. Emperor Showa, overriding the suggestions of the military, decided for immediate action to contact Americans for a conditional surrender. An immediate response was received from the commander of the US forces,

General MacArthur, stating that only an unconditional surrender was acceptable.

On 15th of August, 1945 Japanese Emperor Showa, after many hours of additional intense discussions with his military leaders, his Prime Minister and the senior Cabinet members, decided to stop fighting and agreed to an unconditional surrender to American Forces. He was now ready to announce an immediate end to the all hostilities because of the existence of a highly destructive nuclear capacity in the hands of United States' military would cause further suffering to the people of Japan. The following day, in a public statement Emperor Showa declared the following: *"Japan's enemy has begun to employ a most cruel bomb, the power of which to do damage is indeed incalculable, taking the toll of many innocent lives."*

Even though the Japanese surrender was unconditional, it was General MacArthur's sole personal decision to protect the Japanese Emperor's throne to establish a long-lasting peace with the people of Japan. Soon after the unconditional surrender, Emperor Showa met General MacArthur. During the meeting, the Japanese Emperor, on behalf of people of Japan, sincerely apologized to the American General for the Pearl Harbor attack.

It would have been appropriate that, in return, the American government would also apologize for the unnecessary use of nuclear bombs on the civilian population of Japan particularly when the Japanese was serious about surrendering. The government of the United States never accepted the responsibility for dropping unnecessarily two nuclear bombs on Hiroshima and Nagasaki. The United States Government owes an apology not only to the people of Japan but also to the whole world community for the greatest war crime conducted by the American military against the noncombatant civilians of Japan.

When he returned home to America, the personal enemies of the American General Douglas MacArthur successfully ruined his political chances of becoming the next president of the United States. Former General Dwight Eisenhower won the election and became the president of the United States. American occupation of Japan lasted only seven years. In 1952 American forces, with the exception of Okinawa, withdraw from Japan. In the meantime, Emperor Showa, who foresaw the postwar economic recovery of Japan, ruled Japan until his death in 1989, thus becoming the longest ruling emperor in Japanese history.

Atomic Bomb Explosion over Nagasaki, August 9, 1945

Downtown Nagasaki after Atomic Bombing

A Temple Site after Atomic Bombing of Nagasaki

Omer Ertur

BOOKS BY OMER ERTUR
[on amazon.com/books]

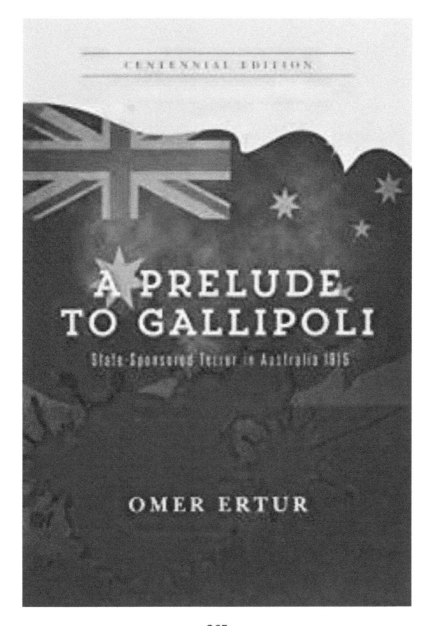

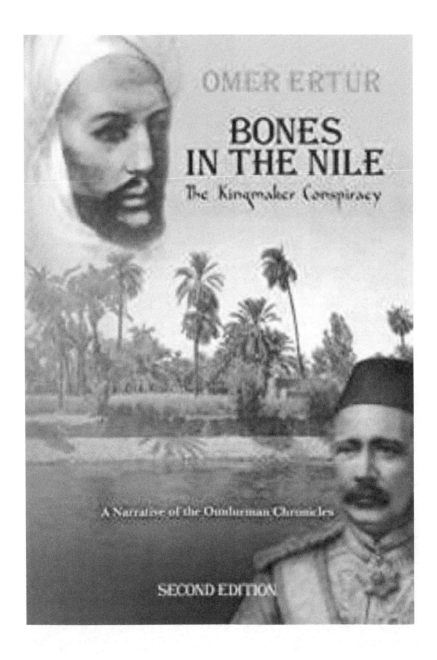

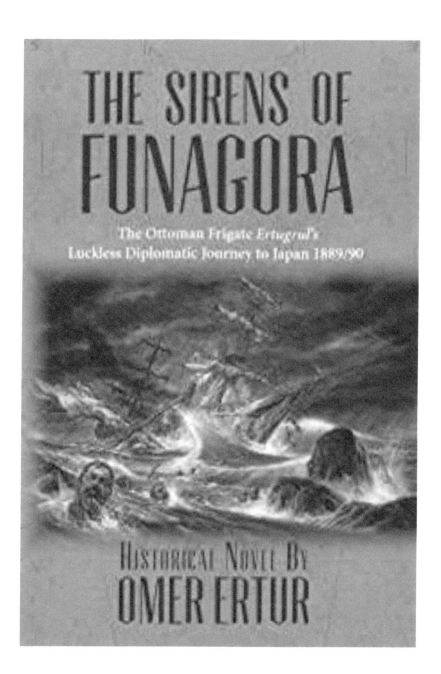

THE SIRENS OF FUNAGORA

The Ottoman Frigate *Ertugrul's* Luckless Diplomatic Journey to Japan 1889/90

HISTORICAL NOVEL BY OMER ERTUR

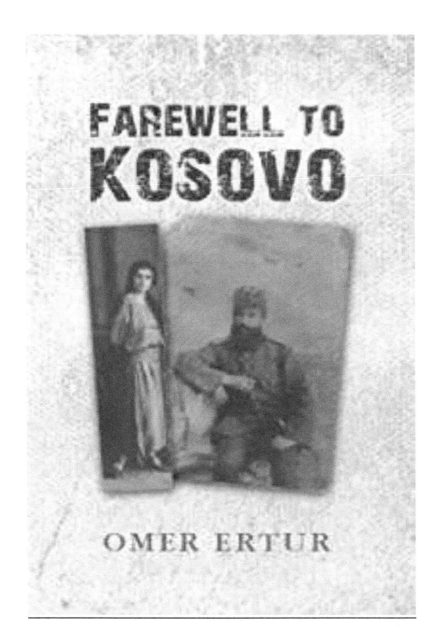

HANNAH'S COLORED PARADISE

A STORY OF SURVIVAL IN AMERICA
DURING THE TIMES OF 'SEPARATE BUT
EQUAL' 1865-1965

OMER ERTUR

Omer Ertur